COLOMBIAN C

OTHER TITLES IN THE SAS OPERATION SERIES

SAS
OPERATION

Colombian Cocaine War

DAVID MONNERY

HARPER

Harper
An imprint of HarperCollins*Publishers*
1 London Bridge Street,
London SE1 9GF
www.harpercollins.co.uk

This paperback edition 2016
1

First published by 22 Books/Bloomsbury Publishing plc 1993

A catalogue record for this book
is available from the British Library

ISBN: 978 0 00 815491 2

Set in Sabon by Born Group using Atomik ePublisher from Easypress

Printed and bound in Great Britain

MIX
Paper from
responsible sources
FSC™ C007454

Prelude

Joss Wynwood reinserted the magazine into the Browning High Power 9mm pistol, and put the pistol back in the cross-draw holster at his belt. After checking that the two spare magazines were in his windcheater pocket, he leaned back on the bench and grinned at his partner.

As usual Richard Anderson was struggling with the shoulder holster, which he, almost alone in 22 SAS Regiment, preferred to the cross-draw. Wynwood got up and helped straighten out the strapping across his back. 'You need a mother,' he added helpfully as he resumed his seat.

'Don't we all,' Anderson agreed, zipping up his windcheater. 'You know what this place reminds me of?' he said, looking round. 'One of those recreation-ground dressing rooms we used on Sunday mornings when I was a kid.'

Wynwood followed Anderson's gaze round the barracks anteroom. 'We used to change behind a tree,' he said, consciously exaggerating the Welsh lilt to his voice.

'What, the whole team, behind one tree?'

Wynwood laughed. His partner seemed in better spirits today, after spending most of the previous day bemoaning the fact that it was Christmas Eve and he was 10,000 kilometres

1

away from Beth and the kids.

The thought was premature.

'What a way to spend Christmas Day,' Anderson said, as if he'd read Wynwood's mind.

The Welshman sighed. 'This *was* your idea.'

'You agreed.'

Yes, he had. After training the Colombian unit for six weeks it had seemed like a good idea to watch them in action. A sort of end-of-term master-class, with two SAS masters and the first Colombian Special Forces Anti-Narcotics Unit as the class. A practical exam. And then he and Andy would be homeward bound in time to welcome in the nineties, Hereford-style.

It was not soon enough for Anderson. 'It just doesn't seem right, not seeing the kids on Christmas Day,' he protested.

'So you keep telling me,' Wynwood said, letting a slight edge into his own voice. He could understand Anderson missing home, but he needed no reminding of what was probably going on in his own house on this particular Christmas Day.

Anderson looked at him. 'What's got into you?'

'Oh, nothing,' he sighed. 'Happy Christmas.'

'Yeah.' It was Anderson's turn to sigh. 'Where the fuck is Gómez?' he growled, getting up and stretching his arms above his head.

As if in reply, footsteps could be heard coming their way. 'I think Gómez the fuck is here,' Wynwood murmured.

The door opened to reveal a smiling officer. He was tall for a Colombian, with typical slicked-back raven hair and neat moustache, and a row of the neat white teeth which Anderson and Wynwood had come to see as the badge of the Colombian middle class. He was, the two Britons thought, an OK guy.

'We're ready,' Wynwood said, getting up.

'*Un momento*,' Captain Gómez said, holding his palms face forward. 'I have to say something you may not . . .' He searched for the right word. 'Appreciate?' he asked.

'Tell us in Spanish.'

Gómez nodded gratefully. 'Señor Muñoz has expressed concern about your presence at the meeting . . . You must understand' – the Colombian shrugged – 'two gringo guards – it makes him look like a tool of the Americans, like he is only saying what he says for the sake of foreigners, that he does not really have the interests of this nation at heart . . .'

'So what's the score?' Anderson interrupted.

'He is happy for you to be there, provided you keep a – how you say in English – a narrow profile?'

'A low profile. OK, we'll be as invisible as we can. Can we go now?'

'Of course.'

The two Britons swapped grimaces as Gómez led them outside into the barracks yard, where the procession was coiled like a snake, its motorcycle head by the closed gate. Behind this three ordinary saloons were sandwiched between the two armoured personnel carriers (APCs) into which Gómez's unit was being loaded.

'You will travel in the third car,' Gómez told them. 'I will be in the first with Señor Muñoz.'

'Which suckers are travelling in the middle car?' Wynwood wondered out loud.

'Oh, just some journalists,' Gómez said absentmindedly. He ushered them into the Toyota's back seat and closed the door.

'Neat,' Anderson said. 'If it all goes well, the journalists will be full of praise, and if it fucks up there's a fair chance they'll all be dead. That's what I call news management.'

3

Wynwood grinned. 'How did an Englishman get so cynical?' he murmured.

'Just paying attention, my son. You ought to try it sometime.'

Up front the motorcycles burst into life, the barracks gates were drawn open and the convoy slowly unwound itself to emerge onto the streets of Cali. It was dusk now, the north-running Calle Ramóna deep in shadow, the fading glow of the sunset visible above the mountains to the east at each intersection. For the moment they were heading towards the centre of the city, but their ultimate destination was the sprawling slum barrio of Malverdes on the city's north-western outskirts. There, in a local sports hall, Señor Muñoz would deliver an election speech to the downtrodden and the dispossessed.

Wynwood examined the view through the open window. He saw lots of concrete, the occasional palm tree, shuttered cafés, rubble, children interrupting their play to watch the convoy go past. Colombia was unfinished, Wynwood decided. The thing about England was that they had had two thousand years to fill in all the spaces, to do the place up properly, to finish the job. Here they had only had a few hundred, and it had been a big place to start with. It would not be finished for a while yet.

Thinking about England took his thoughts back, reluctantly but inexorably, to Susan. The thought of her and her boyfriend – whatever his goddamn name was – sent a shaft of anger surging from his stomach to his throat. It would be about eleven o'clock in England; they would probably be in the middle of a Christmas fuck, probably on his living-room carpet, under the Christmas tree he and Susan had successfully replanted last January. Well, he hoped the bastard got pine needles in his prick.

Why did he think about her? Why torture himself? He didn't want her back any more than she wanted him back. But it stuck somehow, stuck in his throat.

Andy was jogging his arm gently. 'Wake up,' he said.

The convoy was slowing down in the early evening traffic, making it an easier target. But the only immediate threat Wynwood could see was the plumes of toxic waste from the bus exhausts. 'No one's going to attack us before we pick up the Big Cheese,' he said.

'True,' Anderson agreed. 'You know, I don't think I could ever get used to hot weather at Christmas. It's perverse.'

'It's hot in Australia.'

'Everything's perverse in Australia.'

'It was probably hot in Bethlehem.'

'I'm talking Christmas here, not religion.'

'Sorry.'

They were halted at traffic lights, and Wynwood was watching a young boy – he could not have been more than six or seven – juggling balls between the cars on the front row. He had no sooner stopped juggling and offered his battered baseball cap for monetary reward than the lights changed. As they pulled away Wynwood saw first the balls then the cap escape from his clutch. And then the boy was kneeling on the street, tyres hissing past his ear, reaching for the silver pesos scattered on the tarmac.

Wynwood did not know why he always felt moved by such obvious evidence of poverty. Maybe his mother was right when she said it was a good heart. Maybe it just tugged at memories of his family's struggle to stay afloat when he was a kid in Pontarddulais. It did not matter either way, he concluded.

They were threading the more prosperous *avenidas* of the downtown section now, passing rows of shops with armed guards where laundered cocaine money could buy you Japanese technology and French fashions. A few minutes more and the convoy came to a halt in the semicircular forecourt of the high-rise Hotel Torre de Cali. All save the lead car, which had dived down into the underground parking lot to collect its political cargo. It emerged two minutes later, resumed its place as the convoy rolled out onto the Avenida de las Americas, and they were heading north-west again, out of the city centre, towards the wall of mountains which marked the western side of the Cauca valley.

The tropical night had fallen with its usual swiftness, and the dim yellow streetlamps were doing battle with a moonless sky. By contrast the occasional shrieking neon sign seemed to possess an eye-aching intensity. As always in Colombia, Wynwood found the change a forbidding one. Such a friendly place by day, but by night . . .

Away to the left, as if to reassure him, the large white illuminated statue of Jesus which stood on the slopes above the city was intermittently visible through gaps in the buildings.

The streetlamps grew rarer and seemingly dimmer, but it was still possible in the gloom to detect a progressive deterioration in the quality of life. Wynwood wondered what Señor Muñoz was thinking to himself two cars ahead. How did you come out to a place like this in a sharp suit and find something to say that anyone would listen to? It would be like Tory politicians turning up in Pontarddulais the day a local mine closed down. Not that they had, needless to say.

The lights seemed to be getting brighter. And there were more people on the sides of the road. They had reached another world.

The convoy moved down a crowded street and came to a halt outside a large, garishly lit concrete hall. Across the street

the words 'Pool! Pool! Pool!' were flashing in alternate yellow
and green neon, and youths with cues were visible through
the windows. Spanish-American pop music, which Wynwood
had decided was easily the worst music known to man, was
blaring overlapping rhythms from several different directions.
Children were already gathering round the armoured personnel
carriers, some open-mouthed, some happily taking the piss
out of the disembarking soldiers. One child had discovered
Wynwood and Anderson, and was clinging Garfield-like to
the rear passenger window of their car.

'What d'you reckon?' Wynwood asked.

'Sit it out a few minutes before we show our honky faces?'

'Yeah.'

The two of them watched Muñoz hustled professionally
past the welcoming horde and in through the doors of the
sports hall. He seemed taller than they had expected from
photographs, bespectacled, silvering hair glinting in the artificial light. His suit was sharp enough though.

'What do you know about him?' Anderson asked.

'Not a lot. He doesn't seem to have been around long.
But he's been gunning for the drug cartels for the last few
months . . .'

'So now they're gunning for him,' Anderson said dryly.

Wynwood shrugged. 'Who knows what makes those
bastards tick. They may think they're so fucking powerful
that people like Muñoz here aren't worth the time and trouble.'

'Well, we're probably going to get an earful this evening.'
He reached for the door handle. 'Miss Brodie, shall we go
and check out our pupils?'

'Miss Brodie was a fucking Scot.'

They clambered out into the warm air. Cali was slightly
less than a thousand metres above sea level, high enough to

7

take the edge off of the humidity, low enough not to get too cool at night. The smell of cooking filled the street.

'Makes you feel hungry, doesn't it?' Wynwood murmured.

'Anything makes *you* feel hungry. You're going to spread like a balloon in a few years' time.'

Wynwood smacked himself in the stomach with both hands. 'Pure muscle,' he said. 'At least I'm not a borderline anorexic,' he added, eyeing Anderson's willowy frame.

Anderson grunted. 'Ever feel you were in a Western movie?' he asked, surveying the scene around them.

'All the time,' Wynwood said, 'but I know what you mean.'

The street they were standing on arrowed off into distant darkness in both directions, and the bustling, brightly lit restaurants across the street seemed to have nothing behind them. It felt like a film set.

'Let's get inside.'

They went in through the main doors, exchanging grins with several of the men they had been training for the previous six weeks. In the main hall, wooden-floored and marked out for basketball, five-a-side football and other sports, several hundred plastic chairs had been arranged. Most were now occupied by a talking, shouting, laughing, screeching audience. Children roamed wild around and under the seats, though none had as yet got in among the ceiling beams. At the far end, on a raised platform made by pushing about twenty wooden tables together, Carlos Muñoz and a couple of local political heavies were sitting talking in another row of plastic chairs. The red, blue and yellow flags of Muñoz's political party were draped everywhere that flags could be draped.

The two SAS men made their way through to the area beside and slightly behind the stage, where another door led through to what looked like offices.

'When the talking starts I'll do the rounds,' Anderson said.

'You mean I have to listen to the speech?'

'I shall expect a full report,'

They did not have long to wait. One of the local men got to his feet, and after spending several minutes in a vain attempt to secure silence from the audience, finally managed to coax several ear-piercing shrieks from the PA system. That did the trick.

A few introductory words elicited more catcalls, and then Muñoz was on his feet. He knew how to handle an audience, Wynwood soon realized. It was not so much what he was saying as the simple way he had of saying it. The content was mostly predictable – corruption in government, the evil of the drug lords, the malign hand of Washington. All three supported each other, no matter how much they wished or claimed to do otherwise. While the American banks controlled the Colombian economy, drugs were the only way to pay for development. While the drug lords controlled all the profits from the trade the politicians were powerless and even the best of them liable to become corrupted.

In fact, Wynwood decided, Muñoz seemed to be arguing for the nationalization of the cocaine industry. Which did have a bizarre logic to it.

'I don't like it,' Anderson's voice sounded in his ear.

'What, the speech?' Wynwood asked, knowing he meant something else.

'Arsehole.'

Wynwood waited for Anderson to say something else, but he didn't. 'Sixth sense?'

Anderson sighed. 'Yeah.'

'Which way did you go? I'll take a look.'

'Out the front, round to the right and through the back door, which brings you into the office beyond this one. The exits are all covered. I just . . .' He shrugged.

'I'll do it in reverse,' Wynwood decided. He walked through the offices to the back door, where Jaime Morales, one of the friendlier Colombians in the Gómez unit, was in charge of a four-man team. 'No problems?' Wynwood asked him in Spanish.

'No.'

Wynwood eased himself out of the door and into a dark, narrow street. Night goggles would have been useful, he thought. Not that there seemed to be anything to see, even with night goggles. Still, he took Andy's sixth sense as seriously as he took his own, and any other SAS man's. 'The senses take in more stuff than the brain can deal with,' the instructor had told them in one of Hereford's classrooms, 'so it comes back lacking clarity, more of a feeling than a thought. Don't ignore something because you can't quite work out where it's coming from or what it is. It may be nemesis coming to call.'

At which point Ben Young had asked whether nemesis wasn't the first book in the Bible. Ben, a long time gone now, was one of those lost to the freezing South Atlantic waters during the Falklands War.

You're getting maudlin in your old age, Wynwood, he thought to himself. A true son of Owain Glyndwr.

He gingerly turned the corner off the hall and padded down the alley which ran along its side to the main street. The latter looked the same, but it did feel different. Or was he imagining it because of Andy? There seemed to be a stillness in the air, a tension. The three cars shining by the front door seemed vulnerable, the group of soldiers smoking by the armoured patrol car complacently cocky. Wynwood couldn't *see* anything, but . . .

He went back indoors. Muñoz was still talking, the audience still listening with what seemed like interest.

Anderson looked at him quizzically.

'Yeah, I think we should talk to Gómez.'

'And tell him what?'

'That he's going to need some help.'

'Rather you than me.'

'OK.' Wynwood looked round. 'Where is he?'

'Out the back, I think.'

Wynwood walked through one office and into the other. Gómez was sitting on a table, talking on the phone to someone, and at that moment something happened, because he stopped talking, shook the phone and then tried listening. 'It's . . .' he started to say, but the rest of his sentence was swallowed by the sound of the explosion.

Anderson did not just hear the explosion – he saw it. And he had a pretty good idea what had caused it too – a rocket, fired from a mobile launcher, impacting on the front APC outside.

The explosion had blown the windows in, and bits of at least one trooper with them. The flying glass had hit the audience side on, and the sound of a huge collective scream seemed to be rending the air in its wake. Anderson, half behind the makeshift platform on the side farthest from the door, was unhurt, save for a small cut on his cheek. He was just starting forward to check out what had happened to Muñoz when, through the blasted window frames, silhouetted against the lighted windows on the other side of the main street, he saw several figures appear, arms stretched to throw. Recognizing the cylindrical missiles while they were in mid-air, he dropped to his knees, covering eyes and ears with his arms.

The dozen or so stun grenades exploded, searing the eyes with their flaring magnesium, lashing the eardrums with overlapping blasts of sound. Even with his eyes and ears covered it felt to Anderson like the end of the world.

11

The silence which followed was almost as complete, but only for a moment, as whimpers rose to wails and wails to screams for help. Anderson looked round for Wynwood, but found only Muñoz, kneeling not two metres away, shaking badly and looking round blindly, blood flowing from a cut above his eye. Above him, above the whole ghastly scene, the row of phosphorescent lights that hung from the beams were flickering like demented telegraph machines.

The shout 'Fire!' penetrated Anderson's brain, and he turned to see a second shower of missiles rain in through the windows, followed, seconds later, by the hiss of gas.

The echoes of the initial rocket attack were still humming in the air when a shout from the guards on the back door announced the presence of enemies in the alley at the rear. A succession of shots followed. Gómez and Wynwood exchanged glances. 'Take the back door,' the Colombian said, and without waiting for agreement hurried back through the other office towards the hall.

Wynwood was drawing the Browning from its holster when a figure burst through the door in question, carrying a Heckler & Koch MP5 sub-machine-gun. At the same moment the stun grenades detonated in the hall behind him. Which was lucky for Wynwood. The newcomer was facing the flash, and even through two doorways this gave him enough pause for Wynwood to fire a double tap through his forehead.

'Shut the door!' he screamed at one of the troops. 'And keep it covered.'

Wynwood turned and walked swiftly – the temptation to run was almost irresistible, but only Clint Eastwood could aim a pistol on the run. Gómez was struggling to his feet, trying to shake the blindness out of his eyes; behind him Andy was looking round. Gas canisters were coming through the window.

'Andy,' he screamed.

'Yeah.' Anderson was grabbing Muñoz by the shoulder. 'Let's take the prize home ourselves,' he shouted.

Wynwood went to help him, holding his breath as the gas billowed round the hall. Already his nose and eyes seemed to be running. Now. he knew what the terrorists in the Iranian Embassy must have felt like.

They managed to pull the politician into the first office, and to slam the door behind them against the gas.

'Where now, Tonto?' Anderson asked. He seemed to be having the time of his life. The sound of gunfire now seemed to be coming from all round the building.

'Out of here,' Wynwood suggested.

'Sounds good.'

Beside them Muñoz seemed to be coming out of the dis-orientation caused by the stun grenades. 'What is happening? What do you want?' He wiped his face with the back of his hand, looked at the blood as if surprised it was there.

'We're the British trainers of this unit,' Wynwood explained. And not too proud of it at the moment, he thought to himself. 'And we're getting you out of here,' he continued.

'But . . .'

'No buts,' Anderson interrupted, hustling Muñoz towards the back door and almost tripping over the Colombian Wynwood had killed a few minutes earlier. 'Nice shooting, partner,' he murmured, noticing the twin holes in the fore-head. 'What now. Shall we ring for a taxi?'

Wynwood ignored him. 'We're taking El Señor out of here,' he told Morales. 'Straight across the alley and through the door that's dead opposite. You and Jesus here can give us covering fire.' He thought for a second, then knelt down and extricated the MP5 from the dead Colombian's hands.

'OK,' he said, 'open the door.'

Morales pushed it outwards, and a volley of fire stitched a pattern on the inner face. Then there was silence.

'Go!' shouted Wynwood.

The two Colombians almost flew through the door, into the rolls the SAS trainers had taught them, coming to rest face down in the middle of the alley, their M16s opening up in opposite directions.

Wynwood was proud of them. 'I'll take the door,' he told Anderson.

Anderson just nodded. 'Get ready,' he told Muñoz, as Wynwood half ran, half rolled across the alley and landed in the opposite doorway with a thud. Ricochets echoed down the walls.

'Shit,' Wynwood muttered. He was getting too old for this. He allowed his eyes a few seconds to adjust to the darkness, and then searched the door for the lock. But there seemed not to be one. He tried the handle and the door opened. 'Our lucky day,' he murmured, and beckoned to Anderson.

At that moment a volley of fire seemed to kick up dust in front of one of the spread-eagled Colombians. It was Jesús. He seemed to cough apologetically as the rifle dropped from his hands.

'Go!' Anderson told Muñoz on the other side of the great divide.

Muñoz looked at him like he was mad. 'No!' he shouted, turning away towards the door leading back towards the hall. As he did so a gas canister bounced off his foot, rolled away and exploded.

With a sound like a moan Muñoz turned and ran straight out through the door, across the alley and in through the open door opposite, bullets whining round his head. Anderson was right behind him, taking the more professional approach, trying to vary the speed and profile of his body as he made the dash.

'I'll check the back,' Wynwood said, and was gone.

'What now?' Muñoz asked Anderson, who ignored him. 'Keep it slow,' he was whispering to Morales, who was edging snakewise towards the doorway. Jesús's body had the limpness of death.

On the far side someone was unwise enough to silhouette himself against the lighted office. For a second Anderson thought it was Gómez, but the man shouted something to others out of sight in a voice the SAS man did not recognize, and just for safety's sake he put a 'double tap' through the man's trunk. He sank to his knees clutching his stomach.

Morales reached the relative safety of the doorway. 'Two,' Anderson said out loud, counting his shots expended. From each direction down the alley he could hear men gathering; he hoped to God Wynwood had found another way out.

He had. 'This way,' the Welshman shouted, and Anderson half pushed Muñoz after him, Morales bringing up the rear. The building seemed to be disused, just a series of empty rooms bisected by a corridor. Wynwood led them out across a freshly flattened back door, through an overgrown yard to a dilapidated corrugated fence. Through one of the many gaps they could see a steep bank leading down to a river.

There was no time for consideration. Wynwood half scrambled, half fell down the slope and into the water. It was deeper, colder and faster-flowing than he had expected, and for a second he had troubling keeping the MP5 clear of the water without losing his balance. The lack of light was a further complication; from the deep channel cut by the river he could see only the stars above and a far bank which might be ten metres away – or fifty.

Muñoz arrived with a splash beside him, followed by Morales and Anderson. The politician started to say something, but Anderson's finger in front of his mouth made him aware of the virtues of silence. Wynwood struck out across the river, the water up to his chest, the current tugging at his body.

The river was about fifteen metres wide. Once the others were all safely across Wynwood started pulling himself up the steep slope, and was just about to breast the rise when noises across the river told him that pursuers had reached the top of the bank they had clambered down. He froze, conscious that he and the others would be masked by the darkness, praying the enemy did not have a torch.

They didn't. But neither did they seem inclined to retrace their steps. Instead, one of them lit a cigarette, giving a snapshot of his face in the glow of the match, and the two of them started an inaudible conversation.

After half a minute of this Wynwood began to wonder whether it might be worth trying to take them both out with the MP5. It would be noisy, but not exactly difficult, even in light like this . . .

The drone of a helicopter insinuated its way into his attention. It had to be behind him, coming towards them. Was it the police? The Army? The enemy?

'Whatever,' he murmured to himself. The helicopter seemed almost overhead now. Wynwood pulled the MP5 into firing position, and as the helicopter passed across the river, about fifty metres downstream of their position and not much higher, he raked the two silhouettes on the far bank. Both were thrown back into the corrugated fence with a crash, the lighted cigarette flying up and forward before extinguishing itself in the river.

Wynwood turned and climbed over the rim of the bank. In front of him he could see several empty railway tracks running parallel to the gentle curve of the river. Beyond them what looked like a large warehouse stretched for about fifty metres in either direction. Two loading docks were built into its side, and one of them was open, letting out the dimmest glow. There had to be a road beyond it all.

By the time he had taken all this in the others had scrambled up the bank to join him. Above the buildings on the far bank the helicopter's lights were now moving across the sky. It was circling. Wynwood no longer had any doubts about whose it was.

'I'll recce,' he told Anderson, and without waiting for an answer struck off along the tracks to the right.

'You OK?' Anderson asked Muñoz, who was crouching beside him.

The Colombian managed a wry smile. 'Yes,' he answered. 'I think so.'

'Jaime?'

'Yes, boss.'

The helicopter was coming almost directly towards them now, its drone growing louder. As it crossed the river someone switched on its spotlight, just too late to catch the huddled group.

Wynwood was not so lucky. He was just recrossing the tracks when the light went on, catching him almost in mid-spot for one brief, revealing second. Then the helicopter had overshot, and he was invisible again. But not for long. It was already banking, and Wynwood had only a few seconds. 'I'll lead them off,' he shouted in English to Anderson. 'There's a way through to a road off to your right. You look after the Big Cheese!'

The helicopter was flying towards them along the tracks, throwing its circle of light forward like a single huge headlamp beam, reaching out for the running Wynwood, catching him and holding him. But only for a second. As someone opened up with a sub-machine-gun the SAS man swerved away to the right, launched himself up off the nearest rail onto the loading stage and disappeared through the open doorway.

Anderson led the others to the right, round the corner of the warehouse and up a rutted alley to the road. On its far side single-storey houses stretched away up the slope, like a hillside of oversized shoeboxes. Some windows showed a dim light, but there were no other signs of life. It was not yet eight o'clock and the district seemed half dead. Or simply keeping its collective head under the pillow.

Anderson could hear but not see the helicopter. At that moment a wash of light advanced along the wall opposite and then stopped – a car had pulled up round the bend to the left.

Muñoz and Morales were standing waiting in the shadows, both looking as though they would rather be somewhere else. If it had been Cup Final day, Anderson thought, their manager would say they had 'frozen'. Both men were certainly shivering, but then sopping clothes and a cool breeze were hardly a recipe for warmth.

Anderson beckoned with a finger, and the three of them started off to the right, leaving behind the wash of light. Morales was limping, he noticed. And Muñoz just seemed exhausted by the night's excitement.

There was no way they were all going to walk out of here, Anderson realized. They needed transport.

Pausing to look back he could see the helicopter some half a kilometre away, almost motionless in the air, its light shining down like one of those beams flying saucers in movies always used to pull up their helpless prey. As he watched another helicopter appeared in the distance, also trailing its spotlight like a net.

18

'Boss,' Morales whispered loudly. 'Look'.

It was a car.

Wynwood's building had turned out to be an abattoir. He ran headlong down a long corridor, past rows of what looked like refrigerated rooms, out into an office area, through to another landing dock. At its edge, watching his rapid approach like startled rabbits caught in a headlight, were two Colombian men – presumably the nightwatchmen. Wynwood had no sooner taken in their presence than he saw another man, better dressed and gun in hand, halfway between a parked car and the loading dock.

Ignoring the first two men, Wynwood went over the loading dock, into a double roll and opened up with the MP5. The man with the gun sank to his knees, surprise on his face.

As a bullet clattered off the corrugated warehouse wall behind him, and as the helicopter appeared round the rim of the warehouse roof, Wynwood rolled once more, sending a concentrated burst through the windscreen of the waiting car. Then, as the pilot struggled to flood the yard with light, he outran it, out through the gate, across the road and into the alleys of the slum quarter opposite.

The car looked new, and what it was doing sitting on the verge of a minor road with its doors wide open Anderson had no idea.

Morales did. 'Riders of joy,' he said in Spanish. It was obvious really. 'They couldn't take it home' – he indicated the hillside across the road – 'but they saved themselves a long walk.'

Muñoz got in the back, Morales in the front, and Anderson demonstrated one of the many skills he had learned at Hereford – hot-wiring. He started the car, and eased it back onto the road, hoping the sound of the engine would be masked by the two helicopters hovering above them. The windscreen was filthy, and he was just wondering whether to get out and wipe it when lights appeared behind him.

He eased the car forward, and for something like fifty metres the car behind simply followed them. Then, suddenly, as if a decision had been taken, the trailing car accelerated forward, flashing its lights for them to stop.

Anderson reckoned from his rear-view mirror that there were at least three men in it. He pressed down on the accelerator, thinking: Christ, what a place! It was like a mixture of Chicago gangsters, *Miami Vice* and the fucking IRA – and all in a foreign language.

Wynwood made his way carefully through the darkened alleys of the slum barrio. He could feel people all around him, twitching their paper curtains, staring out through candlelit cracks in their doors, muttering to each other. They knew he was passing through, all right.

The real enemy still did not, if the activities of the helicopters were anything to go by. One was sweeping the valley bottom, its spotlight turning the rails into silver arcs and the waters of the river to boiling ink. The other was still hovering above the warehouse. Then, as Wynwood watched, it suddenly veered away to the south, as if yanked by a sudden signal.

He turned and carried on up the hill, a rank smell growing slowly stronger in his nostrils. Reaching the crest a few minutes later, he discovered its source. Here the houses abruptly ended, and in the valley below there was only rubbish, mountains of it, stretching as far as his eyes could see.

A couple of kilometres to the south Anderson accelerated down another dark street, the car like a bucking bronco on the potholed surface. Behind them the pursuit was neither gaining nor losing ground. 'Which way?' he asked Morales and Muñoz. Neither answered. Glancing in the rear-view mirror, he noticed that Muñoz seemed to be praying.

Anderson squealed the car round another corner. Above the buildings on the right-hand side of the road the dark shape of a helicopter loomed across the stars. Why didn't the bastards open fire?

And then it occurred to him how they had managed to get this far. The bastards wanted Muñoz alive. Which had to give him some sort of edge. All he had to do was stay ahead.

Another intersection was approaching. And bright lights. He slowed marginally, decided on a left turn and took the corner on two wheels.

A familiar-looking convoy of cars appeared in front of him, headed by a wrecked APC. Outside the hall the road was covered in people, presumably those brought out since the original attack.

All this took a second to take in. He swung the wheel to the right, towards a side-street opening, just as two children stepped out to cross. Another wrench of the wheel missed them but not the corner building. The front right of the car struck it at an angle, catapulting Jaime Morales out through the windscreen, and slamming Anderson's head against the roof as it slammed his chest again the steering wheel. He had one last glimpse of gunmen walking carefully towards the car before he blacked out.

Wynwood found a mound that seemed suitable and started to dig himself into it. The garbage was fresh, which carried a twofold advantage. For one thing it had not had time to congeal, which would make made it easier to penetrate

21

without leaving obvious signs. For another the stink was so bad it would deter anyone from looking too closely.

The downside was only too obvious to Wynwood as he worked himself into and under the putrid heap. The famed ditch at Hereford, filled with animal entrails, was lavender compared with this.

1

It was a minute past midnight in Bogotá. President Juan
Estrada was happily settled in front of the TV in that part
of the Presidential Palace reserved for his personal use. His
wife had finally gone to bed, and he had three back-to-back
episodes of *Dallas* to watch on his video. He was not sure
what vintage they were – they might even be from the series
which had turned out to be only Pam Ewing's dream – but
that didn't matter.

In fact these days the further he got from reality the better
Estrada liked it. So he was not particularly pleased when his
Filipino houseboy brought news that his Minister of the
Interior had arrived to see him on urgent business.

'I suppose you'd better show him up,' the President said
reluctantly, freezing the video on the Miss Ellie who had
come back from the dead. He smiled to himself.

Luis Quintana was not smiling. 'Juan,' he began, 'I'm sorry
to interrupt your Christmas, but this couldn't wait.' He looked
across at the drinks tray. 'Can I help myself?' he asked.

'What can't wait?' Estrada asked.

'Carlos Muñoz has been kidnapped.'

A faint smile appeared on the President's face.

Quintana poured himself a large neat whisky. 'In Cali. He was out in some slum barrio, talking to the poor, and . . .' He shrugged. 'They snatched him.'

'Who?'

'Not sure. But it looks like either the Escobars or the Amarales. Whoever it was, they managed to kill about twenty people in the process.'

Estrada grunted. 'Ransom, you think?'

'Probably.' Quintana took a large hit of whisky.

'Who'd pay?'

'His family,' Quintana suggested.

Estrada grimaced. Muñoz was standing against him in three months' time for the Party's Presidential nomination. And as matters stood lately it looked like the bastard had a chance of winning, regardless of the fact that Estrada was the incumbent president of the country. 'I could always pay the bastards to keep him,' he said sardonically.

'Some people may think you paid the bastards to snatch him,' Quintana replied mildly. 'And there's more. One of the two English Special Forces people was taken with him. You know, the ones your favourite Mrs Thatcher let you borrow.'

'She's not my favourite! I just enjoyed annoying the Americans by taking English soldiers as advisers.'

'Well, she's not going to be pleased.'

'So she won't be pleased.' He thought for a moment. 'What about the other Englishman?'

'He's missing.'

'Wonderful,' Estrada said wryly.

'Anyway, in a few hours your favourite will probably be on the phone asking you what steps are being taken to find one soldier and release the other.'

'I'll take the phone off the hook.'

24

Quintana sat down opposite Estrada. 'Juan, I agree it doesn't matter a damn what the British want or think. But Muñoz is another matter. You know as well as I do that this nation is like a house of cards. Take one out, any one, and the whole thing's liable to come down on our heads. Muñoz is the acceptable face of our system. You know and I know that he's just a stupid dreamer who wouldn't recognize the real world if it bit him . . .'

'It looks like it just has,' Estrada interjected sourly.

'Maybe. As far as Washington and a lot of our own people are concerned, the Muñozes are the only reason they give us any credibility at all. Muñoz is proof that the cartels don't run the nation.'

'They do, near as damn it.'

Quintana suppressed his exasperation. 'Yes, but as long as it looks like they have some opposition the Americans are not going to turn the country into a free-fire zone to protect their bored children from cocaine and our own people are still going to pay taxes to us as well as the cartels. We may not need Muñoz but we need people like him, and it has to look like we're trying to get him back.'

'It'd be nice to fail.'

'I agree we could find a more satisfactory opponent for you for the election, but . . .'

'So, find me the biggest idiot of a general you can and we'll send him off.'

'No. It would have to be our best people. But anyway I have another idea. Why not let the British do it for you? Their men need rescuing too, and if they fail we have a convenient scapegoat, no?'

'Could they even attempt such an operation so far from England?'

'The Malvinas?' Quintana said dryly.

'That was a full-scale military operation.'

'I know. But they have the capacity, believe me.'

'They might refuse.'

Quintana laughed. 'They are far too arrogant to refuse. Particularly when it's pointed out – tactfully of course – that their men's incompetence was responsible for the success of the kidnap attempt.'

'Was it?'

'They trained the unit who were supposed to be protecting Muñoz.'

Estrada thought about it. 'You said if they fail we have a scapegoat. What if they succeed?'

'We'd be no worse off. In fact, when I think about it, we'd be better off. Who will be able to claim the credit for bringing them in? You. What selflessness! All that ingenuity and effort, just to rescue your main opponent from the cartels. Everyone will be impressed.'

Estrada shook his head. 'I still think I'd rather have Muñoz in a box.'

Quintana was looking at his watch. 'It's 5 a.m. in London. No point in waking them up. You can talk to your favourite first thing in the morning.'

'OK,' the President agreed. 'Now go away and let me watch TV.'

With almost infinite patience Wynwood eased his head out through the top layer of fetid rubbish. For at least a minute he held the same position, not moving his head, eyes growing accustomed to the darkness, ears straining for any sounds of human activity. There seemed to be none. With the same patience he slowly swivelled his head. There was darkness all around. Tilting his head upwards he discovered, thankfully, that the stars he would need for navigation were still twinkling in a clear sky.

Still conscious of the need to make as little noise as possible, he eased himself out of the flank of the rubbish mountain and gingerly descended to the firmer ground around its base. To his surprise he could hardly smell it any more. Doubtless anyone else would be able to smell him a mile away.

There did not seem to be a shower handy.

He brushed himself off as best as he could, thinking it had been worth it. Several times over the last eight hours he had heard dogs not far off, but no dog alive would have been able to trail him through the *mélange* of smells in this place.

His watch, guaranteed to withstand two hundred metres of water – so useful for a time-conscious manta ray, Wynwood thought – had managed to survive one metre of Colombian refuse. It was four after four, which gave him around two hours more of darkness. He had decided against going back into Cali – there was just no way of knowing who could be trusted. No, it had to be Bogotá, where at least the presence of embassies induced a notional sense of one law for everyone. And anyway, it was on the way home to Blighty.

So which way? Memory told Wynwood that Malverdes was north-north-west of the city centre, and that the main north road out of Cali actually ran due north-east across the valley before heading due north along the bottom of the mountains. So, eight kilometres north would take him clear of the city, then the same distance east should bring him to that road. Sixteen kilometres in two hours should not be beyond him, not travelling as light as he was. Keeping one eye on the Pole Star, which nestled close to the horizon this far south, he started wending his way through the valley of rubbish.

It covered another two kilometres before giving way to a stretch of bare hillside presumably earmarked as an extension. Beyond this he found himself pushing through steeply sloping cornfields, the tumbledown shacks of their owners often visible as a dim square of black in the valley below. These in turn gave way to less broken slopes, mostly bare, which reminded him, in the dark at least, of the Brecon Beacons.

For once his SAS training seemed almost too apt. His thoughts went back to that day in Initial Training almost ten years before, crawling on all fours through the trench filled with water and sheeps' intestines and God knew what else. At the end of that day they had pulled the trick of having the waiting lorries drive off just when you thought the agony was over. He had been almost swinging his arm back to belt the officer when someone else had beaten him to it. And had of course been RTU'd – Returned To Unit. Not SAS material.

Wynwood grinned to himself. First the Brecon Beacons, then Mount Kent in the Falklands campaign, now the fucking Andes. Next year, Nepal!

He walked on, gradually swinging his line of march east of north and downhill. Over the next few kilometres he crossed several small dirt roads, passed many small homesteads and one larger-looking *estancia*, reaching the shallow banks of the River Cauca at almost exactly 05.30. To the east he thought he could make out the faintest seepage of light above the mountains. Full daylight was less than an hour away.

As he sat on his haunches a light crossed his line of vision to the east. A car or truck. As he watched another glow moved in the opposite direction. It had to be the main highway, three kilometres away at most.

Wynwood slid into a river for the second time that night. This one seemed even colder, but the current was leisurely, and he had no difficulty traversing its thirty metres with the two guns held above his head. After examining the lie of the land on the far side – an orchard stretching off into the distance – he left the guns on the bank and went back into the water to thoroughly wash himself and his clothes.

He climbed out feeling a lot cleaner. Hot water would have been nice, not to mention a bar of soap, but beggars can't be choosers. Especially after dark in Colombia. He picked up the two guns, thought for a moment, then turned and hurled the MP5 up and out into the centre of the river. It was just a trifle conspicuous for daylight.

A long walk up through orchards and more cornfields eventually brought him to the side of the highway. He waited in the half-light for a few minutes, watching two cars, one bus and one truck go by, then hurried across and up the opposite slope. While the invisible sun rose beyond the mountains he followed a course out of sight of, but parallel to, the highway. After about five kilometres he found what he was looking for – a roadside eating-place. On the slope above it he stripped, laid his clothes out to dry in the sun, and settled down to wait and watch. It was just past nine o'clock.

In London it was already four in the afternoon. Barney Davies was not sorry to leave the house in Bloomsbury where his wife, their three children and her new husband were celebrating Boxing Day. In fact the mixture of polite chatter, unserious drinking and repressed anger was likely to give celebration a bad name. It was all for the kids, of course, and predictably enough they had shown their appreciation

29

of this sacrificial get-together by disappearing into the remotest corners of the house. Happy families.

It was a cold day, and not exactly bright, but the clouds were high enough to ward off a depressing gloom. And at least it was a pleasure to drive through London's near-deserted streets. The city had an almost post-holocaust feel to it – all that was really needed was a few cars skewed across the pavement, the odd body.

You cheerful bastard, Davies told himself, guiding the BMW down the half-empty Strand. He wondered if any more news of Joss and Andy had come in, and whether their disappearance was the reason he had been summoned to the Whitehall conference room. He would soon find out.

He parked off Horse Guards Road and walked through the maze of buildings and covered walkways towards the back of Downing Street. His pass was examined three times, the final time by a doorkeeper who recognized him from his last visit. That had been several years ago, and his lads had ended up taking back an African country for its rightful government. Whatever that might be in Africa.

He climbed the stairs to Conference Room B, wondering, as last time, where Conference Room A might be. Two men he did not know were already sitting on one side of the table. Unlike him they were wearing suits and ties. He smiled at them and sat down. Half a minute later a more familiar figure arrived – one of the Foreign Office ministers, Davies knew, though he could not remember the name. And on his heels the Prime Minister, who treated them all to a wide smile and a hint of gardenia.

She took her seat at the head of the rectangular walnut table, and introduced everyone. Across from Davies were Pennington (young and studious-looking, from the Foreign

Office's Latin America section) and Spenser (fair and harassed-looking, from MI6). The tall, patrician man he had recognized was Alan Holcroft, a junior minister at the Foreign Office.

'And you all know who I am,' the Prime Minister added without apparent humour.

'Very well,' she went on, 'I'm sorry to have to drag you all in here on Boxing Day' – she looked about as sorry as a cat with a bowl of fresh cream, Davies thought – 'but something has come up that requires immediate attention. All of you, except perhaps Lieutenant-Colonel Davies here' – she gave him a brief smile – 'have some idea of what this is about, but for the Lieutenant-Colonel's sake I'll summarize what we know for certain at this moment. Please correct me if I make any mistakes.' She glanced around, as if daring anyone to show such temerity.

'Two of Lieutenant-Colonel Davies's men, Sergeants Wynwood and Anderson, both I believe of 22 SAS's Training Wing . . .?' She gave him a questioning look.

'That is correct,' Davies agreed. So it was about Joss and Andy.

'These two men have been on secondment in Colombia, training a new Anti-Narcotics Unit at the express invitation of the Colombian President. As you know, this is the sort of job the SAS has fulfilled, with great success, in many parts of the world over the last thirty years. And of course it's in all our interests to strengthen the forces fighting against the drug trade in South America.'

She paused for breath. 'Their ten-week term of secondment was due to end this coming weekend. However, yesterday – Christmas Day – they accompanied the Anti-Narcotics Unit on an operation. This had nothing to do with drugs apparently – it

involved ensuring the security of a prominent politician' – she
checked the memorandum in front of her – 'one Carlos
Muñoz, at a meeting in the town of Cali. This meeting was
attacked, either by guerrillas or gangsters of the drug trade,
and at least fifteen people have been killed. Muñoz and the
two SAS men were apparently not among them. They have
simply disappeared, and the presumption is that they have
been kidnapped.

'Are there questions at this stage?' she asked.

'What do we know about this Muñoz?' Holcroft asked
his minion from the Latin American section.

Pennington adjusted his glasses and started off on what
seemed a prepared speech. 'He is a prominent member of the
Colombian Liberal Party, and the signs are that he intends
to challenge Juan Estrada, the current national President, for
their Party's nomination for the next Presidential election this
summer. He's a liberal with a small "l" too, almost a social
democrat by Colombian standards, so he's critical of the
current Government, and he's also talked a lot about the need
for stronger action against the drug cartels. In fact, more than
once he's hinted at high-level connections between the current
Government and the cartels . . .'

'How do the Americans feel about him?' Holcroft
interrupted.

'Er . . . That's hard to say. They distrust him because he's
rather left-wing, but they like his anti-drug stance, so . . .'

'So they haven't got a clue,' Holcroft half sneered.

The Prime Minister frowned at him.

'If he's such a threat why wasn't he simply killed?' the
MI6 man asked Pennington.

'He may have been by now. But there's a long history
of kidnapping politicians for ransom in Colombia. They

– whoever they are – may just want money. Or they may want to use possession of Muñoz as a means of exerting pressure on his liberal friends.'

'And our SAS men?' the Prime Minister asked, taking the words out of Davies's mouth.

'Again they may simply want money. Or perhaps they intend to use the SAS men as bargaining counters. We have several minor cartel people in prison here. They may want them released.'

'Well, they can forget that idea,' the Prime Minister said, half to herself. 'Thank you, Mr Pennington. Now, there is one further fact of which you are all unaware. This afternoon, an hour or so after the first news had come through from our embassy in Bogotá, I received a personal call from the Colombian President. He expressed his regrets, but doubted whether the forces at his disposal would prove equal to the task of rescuing either Muñoz or our men . . .'

'That seems likely,' Pennington muttered.

'. . . and then, well, not to put too fine a point on it, he invited us' – her glance came to rest on Davies – 'to go and get our men back ourselves.'

'What?' Holcroft half spluttered.

She shot him a withering glance. 'Before we ask whether this *should* be done, I'd like an opinion on whether it *could* be done. Lieutenant-Colonel Davies?'

All Davies's military instincts revolted against giving a snap judgement. He knew next to nothing about either Colombia in particular or South America in general. But he also knew this was a crucial moment, that the Prime Minister expected a yes, perhaps even needed one to get the possibility past people like Holcroft. And damn it, if anyone could do it, 22 SAS could.

33

These thoughts occupied about two seconds. 'Yes, it could be done,' he said. 'With one obvious proviso – we'd have to know where they're being held.'

'What base would you use?' Holcroft asked.

'Belize,' Davies said, almost without thinking. It was probably close enough. If not, they would have to think again. But in the ops room at Hereford, not in Conference Room B with the PM looming over the table.

'Will finding them prove a problem?' the Prime Minister was asking the MI6 man.

'Hard to say,' he said diffidently. 'We have a reasonable network in Colombia, and our friends have an even better one.'

'I wouldn't like to be the one to tell the Americans we're envisaging military action in Colombia,' Holcroft said.

The Prime Minister stared at her memorandum for a few seconds. 'Very well,' she said at last. 'Let us assume it could be done. What do we risk and what do we potentially gain, apart from the rescue of our men, by trying? Alan, could you describe the risks. Then perhaps Mr Pennington could describe the potential gains.' She smiled at the latter, as if to encourage him.

Holcroft was silent for a moment, wondering, Davies guessed, how to present his case in the light most likely to please his boss. 'I don't wish to cast doubts on our forces' ability to overcome the military problems inherent in such an operation,' the Foreign Office man began, 'but I have to point out that the perils of failure would be immense. For one thing we would look like a colonial power all over again, undoing all the good repair work our people have done in Latin America since the Falklands. The cost in trade would probably be severe . . .'

'Even if we're there by invitation?' the MI6 man asked.

'It won't be by *public* invitation,' Holcroft said acidly. 'I repeat, the trade consequences will be severe. Secondly, our relations with the Americans will be damaged whatever happens. Latin America is *their* backyard, and they never forget it. If we inform them of any upcoming operation it will probably be leaked, and if we don't they'll accuse us of not even having the courtesy to tell them when we're trespassing on their turf.'

He leant back in his chair. 'I need hardly add that we will be risking the lives of many soldiers for the sake of two men whose lives, as far as we know at this moment, are not in immediate danger.'

The Prime Minister nodded. 'Mr Pennington?'

'I agree with everything Mr Holcroft has just said,' he started diplomatically. 'However, Colombia is potentially one of our most important trading partners in South America, and gaining the goodwill of the next President – whether it be Estrada or Muñoz – would be worthwhile in this respect. If successful, the operation would add to the prestige of both Britain and the SAS. The latter, if I may put it so' – he glanced almost apologetically at Davies – 'is a saleable commodity in its own right these days, and new demonstrations of prowess and efficiency make it more so. I realize such an operation won't be front-page news, but I imagine those who matter will hear of it. And, with all due respect' – another nod in Davies's direction – 'the same can be said of what appears to be yesterday's failure . . .'

'Señor Estrada seemed to hold the same opinion,' the Prime Minister said dryly.

Pennington shrugged. 'As for the Americans, such an operation would doubtless irritate some of them, but I think the added respect we'd get from others would probably more than compensate.' He too leant back in his chair.

'Do you have anything to add, Mr Spenser?' the Prime Minister asked.

'No.'

'I do,' she said. 'I think the successful conduct of such an operation would increase our respect for ourselves. But, we cannot reach a final decision at this moment. In the meantime – Mr Spenser, please get your people in Colombia moving. Thank you, gentlemen, that is all.' She got to her feet. 'If you could stay behind, Lieutenant-Colonel Davies.'

Davies looked at the framed picture of a tea schooner as the others filed out. In Victorian times Palmerston would just have sent a gunboat, he thought to himself. Nowadays they'd send the SAS. It felt desperately old-fashioned, and it made him feel proud just the same.

'Lieutenant-Colonel . . . Barney,' she corrected herself with a smile. 'Start planning. And assume it's on unless and until I tell you it's off.'

'Yes, Ma'am,' Davies said to her disappearing back.

He walked thoughtfully back to his car, and sat staring out through the windscreen at the tops of the bare trees in St James's Park. 'Hereford!' he said suddenly to himself. He'd ring the kids on the car phone once he was on the M40. It was only a couple of hours since he had seen them – they would still remember who he was.

Joss Wynwood, now dressed in dry clothes, albeit ones that looked like they had been danced on by horses, carefully descended the hill beyond the roadside restaurant, taking care to keep whatever tree cover there was between him and the back windows. For three hours he had been waiting and watching a long line of trucks pull into the parking area, and at last one had parked in the exact place which he had been hoping for.

Reaching the foot of the hill Wynwood found he had got his angles right. Anyone crossing the ground between the trees and the truck's cab could not be seen from the restaurant's windows. He walked swiftly across, found the cab door open, and slid into the sleeping space behind the two seats.

About twenty minutes later the driver returned, opening the door and pausing to belch loudly before climbing up into the driving seat. He pulled the door to, belched again, rather more softly, and caught sight of Wynwood in his rear-view mirror.

'*Qué?!*' he exclaimed, turning round angrily. '*Qué . . .?*' he started again, breaking off abruptly when he saw the Browning.

'I need a lift,' Wynwood said softly in Spanish.

'Sure, sure,' the driver said, his hand reaching almost involuntarily for the door. 'But please, no guns.'

'If you open the door I shall shoot you,' Wynwood said steadily. 'Now start the engine, and let's go.'

'Yes, yes. Where? Where do we go?'

'Where are you headed?' Wynwood asked.

A look of cunning flashed across the driver's face. 'Cali,' he said. 'Cali.'

'You just came from Cali,' Wynwood said patiently. 'You're going north. Where to?'

'Ibagué.'

'That will do fine. Drive. In the meantime . . .' He reached past the Colombian for the paper bag. 'I think my need is greater than yours.'

'If you are hungry I can go back for more.'

'Nice try, bozo. Drive.'

'I am Manuel,' the driver said indignantly.

'Figures,' said Wynwood.

'*Qué?*'

'Drive!'

Manuel pulled the truck out onto the highway.

'Jesus, she's gorgeous!' Kilcline almost groaned.

'You could say that,' Bourne agreed, licking the Guinness head off his upper lip and following his partner's gaze. Its object was sitting at a table on the other side of the Slug and Pellet: a girl in her late teens with pale skin and lipstick which matched her billowing dark-red hair. Her black dress seemed to be unravelling at both ends, revealing extra yardage of both creamy breast and black-tighted thigh with each subtle shift of position.

'Jesus!' Kilcline repeated. He was on his fourth pint and it was beginning to show. The Killer just could not take his drink like he used to, Bourne thought. Which was hardly surprising: their wives only let them out like this on Boxing Days.

Kilcline groaned again, causing the girl to flash him a smile.

'Down, boy!' Bourne said, but he need not have bothered. The girl's boyfriend, a large and probably harmless oaf, had had enough. He approached their table, looking like a wing forward come to investigate a suspicious ruck.

He leaned forward across the table, hands palm down, his face no more than a foot away from Kilcline's. 'You want a photograph, grandad?' he said with a startling lack of originality.

Kilcline smiled at him. 'Naked?' he asked.

The boy's face tightened still further. 'OK,' he sneered. 'I know you're probably too old to get it up any more, but I think I'm gonna kick the shit out . . .' His friend was tugging at his sleeve. 'What?!'

'We need to talk,' the friend told him, offering Bourne and Kilcline the hint of an apologetic smile.

'Now?!'

'Yes, now!' He pulled him away.

'I'll be back in a minute,' he snarled over his shoulder.

'Mine's a pint of Dark Star,' Kilcline shouted after him.

'Why do boys that age think boys our age are beyond sex?' Bourne asked himself out loud. The letters 'SAS' could be heard in the conversation taking place across the bar.

'I'm almost inclined to kick the shit out of him anyway,' Kilcline mused. 'I don't like being called grandad.'

'You'll be one in a few months.'

'Maybe, but I've only been forty for a few weeks, and I could still wrap that shithead round a lamppost.'

'That's what they've just told him,' Bourne observed. The offended party, friends and girlfriends were on their way out, all eyes on the door, save for the vision in red and black, who could not resist giving them a farewell smile.

'I was enjoying that,' Kilcline said.

'It's called voyeurism,' Bourne said. 'She's a lot younger than your daughter.'

'So was Lolita.'

'How's the other one?'

'The other daughter? Oh, Kate's fine – she won a couple of medals last weekend at the county championship. Four hundred metres and long jump. It's the West of England next. I think she could go all the way.'

'Sounds good. And Jill?'

'I thought wives were out of bounds on this occasion.' He sighed. 'She's fine – sent her love. How's Lynn?'

'Same. Are we getting old, do you think?'

'Yes, grandad. One more for the road, I think . . . Same again?'

Bourne nodded, and watched his friend shoulder his way through the scrum to the bar. Nearly twenty years they had known each other. They had met in Oman, high on the Jebel Massif in the middle of an operation against the *adoo* terrorists. Kilcline had been working his way through every known Elvis song at the time, and if the *adoo* had not shot him his own side probably would have. It was not a serious injury though, and through later months of fly-blown boredom they had become good friends. Both had spent three terms in the SAS before returning to their original units – in his case the Royal Signals, in Kilcline's the Royal Engineers – and they had wound up back together in the SAS, both Majors, commanding the Counter Revolutionary Warfare and Training Wings respectively. Bourne still preferred Otis Redding to Elvis, but otherwise they got on pretty well.

Kilcline was on his way back, when Bourne felt a hand on his shoulder. For a second he thought it was the oaf come back, but it wasn't.

'This is the fifth pub I've tried,' Barney Davies said, sitting down.

'Hi, boss,' Bourne greeted him, with that lack of formality which characterized most SAS conversations between ranks.

'What would you like, boss?' Kilcline asked, placing the pints of Guinness and Dark Star on the table.

'Nothing, thanks,' Davies said. 'I need to talk to you both.' He looked round. 'But not here. Can I invite you back to my place? For a coffee perhaps,' he added, watching Kilcline's difficulty in completing the journey from upright to seated.

'Now?' Bourne asked.

'Yes, if you don't mind.'

It was not exactly a request, and within a minute they were emerging from the pub into the cold air, then diving into the warmth of the CO's BMW. Jazz came on with the ignition, and no one spoke during the ten-minute drive to his cottage on the western outskirts of the town.

Davies deposited them in the living room, apologized for there being no fire – 'I've just got back from London' – and went out to the kitchen to make coffee. Kilcline and Bourne exchanged glances. 'What the fuck's happened?' Kilcline murmured.

'I expect he'll tell us when you're sober enough.'

'I'm not that pissed!'

Davies came back with three mugs of black coffee and a packet of sugar. 'Right,' he said, sitting down. 'Sergeants Wynwood and Anderson have gone AWOL in Colombia. Probably kidnapped. At least, we hope so because if they haven't been then they're probably dead.' He stirred two spoonfuls of sugar into his coffee.

Bourne and Kilcline waited for him to continue, suddenly feeling much soberer.

Davies recounted what was known of the events in Cali.

'I don't suppose the Government are going to *do* anything about this,' Kilcline said bitterly.

'That was my expectation,' Davies agreed, 'but for once we may be wrong. The possibility of action *was* discussed.' He went over the political arguments that had been put for and against. 'As far as I could tell the PM is determined that we should take action. She told me the rescue operation – *our* rescue operation – would be on until such time as she called it off . . .'

'That's great,' Bourne said.

'Brilliant,' Kilcline agreed.

41

'Yes, but I also got the feeling that she's going to need all the help she can get. The Foreign Office don't like the idea – that was obvious enough – and God knows what the Cabinet will say, if she ever puts it to them. I think she'd like a little help . . . What do the Israelis call it when they plant a few more settlements on the West Bank? – "establishing facts". The more "on" we make this, the harder it'll be for anyone to call it off.'

For a moment there was silence.

'A four-man team inserted by land, right away,' Bourne said, as if to himself. 'Then anything up to a couple of dozen troops for insertion by air, depending on what the ground team reports back.'

'Sounds good,' Davies said. 'Now go home and get some sleep, both of you. I want something on my desk by noon tomorrow.'

The road ahead seemed clear of both other traffic, houses and possible phones. The last sign had announced that Ibagué was only eight kilometres away. 'Pull over,' Wynwood said.

'Why?' Manuel wanted to know.

'Just do it.'

The truck shuddered to a halt. Manuel looked distinctly nervous.

'Do you know the bus station in Ibagué?' Wynwood asked him.

'Of course. It is my town. I will take you to it,' he added eagerly.

'No. I'm afraid this is where we part company.'

'You are leaving?' the Colombian asked hopefully.

'No, you are. I'm afraid you're going to have to walk the rest of the way.'

'*Qué?!*'

'It's not far.' He reached into his pocket, and counted out the peso equivalent of twenty pounds, which he guessed would be a week's wages to someone like Manuel. 'This is for your trouble,' he said. 'Of course if I'm arrested I'll have to tell them I gave it to you,' he added, hoping that would prove a sufficient deterrent should Manuel find a phone round the next corner.

'But my truck!' the Colombian protested.

'I'll leave it as close to the bus station as I can,' Wynwood promised. 'Now out!'

Manuel got reluctantly to the ground, and looked up woefully at Wynwood as he slammed the truck into gear. Glancing in the rear-view mirror as he pulled back onto the road Wynwood could see the Colombian busily counting the money.

It was beginning to grow dark now, and the lights actually flickered on beside the road as he drove in through the outskirts of Ibagué. They had come less than three hundred and twenty kilometres in eight hours, but like every cross-country Colombian journey Wynwood had ever taken, it had seemed like there was a mountain to cross every couple of kilometres, and most of them seemed at least that high.

He parked the truck as promised, no more than a hundred metres from the bus station, bought a ticket for Bogotá on the fast night bus and found a table at the back of an anonymous-looking restaurant. Steak, cassava and potatoes restored his sense of well-being, and over a large cup of coffee he thought about Susan for the first time that day.

Damn the woman! He wondered where and how Anderson was. A phone on the wall suggested the possibility of calling the embassy in Bogotá and finding out, not to mention telling someone he was alive himself, but the risk, though probably minimal, did not seem worth taking. He would be in the capital by six in the morning and, if he had any say in the matter, on a plane for home not many hours after that.

2

A freight train rumbled across the North London Line girder bridge as Eddie Wilshaw jogged towards it along the River Lea towpath. The diesel wore a different livery from that of his childhood train-spotting days, but he still recognized it as a Class 47. The train was probably on its way from the freight terminal at Felixstowe to the marshalling yard at Willesden.

It was strange what crap the brain kept filed away, he thought, passing under the bridge. A couple of hundred metres ahead of him three black youths were standing in a circle astride the path, apparently deep in conversation with each other.

Eddie wondered. This stretch of the towpath between Carpenter's Road and the Eastway was notorious for muggings and – if you were female – worse. There was no exit between the two roads, just the canalized river on one side, high wire fences on the other. There weren't even any homes overlooking the river, just grimy industrial premises. If he were the nervous type, Eddie thought to himself, he would do a rapid U-turn and get the hell out of there.

As it was, he had never really been afraid of anyone in his life, and two and a half years in the SAS had done nothing to undermine such confidence. He jogged on, wondering if the boys on the path ahead had suffered a worse Christmas than he had.

He was twenty metres away when the tallest of the youths turned in his direction. A long, unbuttoned black trenchcoat revealed red baggy trousers and a bright-green sweater. Dreadlocks spilled out of a Rasta beret to frame a handsome face. The mouth broke into a wide smile. 'Edward, my man!'

Eddie laughed. 'Lloyd, my man,' he echoed, offering his palms for the ritual greeting.

'These is Martin and Stokely,' Lloyd said, introducing the others, who nodded without much enthusiasm. 'You still defending the British Empire?' Lloyd asked.

'You still worshipping a dead Ethiopian president?'

'I reckon,' Lloyd said, smiling. 'You home for Christmas?'

'Yeah. See my dad, you know.'

'He still live in Keir Hardie?' Lloyd asked, looking back over his shoulder at the tower blocks rising beyond the Eastway bridge.

'Yeah. There's no way he can get out.'

'No job?'

'You're kidding. My dad was unemployed when there was full employment.'

Lloyd laughed.

'How're you doing?' Eddie asked.

'Not too bad, you know.' He waved one hand in the air, seemed about to say something, but decided against it.

He was realizing his friends were uncomfortable, Eddie thought. 'I'll see you around,' he said.

'Yeah. Hey, there's a party tonight, at Brian's. Brian Richards – you remember him? Why don't you come? Two-four-five Graham Road.'

'Dalston?'

'Yeah.'

'I might well.' He probably would – anything was better than another evening in front of the TV with his stoned father.

'Right, man, we'd gotta be going,' Lloyd said, giving him another huge smile. The other two were already walking on. 'See you tonight.'

'Yeah.' Eddie stood there for a minute, then turned and broke into a jog, then slowed to a halt again. He had had enough exercise for one morning, and had no great desire to be back at his dad's flat. Instead he walked on, under the Eastway and Homerton Road, before turning off onto the vast grassy expanse of Hackney Marshes. He found a seat and sat down, staring across the river at the tower block he had once lived in, along with his parents and sister.

Clare was long gone, all the way to Epping with her solicitor wanker of a husband. And his mother had died three years ago, just before he had been tested for the SAS. So now there was just him and his dad, two males who had never known how to talk to each other and never would. Football was their only mutual topic of conversation, and since both of them were Tottenham supporters that tended to be just one long moan.

Which reminded him. Yesterday the stupid bastards had thrown away a two-goal lead in the last four minutes. He thought about Lloyd Walker. The two of them had gone to both primary and secondary school together. Lloyd's family had also lived in Keir Hardie, three floors further up. His father had been a porter at Homerton Hospital, probably still was. Assuming – a big assumption these days – that the hospital was still there.

He and Lloyd had really become friends because they had shared a secret – each knew the other was clever. It was not the sort of thing you wanted spread around, not in Homerton Grove Comprehensive. It got you resented, the way being good at football or good with your fists did not. If you were clever you hid it well, sometimes even from yourself.

Despite everything Eddie could have gone on to higher education. He had managed enough 'O' levels to get into a Sixth Form College, and after eighteen months there he had landed interviews at several universities. At the first of these he had found himself in front of two snotty wankers who wanted his views on multiculturalism. That had not been so bad – at least he had wiped the smiles off their faces – but a cup of tea in the student canteen afterwards had killed any scholastic ambition he had. A group of students – middle class, every last one of them – had been arguing about politics in general and the causes of poverty in particular. He had listened, with interest at first, and then with growing anger. The conversation was full of long words and complex socio-logical theories, but it had not made him feel inferior. On the contrary, it had made him realize that he had already learnt more about the real world growing up in Hackney than this bunch were likely to do in their whole lives. He had taken the train back to London, spent the weekend brooding about it, and on Monday morning walked through the doors of the Army Recruiting Office that he had so often sneered his way past.

The Welsh Guards had taken him on. Three years later he had made it into the SAS. And he had not regretted a minute of it.

Wynwood's bus pulled in to Bogotá's central bus station soon after seven in the morning. He had not had much sleep, but there had been no major scares either. The one military roadblock had been manned by soldiers who seemed more asleep than he was, and once again the habit of carrying his passport with him at all times had proved its worth.

He clambered stiffly down to the ground and went looking for a coffee in the bus station. Two cups and a stale pastry later he found a telephone that worked. It seemed to ring for ever. Didn't the goddamn embassy have a twenty-four-hour answering service? At last someone picked it up. Wynwood asked for the Military Attaché.

'Who's calling?' the voice asked.

'Wynwood's the name,' he said.

'Hold on, please,' the voice said. With rather more interest, Wynwood thought.

Another voice appeared. 'Sergeant Wynwood?' it asked.

'Yeah, look . . .'

'Where are you?'

'The bus station . . .'

'In Bogotá?'

'Yeah.' Who was this moron?

'Are you OK?'

'I'm still standing.'

'Is Sergeant Anderson with you?'

'No. Why . . .?'

'When did you last see him?'

'About thirty-six hours ago. In Cali.'

'Right. Can you call again in fifteen minutes, please?'

'What!? Look . . .'

The line had gone dead.

Kilcline strode into Bourne's office with a wide grin on his face. 'Wynwood's OK,' he said. 'He's in Bogotá.'

'Fantastic!' Bourne agreed. 'But no sign of Anderson?'

49

Kilcline perched himself on the corner of Bourne's desk. 'No, it looks like Andy's in the bag. Still, one's a bloody sight better than none. How are you doing?' he asked, surveying the various files and books strewn across Bourne's desk.

'Not bad. There's only one real problem, as far as we can see. Getting them out.'

'Not an insignificant part of the operation.'

Bourne smiled sardonically. 'No.'

'What are the options?'

'Helicopters off a British carrier, helicopters out of Panama or off a US carrier, helicopters out of a Colombian airfield.'

'You seem to have a helicopter fixation,' Kilcline said.

'I suppose they could walk to Brazil,' Bourne added sarcastically.

'OK, I just don't like helicopters.'

'I'm not that fond of them myself,' Bourne conceded, his mind going back, as it too often did, to the nightmare minutes that had followed the crash in San Carlos Water seven years before. Both he and Kilcline had survived – many friends had not. And all because some stupid bird had chosen to commit hara-kiri in the rotor blade.

'Is there any British carrier available?' Kilcline asked.

'Nope. At least not in the timespan we're looking at. And anyway we could hardly send one through the Panama Canal without attracting attention.'

'American?'

'Probably not, and in any case it's not an attractive option. For one thing it would put them right in the picture, with all that would do for security . . .'

'What security?'

'Exactly. For another, it wouldn't fit too well with the PM's DIY approach to sorting out the world. And lastly, they'd probably turn us down anyway. Or spend so long thinking through the diplomatic collaterals that Anderson would have died of old age before we got to him.'

'The Colombian airfield.'

'Yeah,' Bourne sighed. 'It all depends on the sort of guarantees we could get. And I don't just mean from the Colombian Government. I want to hear from whatever security people we have out there. I'd want *them* to say we can trust the military.'

'There must be some good guys in the Colombian military, or why were Joss and Andy out there in the first place?'

Bourne shrugged. 'The problem is knowing who they are. Still, if we get some satisfaction there, then the logistics aren't a problem. The Colombians can provide the transport, and ride shotgun if they think it's necessary. And there won't be any range problem.'

'What about insertion?'

'Depends on the terrain, but probably HAHO out of a Hercules from Belize.'

Kilcline nodded. 'No word of where yet?'

'Nope. Are those the files on Anderson and Wynwood?'

'Yep.' He passed them across.

'I'll bring 'em back over when I've read them,' Bourne said, 'and ask you any questions then. OK?'

'Sure.'

Kilcline disappeared, and Bourne started working his way through the top file. Richard Anderson was twenty-nine, and a Staff Sergeant in the Training Wing. His primary area of expertise was engineering, but he also specialized in weaponry, signalling, and was reasonably fluent in Spanish.

Impressive, Bourne thought.

Anderson had served in the Falklands as a para, winning a mention in dispatches for Goose Green, and joined the SAS the following year. He had several tours of service in Northern Ireland, and had been one of the back-entrance team in Operation Nimrod – the breaking of the Iranian Embassy occupation. He had just begun his third three-year term with promotion to his current rank.

After completing his second tour in Ulster he had undergone a brief course of psychiatric counselling. Successfully.

His background was middle class: the third son of a Congregationalist minister in Southport. He had attended a minor public school, joining the Parachute Regiment straight from there at eighteen. He was now married with two children, one of each gender. His hobbies were listed as rugby, cricket, motorcycles, opera and stamp-collecting.

Bourne closed the file. Given that the man was being held in God-knew-what conditions the reference to counselling was somewhat worrying. Though of course it could work the other way. The people who survived best in such circumstances were usually those who knew themselves best. Maybe Anderson had learnt something about himself.

The photograph showed a pale-skinned Germanic face with rapidly thinning hair. Joss Wynwood's, by contrast, showed a face torn between rugged and cheeky, with almost twinkling brown eyes peering out from a mass of dark, curly hair. He was thirty-two, and also a Staff Sergeant in the Training Wing, now approaching the end of his third term in the SAS.

His first major action had been as a member of the three-man team sent into the Gambia to rescue the deposed President's family in 1981. He had served with the Regiment in the Falklands, taking part in both the recapture of South Georgia and the Long Yomp from San Carlos to Port Stanley. Since then he had done the usual tours in Ireland, without,

Bourne noted, any need for psychiatric counselling. He was married too, but without children. His hobbies were rugby, photography and music. A nice mixture, Bourne thought. Somehow he had confidence in Wynwood.

He gathered up the files, left the office and building, and walked through the sunlight to the adjoining building where the Training Wing administration was housed. Kilcline was gazing moodily out of his window. 'Wish I was going,' he said to no one in particular.

'Yes, grandad,' Bourne said, placing the files on Kilcline's desk and taking a seat. 'Tell me, should I be worrying about the fact that Anderson had psychiatric counselling?'

'I've been thinking about that, and I'm not sure. I don't think so. You won't find a cooler man under pressure, but he does tend to bottle things up. He had nightmares for a long time after his second tour in Ireland – couldn't express what was getting to him any other way.' He paused. 'I guess a lot depends on how he's being treated. It sounds crazy, but I'd say he'll hang together better if he's treated badly. Within limits, of course.' He looked up. 'But does it really matter – you've only got to drag him out and throw him into a helicopter, haven't you?'

Bourne sighed. 'I guess so.'

'Do I detect signs of compulsive perfectionism? Maybe *you* should have some psychiatric counselling.'

'Maybe I should,' Bourne agreed with a smile. 'Is Wynwood as together as he seems to be?'

'Pretty much. I can't think of anyone I'd rather have with me in the wilds of Colombia.'

'Good.' Bourne started to get up.

'Except . . .' Kilcline paused.

'What?'

'This is only hearsay, and it may have nothing to do anything, but his marriage seems to be in trouble.'

'Whose isn't?'

'Mine isn't. Neither's yours, you cynical bastard. I just have the feeling that – if it's true – Wynwood's someone who'd take it badly, that's all. It's just a feeling.'

'OK,' Bourne agreed. 'Thanks. I'll see you later.'

He walked back to his own office, where an orderly was placing four new files on his desk. Bourne looked through them, extracted one and handed it back to him. 'Even the SAS doesn't send men with broken legs on overseas missions,' he said.

'No, boss,' the orderly agreed and made a swift exit.

Bourne looked at the three photographs pinned to the front covers. The first showed a pleasantly ugly face, with blue eyes, fair hair and a large mouth. The expression was almost insolent. That was Trooper Edward Wilshaw.

The second showed a more compact face, with almost hooded dark eyes and short, straight, black hair. There was hardly any expression, just the hint of an embarrassed smile. That was Trooper Damien Robson.

The third showed a slightly Slavic face beneath spiky hair, smiling cheerfully at the camera as if he didn't have a care in the world. That was Corporal Chris Martinson.

They looked so young, Bourne thought.

Wynwood rang back twenty minutes later – it took him that long to find someone prepared to admit they had any change.

'Listen,' the same voice told him. 'Your partner's missing, probably kidnapped by one of the cartels. The Government's response – our Government's, that is – is still being discussed in London, and until we have some clearer idea what's going on we think you'd better not come to the Embassy. So we've got you a room at the Segovia Hotel on Carrera 7. It's paid for. Can you afford a taxi into the centre?'

'Yeah, just about.' He'd given most of his money to Manuel.

'I'll have some cash sent round. As soon as we know anything I'll let you know. OK?'

'I guess so . . .'

The line went dead again.

Chris Martinson raised the binoculars to his eyes and lowered them again. They were only redshanks on the distant mudflats; he thought he had caught a hint of green. Below him a posse of oyster-catchers were drawing crazy patterns in the mud; in the sky above a huge flock of Brent geese was swirling out towards Northey Island.

He remembered his great-grandfather's stories of the island, of the temperance colony which had settled there early in the century, and how a thriving local trade had grown up to supply the inhabitants with illicit liquor. 'You could hardly move at night for rowing boats crammed with bottles,' the old man had used to say, before cackling himself into a coughing fit.

At least, that was how Chris remembered it – his great-grandfather had died in 1969, aged ninety-two. Chris had been seven.

The sun was at its zenith now, the wide expanse of the Blackwater a piercing silver-blue. It was time to head home for lunch, though he was not sure he had room yet for another helping of his mother's cooking. Three days of over-indulgence had left their mark.

He started walking along the path which followed the winding northern shore of the estuary towards Maldon. In the first couple of kilometres he encountered several family parties and a couple of lone men; all greeted him with a smile, echoing the day perhaps, but also the simple friendliness of country life. Whenever he was at home, and particularly on days like today when he was out walking, Chris offered a silent prayer of thanks for having grown up in a place like this.

Eddie had called it 'a mudflat too far', but then how would someone from Hackney know any better? He'd liked The Carpenters well enough, and given time . . . You couldn't understand the countryside by making day trips into it.

Chris's parents had not liked Eddie – that was certain enough. Too clever, they had thought; too pleased with himself. The killer had been the last argument with his father, and Eddie calling patriotism a heap of crap. Hearing something like that from one of the town's token socialists was one thing; getting it from an SAS man was another. It had not so much annoyed his father as shaken his sense of the world, Chris thought. Eddie had some strange views.

He did not like animals either, which Chris, who loved just about all of them without reservation, found almost stranger than strange. The two of them were so different in so many ways, yet they were friends. And it was not just being in the SAS together. There was something else they had in common, something about who they were which he could not put his finger on.

He would like a dog himself, he thought, as a couple with a huge golden retriever walked by in the opposite direction. But not for a few years yet. You could hardly keep a dog properly in the Army, and he intended to spend most of his annual leave outside England. The previous year he had blown most of his savings on a fortnight in Costa Rica, visiting all the wildlife reserves. It had been like heaven. So many different species of bird. Such beautiful colours. Six months later he was still revelling in mental flashbacks of the trip. The best thousand pounds he had ever spent. The only thousand pounds he had ever spent. He had even got a Spanish proficiency mark on his skills dossier for his troubles.

Where could he go this year? He fancied Lapland, but it would probably be too expensive.

Another flock of Brent geese smudged the sky as he passed The Ship and started up the canal. He thought about Molly, and their date that evening. He had met her only three days before, at a Christmas Eve party in Goldhanger, but somehow he already expected something good. She was older than him, about thirty-four he guessed from things she had said, but what did a seven-year age gap mean these days?

One thing it meant was that he did not feel she needed him – or the 'relationship' – to make sense of the world for her, the way so many of the younger women he had known seemed to. And finding out that he was in the Army had not thrown her in either of the two usual directions. She had neither been impressed nor appalled – just taken it on board.

And she had let him talk. No, now he thought about it, she had actually encouraged him to talk. And having several pints inside him, he had obliged. About being in the Army, being in the SAS. 'I love it,' he had said. 'It stretches me.' And it did. Like nothing else he had ever come across. Stretched him physically, mentally, every which way.

'Are you married to it?' she had asked, and to his surprise he had realized that he was not. It had been his life for eight years, and would be for a few more yet, but it was not the limit of his ambition. Another five years perhaps, and then he would quit, spend a couple of years seeing all the wild places of the world while he was still young enough, find the few places people had not managed to fuck up yet. And he would not just be in the way: with the medical experience he had picked up in the Army he could make himself useful.

'I think you're the first man I've met who knows what he wants to do,' Molly had said. She had also had rather a lot to drink. It had not affected her kissing, though.

Chris smiled at the memory. It promised to be a good evening. He strode up Chilton Street, remembering his mother had asked him to buy bread.

Damien Robson – 'the Dame' to all his comrades in the SAS – inserted the last inch of Mars bar into his mouth and stared out of the Renault's window. The drizzle was still coming down – a cold drizzle – he imagined standing out there in the street would be like standing under a half-hearted cold shower. Which was almost attractive when you had been cooped up in a car seat for four hours with nothing to do but watch and wait.

It would be better if he was alone, but the guy from 14 Intelligence was sitting next to him, also eating a Mars bar. The Dame had already forgotten the man's second name – his first was Alan – but at least he had finally got the message and stopped trying to start conversations.

Through the drizzle the lights of the Turf Lodge estate were dimly visible above the roofs of the terraced houses on the other side of Kenneally Street. Out of sight, round the corner at the end of the street, two more 14 Intelligence men were sitting in a battered Fiat. Another three were staked out inside number 36, where the terrorist arms cache awaited collection.

And tonight was the night, according to someone or other's tout. The Dame doubted it, but he was only playing the odds. For every successful stake-out he had been on in Northern Ireland, he had been on half a dozen wastes of time. And this was beginning to look like one of those.

A pair of young girls walked past on the pavement, laughing under their shared umbrella, apparently oblivious to the watchers in the car, though you could never be sure. In a few minutes they might be telling their Provo brothers that two suckers were asking for it in a Renault on Kenneally Street.

Or they might be watching *Coronation Street*, like his sisters back in Sunderland. Innocent people living innocent lives, no threat to anyone.

The Dame had to admit it though – he liked Belfast. He did not like working there, and he felt sorry for all the people who had to live with it the way things were, but just as a town, as a bunch of people, it reminded him of Sunderland. The same brick streets and derelict docks, the same smell of the sea on the breeze. Like Sunderland it sometimes felt a bit sorry for itself, but the people were not beaten, not really. They held their strength inside, only brought it out when they needed to. Which was the way it should be.

His companion nudged him, and pointed over his shoulder. In the rear-view mirror he could see a youngish man in a leather jacket making his way up the other side of the street. He did not recognize him.

'No,' he said.

'Our man's darker, right?' Alan asked.

'Yes. And older than that.' The Dame was only there, rather than sitting around the TV in Sunderland with his mother and sisters, because the year before he had been one of the few to clock a sight of – and live to remember – the Provo that the tout had claimed would be coming for the cache. His name was Eamonn O'Hanlon, and he was wanted for three murders and more kneecappings than anyone could count.

The Dame had almost been the fourth victim, and he was not about to forget O'Hanlon's face.

It was almost half-past eight – half-time at Filbert Street. Jesus, Sunderland could do with three points . . .

The sound of a motor accelerating drew his eyes to the rear-view mirror. A Toyota van was accelerating up the street, rather fast . . . If this was the men coming to pick up the Armalites surely they would be trying to look less conspicuous . . .

An explosion spun the Dame's head round. The air seemed to be full of flying objects, and number 36 was hidden by a billowing cloud of smoke. As he watched, a flowerpot, still containing its spider plant, landed right way up in the road ahead, and stood there shaking, as if traumatized by its flight.

The Toyota!

He turned his eyes right just at the moment it scraped past and round the front wing of the Renault, squealing to a halt almost dead in front of them, not five yards away, the back doors swinging open. The Dame threw himself down as two hooded figures were revealed, each holding a sub-machine-gun. The windscreen blew away and Alan sank back into his seat with a deep sigh.

The Dame extracted the Browning from its cross-draw holster and waited for the sound of the Toyota moving away. It did not come. Instead there were footsteps.

He had less than a second to make a decision, but it was not difficult. To do nothing was to die.

Using one foot on the bottom of the nearside door as leverage, he pushed himself up and across the dead Alan, the Browning aiming out through the windscreen. Like a duck coming into the sight of a fairground rifle, aim and target came miraculously together. The Dame pressed the trigger twice in quick succession, and whirled the Browning round in search of the other target just as something seemed to hiss across the shoulder of his windcheater. The sounds of the terrorist's shots were still echoing when the Dame sent two bullets through the upper centre of his body.

A third man appeared around the side of the van, and disappeared just as quickly. The Dame could see nothing through the open back doors of the van, but he fired anyway, and thought he heard a cry of pain. The van roared away into the drifting smoke and disappeared.

Sirens seemed to be opening up from all directions. An ambush, he thought. An ambush within an ambush. The cache had been bait, planted over a bomb, which someone had detonated at exactly the right moment to disorientate those in the watching cars.

He wondered whether the occupants of the other car had been any quicker than Alan.

He checked the latter's heart just to make sure, then cautiously climbed out of the car. The two men he had shot were lying a few feet apart. Both were young – young as he was. The first had died instantly, the second had taken time to spill a trickle of blood onto the wet road.

Neither of them was Eamonn O'Hanlon.

'You look sharp,' Eddie's dad remarked from the living-room doorway.

'Yeah,' Eddie said, examining his tie-knot in the hallway mirror. 'What are you doing this evening?'

'Oh nothing. You know. There's a good film on the TV – one of the *Star Treks*. *Five*, I think. Not that it makes much difference.'

Eddie smiled at him. Behind his father he could see the papers, tobacco and dope tin all laid out on the arm of the sofa. 'Don't get busted while I'm out,' he said.

'Some chance,' his father said. 'They'd have to mend the lifts first.'

That was probably true, Eddie thought, as he walked down the seven floors to the ground. His dad's car, a second-hand Nissan Cherry, still had all its wheels. The local kids probably knew whose it was.

He pulled out into Glyn Road and headed west towards Mare Street. He had told his father the party started at eight, but one in the morning was more like it. First off he would have a decent meal in a wine bar he knew under the railway arches.

It was the third time he had been there over the furlough week and this time the waitress recognized him. She was quite small, with dark hair tied back in a bun, and a face that managed to be both decidedly European and vaguely oriental. And she had a lovely walk, Eddie thought, watching her cross the room.

He wondered what her name was.

He studied the menus, and decided on Chicken Chasseur with a Portuguese red. He could really get into wine, he thought. If he ever had any money, building up a good cellar would be really interesting.

The waitress took his order.

'Can I ask your name?' Eddie asked.

'Lisa,' she said. 'As in Mona.'

He liked that. When she brought the meal he asked her when she got off. Midnight, she said. And yes she did fancy a party. But he would have to put up with her dressed the way she was.

Eddie took his time with the bottle of wine, watching the other customers of the wine bar – mostly yuppie wankers as far as he could see – and enjoying Lisa's occasional passage across the room. He would put up with her dressed the way she was, he thought, but he would rather have her naked.

Who knows, he thought. He visited the men's toilet and found a condom machine that actually worked, which had to be a good omen.

She was not just sexy, he discovered on the way to the party. She was a student at Hackney College, planning on going round the world for a year when she was finished, and on an eventual career in some area of conservation.

Despite his fears the party was already in full swing when they arrived, and after sinking two glasses of wine in quick succession Lisa announced her desire to dance. They danced. First like dervishes, then like robots, finally in each other's arms.

She smelt good. Too good. He could feel an erection coming between them. So could she, and pulled him closer. They kissed for a while.

'Do you have a home we could go to?' she asked.

''Fraid not. Do you?'

She giggled. 'No. Can we go for a drive?'

'Sure.'

'I have to go somewhere first.'

He waited in the hall, looking around him. There was no sign of Lloyd, but maybe it was too early for him. The party seemed about seventy per cent black and thirty per cent white. But no Pakis, Eddie thought. They just did not mix, the Asians. Funny that – everyone had this bugbear about the blacks, the West Indians, but most of them were quite happy to be British. They were pissed off about being poor, not about being British.

63

The Asians, on the other hand, just wanted to keep to themselves. Which pissed everyone else off.

'I'm ready,' Lisa said behind him.

It was cold outside now, and it took the car heater a while to warm up. Eddie drove east, her hand on his thigh.

'Where are we going?' she asked.

'Somewhere quiet?' he said. A tiny voice in his head told him she should not be putting herself at the mercy of a stranger like this. He would tell her so. Afterwards.

He found the industrial lane he knew, and drove to the end where a circular turning space fronted a corner of the Marshes. There was no one else there. Eddie had never been very enamoured of back-seat fucking, but Lisa made it a very pleasant experience. By this time the car heater had done its job, they had managed to strip each other of everything but socks, and Tina Turner's 'Steamy Windows' was playing in Eddie's head.

'I liked that,' she said, as they helped pull each other's trousers on.

'Yeah,' he agreed. Seeing her again would be nice, he thought. He had four more days to survive in Keir Hardie Tower. 'Where do you live?' he asked.

'Stoke Newington.'

'I'll take you home.'

'Oh.'

'I didn't mean it as an insult. I'd like to see you again. Soon.'

'Yeah, OK.'

They climbed back into the front seats.

'I don't do this all the time, you know,' she said.

'What?'

'What do you think? Fuck perfect strangers.'

'OK.'

'But I noticed you when you came in on Christmas Eve, and . . .'

'I'm glad.'

'What do you do, anyway?'

Eddie hesitated. He often lied at this point, because the true answer usually led the questioner to draw all the wrong conclusions about him. But this time he decided on being straight. 'I'm in the Army,' he said.

She said nothing.

He looked at her in the half-light. 'Surprised?' he asked.

'Yes,' she said.

'The Army's like most things,' he said. 'Everyone's different, and everyone's in it for a different reason.'

'What's yours?' she asked.

'I wanted to get away from Hackney,' he said. When he knew her better he could try and explain it properly.

She smiled. 'It'll take some getting used to,' she said. 'Most of the people I know think the Army's just a bunch of trained thugs.'

'They're wrong there,' Eddie said. 'We're *highly* trained thugs.' He started the engine, turned the car and slowly drove back down the lane to the road. 'Whereabouts in Stoke Newington?' he asked, wondering whether to tell her he was SAS. No, he decided.

She didn't seem too worried about his occupation, leaning her head on his shoulder all the way back to Shacklewell Lane, where she shared a first-floor room with another girl. He took down her telephone number, and they kissed with a tenderness which almost surprised him.

He took the drive back to Hackney slowly, realizing he had to be over the limit. He was nearly home, stopped at the lights on Chatsworth Road, when a familiar figure burst out of the road to his left, and stood, holdall in hand, looked wildly around, not five metres away.

'Lloyd!' he shouted.

His friend almost jumped out of his skin. The swelling whine of a siren suggested an explanation for the nervousness.

'Give us a lift, man?' Lloyd asked.

Eddie sighed. 'Get in,' he said.

Lloyd climbed in with alacrity, but still almost managed to fall out again as Eddie accelerated away up the road.

'What's in the bag?' he asked.

'Er, party things.'

'Try again.' The police car had swung round behind them.

'Just a few watches.'

'Shit!' Eddie gripped the wheel harder. 'OK, they're going out the window.'

'No, man . . .'

'Either the bag goes, or you and the bag. Choose.'

'All right man, don't get your white knickers in a twist.'

'Open the window. Once we're round the next corner.' They took it on squealing tyres. 'Here, look, there's a skip.'

Lloyd leant out and propelled the bag with perfect accuracy. 'Magic Johnson – eat your heart out,' he said exultantly, falling back into his seat.

Eddie took another tight turn, then another, then dramatically slowed down as he reached Chatsworth Road again. Which was fortunate, because a police car was flagging them down.

'Evening, officer,' Eddie said.

The constable stared at him while another stared at Lloyd from the other side. 'Can I show you some ID?' Eddie asked, finger poised over his pocket.

'How kind,' the constable said sarcastically. 'Mind if we look in the back?'

'Not at all.'

The second constable had a look, while Eddie showed his 22 SAS identity card.

'One used condom on the floor,' the second constable reported.

'Couldn't you afford one each?' the first one said with a grin. 'Go on, get out of here.'

'I must have one of those magic cards printed,' Lloyd said as they drove off.

Eddie turned a corner and pulled over. 'Why don't you go robbing in Hampstead or somewhere like that?' he demanded.

'I'd get caught, brother, that's why.'

'You'll get caught here.'

'Yeah, I know. But a black boy gotta do what a black boy gotta do. We can't all play Lone Ranger for Queen and Cunt. And besides, if every poor black boy went over Hampstead it'd be like the Notting Hill Carnival every night of the week.'

Eddie smiled. 'Yeah, right. Have you ever considered planning anything?'

'I had the brick with me, didn't I?'

They both burst out laughing.

Eddie was still grinning as he began the climb to Flat 26, but somewhat less cheery when he let himself in. The TV was still on, the smell of marijuana thick on the air. His dad looked at him with glazed eyes. 'Message by the phone,' he said.

Eddie went and looked. 'Report Back Hereford Souness,' it said.

So either the Glasgow Rangers manager was getting messages, his dad could not spell 'soonest', or it was a joke.

There was a stoned giggle from the living-room.

3

Eddie's alarm went off at 7.30. He had a quick shower, and sat in the kitchen with a bowl of cereal and a cup of coffee. The whole flat still smelt of dope, but if he opened a window his dad would probably die of hypothermia. At ten to eight he switched on the local radio to get the weather forecast – clear but cold – and find out which BR and Underground lines were fucked that morning. The answer was none that he intended to use. At eight o'clock, with his father still snoring loudly in the bedroom, Eddie left a note saying 'Gone To War' on the kitchen table and started down the fourteen flights of stairs which led to the outside world.

It seemed deserted – as usual the people of Britain had decided that the period between Boxing Day and New Year's Eve was a national holiday. The trains were running though, and Eddie took the overland to Liverpool Street, changing there onto the Circle Line for Paddington. He arrived with more than half an hour to spare before the Hereford train, and was in the queue for a coffee in Casey Jones when a hand grabbed his shoulder.

He turned to find a familiar, cheery face. 'Christ, I thought they might want me for something important,' Eddie said. 'But if they want you as well . . .'

'Get me a coffee while I get my ticket,' Chris said. 'And watch my bag,' he added, dropping it within an inch of Eddie's foot.

'Yes, Corporal.'

'Bollocks,' Chris said over his shoulder.

He came back five minutes later. Eddie handed him his coffee.

Chris examined the cup, then the giver. 'Christ, you must have had a good Christmas. You look bloody awful.'

'Thanks. I didn't get much sleep last night, that's all. I'll kip on the train.'

'And why didn't you get much sleep?'

'I was deep in sexual ecstasy. There were these four nympho-maniacs – one blonde, one Chinese, one black and one Arab princess – and they were passing me round.'

'I expect they were all trying to get rid of you.'

Eddie laughed. 'How was yours? You don't look that good yourself.'

'I think I'm in love.'

Eddie groaned. 'Not again. Another simple peasant girl, is it? A shepherdess, something like that?'

'Something like that. She works at Essex University, some sort of admin job, I think. We didn't have much time for talking.'

'Well, country folks do speak slowly. Funny that – you'd think with a smaller vocabulary it'd be easier to find the right words, not harder.'

Chris eyed him with affection. 'Have you finished? Molly is about as slow up top as Nigel Mansell's gear-stick. And gorgeous.'

'Breasts like peaches?'

'Yep.'

'Thighs to die for?

'Yep.'

'And you're in love.'

'Yep.'

'How'd she take the news of your sudden departure?' Eddie asked.

Chris grimaced. 'She doesn't know yet. I'll ring her from Hereford.' He sighed. 'We were going out tonight.'

Eddie patted him on the shoulder. 'Cheer up. Let's go and find this train.' He picked up his bag, thinking he would ring Lisa when they arrived.

Ramón Amarales was watching from the upper verandah when the red car came into view on the valley road. He had a shrewd idea why his brother was paying him a visit so early in the morning, and was not exactly looking forward to the confrontation.

Not that he ever really looked forward to seeing Miguel. Or his sister Victoria, who was due back in Popayán from Bogotá that day. Though he, Ramón, was the head of the family, neither sibling had ever given him any respect. They just spent the money he made for them.

Miguel was supposedly the good-looking one, the sociable one. And, by his own reckoning, the intelligent one. Ramón did not deny his brother was handsome, but anyone with any intelligence would have thought twice about tying himself to that Escobar bitch. He wondered if the woman stopped shopping when they were in bed. She had to have more dresses than Imelda Marcos had shoes. Victoria, he admitted, was intelligent. But what had she done with her brains? She had married an idiot too, albeit one who was rather more useful to the family than Maria Escobar. He bored her, and presumably she had affairs. Otherwise, as far as Ramón could see, she did nothing but read French magazines, ski and paint her toenails.

He poured himself another coffee from the silver jug on the tray, added two spoons of sugar and resumed his position, leaning against one of the verandah supports.

Miguel's car was being allowed through the outer perimeter gate. Against the sweep of green mountains the red car seemed almost like an insult. But then Miguel had always preferred the city to the real Colombia. Maybe he was intelligent in his way, but he had about as much wisdom as his wife.

'Juanita,' Ramón called through the open door. 'Fetch Chirlo for me.' He liked having his chief *sicario* with him at such times, mostly because he knew Miguel disliked the man.

The car cruised up through the paddock towards the second gate, causing the two Arabian horses to canter away towards the stream.

'Yes, *patrón*,' a soft voice said behind Ramón.

'Chirlo, have some coffee. Miguel has come,'

Rodrigo Sepulveda smiled and helped himself. He was twenty-four years old and looked younger, with clear blue eyes that looked out from under long, light-brown hair. The scar which gave him the nickname Chirlo ran horizontally across his left cheek like an African tribal mark. He sat down in one of the two rocking chairs, idly stirring his coffee.

The sound of footsteps on the stairs preceded Miguel Amarales's appearance in the doorway. He looked, Ramón thought, more than ever like a male model. Long black hair framed his Castilian features, the luxuriant moustache was cut to perfection, the sleeves of his white shirt were rolled up to reveal a gold watch on one wrist, a gold bracelet on the other. He might not have been a resounding academic success at UCLA, but his fashion sense had been honed to perfection.

'Why?' he asked angrily, shaking his head and causing a snake-shaped gold earring to dance out from under his hair.

'Have some coffee,' Ramón suggested. Maybe he should grow a moustache himself, he thought.

'Why didn't you consult me first?' Miguel demanded to know.

'You were in Miami, and . . .'

'I was on my way back.'

Ramón shrugged. 'We couldn't wait.'

Miguel poured himself a cup, scowling first at his brother, then at Chirlo. 'So why?' he asked.

'Leverage,' Ramón said. 'And example. If we send Muñoz back he'll think twice about sounding off quite so much in future. Whatever we do with him, others will think twice.' He tinkled the ice in his glass. 'Everyone knows deep down that there's two sources of power in this country, but we have to remind them occasionally, bring it to the surface of their minds, so to speak. The moment politicians think they can ignore us with impunity we're finished.' He shrugged. 'It was an exercise in *realpolitik*. And an interesting military exercise, too.'

'Was that the real reason?'

'I've given you the real reason,' Ramón said angrily.

Miguel half smiled. 'OK, OK.' He knew his brother too well. 'But what made it interesting?'

Ramón smiled. 'We based it on the British SAS attack on that embassy in London,' Ramón said. 'Which turned out to be somewhat ironic. We caught an SAS man with Muñoz.'

'What are you going to do with him?'

'I don't know. Maybe ransom him back to the British. Maybe offer him work helping to train our men. The SAS are the best, you know.'

'Better than the Americans?' Miguel asked, surprised.

'Oh yes.'

Miguel looked round. 'Where are they?'

'Upstairs. They only arrived this morning.'

'Have you talked with Noguera?'

'Of course. He and Victoria should be coming to dinner tonight.'

Miguel grimaced. 'With an open pocket, no doubt. Our brother-in-law's needs seem to keep rising.'

Ramón smiled. 'He's the only Military Governor of the province we have. At least for the moment.'

'Maybe. How much are you asking for Muñoz?'

'I haven't decided yet. Chirlo, what do you think?'

'*Patrón?*'

Ramón repeated the question and Chirlo allowed half his mind to consider it. The other half was still busy absorbing the news that his mistress would be coming to the ranch that evening.

Eddie and Chris took a taxi from the station to Stirling Lines, the SAS headquarters in the Hereford suburb of Redhill. On arrival soon after two they were told there would be a preliminary briefing at 1600 hours in the 'Kremlin'.

'Who else has been called back?' Chris asked the orderly sergeant.

'Just you two, the Dame and Monkey. But . . .'

'They here yet?'

'No. The Dame's being flown in from Belfast. But it looks like Monkey's not going to make this one. He broke a leg playing rugby yesterday.'

'Probably on someone's teeth,' Eddie murmured. He got on OK with Monkey on a superficial level, but he had never been in a tight spot with the man, and he was not sure he wanted to be. He might be wrong – others had found him all right – but he had no great desire to find out. The myth about the SAS – that all three hundred of them got on with each other like best buddies – was just that, a myth. They got on with each other because they all had the self-discipline not to let the ones they did not like get too far up their noses.

'You know what this is about, boss?' Chris was asking the order sergeant.

'Yes thanks,' the sergeant said with a smile. 'And so will you come 1600 hours.'

'C'mon,' Eddie said. 'Let's do an hour in the gym.'

They walked back to their adjoining rooms, and met outside again ten minutes later in shorts and singlets.

'If Monkey's kaput we'll need another signaller,' Chris mused.

'Looks like it.' Each four-man team had a specialist signaller, medic, engineer and linguist. Most had an array of secondary skills, more so with each year of service.

Eddie was the linguist in this proposed team – thanks to two long summers in his teens working as a bouncer on the Costa del Sol – but he had also acquired a good grounding in communications during a stint in Northern Ireland the previous year. Chris was primarily the medic, but there was not much he didn't know about boats, and he had more than a smattering of Spanish. Damien – the Dame – was the engineer, with special expertise in laying and defusing explosives.

'The Dame's got Spanish too, hasn't he?' Eddie said, as he set the weights on the backbreaker.

'I hope to Christ it's not Gibraltar,' Chris said.

Wynwood climbed out of the shower, pulled on his shorts, carefully sniffed himself, and pronounced himself satisfied. The stiff nail-brush someone had abandoned in his hotel bathroom had removed the last traces of the Cali rubbish mountains.

He unfastened the window and examined the outside world. The sky was clear, the air delightfully warm, like an early summer day on the Gower. He had grown to like Bogotá in the two or three days he and Andy had spent there after their arrival back in November. Maybe they had only seen the nice bits, but the place had a good feel to it.

If he could only get his wife out of his head he could enjoy his last few days there as well.

Having something to do would help. He checked his watch – twenty minutes till he was supposed to meet the man from the British Embassy. Oliver his name was, though whether that was his first name or last Wynwood did not know.

Wynwood dressed, left his room and made his way downstairs. The man on the desk gave him a cheerful '*buenos dias*'. He smiled back and walked out onto Carrera 7. Across the street a white-towered church almost blazed in the sunlight.

The Museum of Gold was only a ten-minute walk away. Oliver had said it opened at ten, and a queue had already formed by the time Wynwood arrived. Rather than join it he sat down on a wrought-iron seat in the square across the street, watching for anyone who might look like his contact.

He had only been there a few seconds when a soft voice echoed in his ear: 'Wynwood?' He turned to find a slightly plumper version of Bobby Charlton, a smattering of long fair hairs twisting in the wind above a bald pate. 'That's me,' he replied.

'Oliver,' the man introduced himself, with what sounded like a faint West Country accent. 'Pleased to meet you. And congratulations on your escape,' he added dryly. 'Shall we go in,' he said, indicating the museum across the street.

'We could just talk here.'

'Have you been already?' Oliver asked, sounding disappointed.

'No, but . . .'

'Well, in that case . . .' The embassy man got to his feet. 'No one should miss the Museum of Gold – it's Bogotá's one great attraction.'

Oh well, in that case, Wynwood thought sarcastically.

At least Oliver paid for both of them. 'I have money for you,' he said as the two walked past a posse of armed guards and up the wide flight of stairs which led to the first-floor galleries.

'Good,' Wynwood said, and waited for more.

He waited in vain as Oliver examined an exhibit. Inside a large glass cabinet a skeleton reclined on the earth floor of a tomb, grinning at the ceiling. Gold trinkets hung from its neck, small gold ornaments lay all around – the treasure it had taken, literally, to the grave. And as if to underline the dead man's failure to buy the intended immortality, spindly roots were writhing in through the walls and ceiling. It was strangely moving, Wynwood thought. It made him think of his father.

Oliver was already moving on to the next exhibit, a life-sized model of two Indians heating gold in a crucible. A few feet away a mixed group of tourists were having a selection of gold-filigree ear ornaments explained to them in both

English and Spanish. Beyond them, ten or more uniformed guards toting automatic weapons and communication devices paced up and down in front of a huge mural of palms and mountains.

I wouldn't fancy trying to rob this place, Wynwood thought; though planning such a robbery would make a good exercise for continuation training back home. Getting hold of the plans might be somewhat difficult.

'I don't have much to tell you,' Oliver was saying by his side. They were now standing in front of the mummified remains of a pre-Columbian woman, who could not have been much more than four feet tall. 'There is a good chance that your people will be attempting a rescue,' Oliver continued, so quietly that Wynwood was not sure he had heard him correctly.

'Did you say rescue?' he asked after a moment.

'Yes. I'm sure you'll have at least as much idea of what that entails as I do. I'm to tell you that nothing is finally decided. If, I repeat *if*, London gives the green light, I understand that three men will be sent in to join you for surveillance and preparation. In the meantime, you're to stay out of sight. Be a tourist.' He looked at his watch. 'Come, they only open the Sun Room once an hour.'

Wynwood followed him up the stairs, absorbing the information he had just been given, working out which questions he should ask. There seemed only one that was relevant. 'Do you know when the final decision is being taken?' he asked.

'Probably today,' Oliver said. 'There's a meeting this evening – 8 p.m. London time – so if a decision is taken the embassy should be informed today.'

The Sun Room occupied the centre of the third floor, and a small crowd was already gathering at its doors. A host of uniformed schoolchildren, all with shining black hair and bright-red uniforms, giggled and poked at each other. Several paler-skinned tourists, most of them looking significantly shabbier than the Colombians in the crowd, chatted to each other in English and German.

His mind still racing through the possibilities, Wynwood waited with Oliver for the doors to open, then filed in with everyone else. The doors clanged shut behind them, causing one of the tourists to gasp, but a split second later the lights came on in the glass cabinets that lined the walls. Each was top-lit, revealing a shining, beautifully crafted gold headpiece against a blue-black surround.

Wynwood had to admit to himself it was magical. He turned to find Oliver watching him, a faint smile on his face. 'OK,' the SAS man said, 'you were right, it's amazing.'

Oliver half bowed.

On their way round the rest of the third floor he asked if Wynwood had recognized any of the opposition in Cali.

'Didn't see a single face,' Wynwood said. 'You don't have any news of Andy – Sergeant Anderson?'

'Not yet. But I'm expecting something on that today as well.'

'Where from?' Wynwood asked innocently.

'Sources,' Oliver said curtly. 'I shall be leaving you now. Your hotel is all right? Good. I'll be in touch.'

'Today?'

'If I have anything to tell you,' Oliver said over his shoulder.

Wynwood spent another ten minutes desultorily examining the exhibits, but his heart was not in it. He made his way outside into the sunshine and started walking. Down a nearby street he found an outdoor café, with several metal tables in primary colours spilling across the pavement. He sat down, absent-mindedly studied the menu and watched the world go by.

Oliver, he guessed, was better at his job than he looked. And Colombian women tended to be on the plump side. How the hell was he going to fill up the rest of the day?

His mind was a blank, he just sat there. As usual, thoughts of Susan came to fill the vacant space. The two of them were through, and they both knew it, and though both felt sad about it – at least he thought she did – neither of them really wanted to turn back the clock. The marriage had run its course – that was all there was to it. They had both accepted it in their heads, and she seemed to have accepted it in her heart as well. Why the fuck couldn't he?

She can accept it, a voice in his head reminded him, because she's fucking that bastard teacher she met at her fucking watercolour fucking painting fucking evening class.

'What would you like, sir?' a waiter asked, apparently not noticing the anger still infusing his customer's eyes.

Wynwood ordered a black coffee. It was the sense of failure that he found hard to cope with, he decided. And losing Andy as well. Oliver had congratulated him on his escape, but he knew better. They had fucked up somewhere along the line, and he had had the luck which had obviously deserted his partner. He wanted the chance to do something right.

Several shoeshine boys inspected his boots with optimistic interest, but he sent them all away – there was something he didn't like about the idea of someone kneeling at his feet. Something demeaning, though who it demeaned he was not sure. The boys certainly showed no signs of embarrassment – in fact they carried their little wooden boxes with a definite swagger.

A trio of Colombian girls – young women really – probably secretaries – sat down at a nearby table. An Indian walked by, wearing a black hat with an embroidered headband. He stopped to look back at the woman trailing twenty metres behind him, who was carrying a huge pile of similar hats in a polythene sack on her back. The noble savage, Wynwood thought.

Yellow taxis went by in profusion. A man suddenly appeared alongside his table, one arm outstretched towards him, the other cut off in a neat stump. 'No,' he said instinctively.

The coffee finally arrived.

'How are you doing, lads?' a voice said from the doorway.

Eddie and Chris turned to greet the owner of the Wearside accent. The Dame plonked himself down on Eddie's bed.

'You just got in?' Eddie asked.

'Yeah. Just come over from fuckin' Belfast.'

'I thought you were on leave like the rest of us.'

The Dame sighed. 'I was. Enjoying it too, getting looked after hand and foot by my sisters. But the bosses needed me for a special job . . .'

'Oh, listen to him – special job!' Chris said.

'We're not fit to tie his shoelaces,' Eddie agreed.

'It was tied up with something happened over there last year,' the Dame said placidly. 'What are we doing here, anyway? I thought I'd be back in Sunderland tonight, not listening to you two wankers mouthing off.'

'Fuck only knows.' Chris looked at his watch. 'It's five to six – we'd better get down there.'

The Kremlin's briefing room boasted all the usual paraphernalia associated with such rooms, plus a huge mounted water buffalo's head which dated back to the regiment's time in Malaya, and whose large, serene eyes gazed down benevolently on Eddie, Chris and the Dame as they took their seats. It was a minute before six, and Chris's stomach was already rumbling. It had to be true, he reflected – the more you eat, the more you need.

'Did I hear thunder?' the Dame asked.

'I doubt it,' Chris said.

'Do you know how Major Bourne got the name "Roy"?' Eddie asked.

The other two shook their heads.

'When he was in the Oman the food used to make him fart like there was no tomorrow. So first they called him "Bourne on the Wind" – get it? – and that got shortened to "Roy" 'cos it's a song by Roy Orbison.'

'That sounds almost stupid enough to be true,' the Dame observed.

'It is true.'

'Have I died and gone to hell?' Chris asked the ceiling.

'You should be so lucky, Trooper,' Bourne said, brushing past him and putting his papers on the table next to the overhead projector. Another four men filed in: Captains Mike Bannister and Rory Atkins, officers commanding C Squadron's Air and Mountain Troops respectively, Training Wing's Major Kilcline, and a man in civilian clothes whom Bourne introduced as 'Mr Pennington from the Foreign Office'.

Bourne started things off. 'Right, unless our security's even worse than I think it is, you four' – he indicated Eddie, the Dame, Chris and Mike Bannister – 'have no idea why you've been dragged out of the bosom of your families halfway through the season of good cheer. I'm sure your families are glad to be rid of you, but . . .'

'Is it true you need a diploma in stand-up to be an officer here, boss?' Eddie asked.

'Yes, Trooper, it is. But to get serious . . .' Bourne went through what they knew of what had happened in Cali. 'We thought Joss Wynwood had been taken as well,' he admitted. 'We only heard this morning that he's alive and well in the capital.'

'That big Welsh bastard would survive a night with Cilla Black,' Kilcline observed.

'Perhaps,' Bourne agreed, 'but what sort of shape would she be in?'

Everyone laughed.

'So,' Bourne went on, 'the job is to get Sergeant Anderson back. And, if we can, recover Muñoz as well.'

'Any particular reason?' Chris asked. 'For Muñoz, I mean.'

'Yes, there is. The unit which was supposed to be protecting him from something like this blew it. Since they were at least partly trained by us, *we* blew it. OK?'

'Yes, boss.'

'OK. Colombia. I don't suppose any of you have been there?'

They all shook their heads.

'Or know anything about the place?'

'Wasn't that where Bobby Moore got accused of stealing a bracelet or something?' the Dame asked.

'Very useful,' Bourne said. 'Well, Bobby can't be with us today . . .'

'We could give him a buzz, boss,' Eddie suggested.

Bourne ignored him. 'But we do have Mr Pennington here from the Foreign Office.'

Pennington was pinning up a large-scale map of northern South America. 'Colombia,' he said, a little nervously, pointing it out on the map. 'It's a big country. About thirty-five million people in an area five times that of the UK. The vast majority of the population, about seventy per cent, are *mestizos* – people of mixed Spanish/Indian descent. Another twenty per cent would consider themselves of pure Spanish blood, while seven per cent are pure Indian and three per cent negro. Nearly all the power is in the hands of the pure Spanish twenty per cent, but the country doesn't have a race problem the way we would understand it. The majority is in the middle, so to speak, which makes for stability, at least in that regard.'

He turned to the map. 'As you can see, Colombia is only just north of the Equator, so those areas close to sea level, the coastal plains and this huge area of jungle in the south-east, have a tropical climate – hot and humid the whole year round.'

Eddie groaned.

'But don't despair,' Pennington went on with a smile. 'About ninety-five per cent of the population live in these mountains' – he ran his finger down the map – 'which give the country a kind of dual spine running north to south. Most of the population lives over 1200 metres above sea level, where the climate is much kinder.

'One last point, before I abandon the geography lesson. You can see from the way the country's made up how hard overland communication must be. And of course this has made it almost impossible for anyone or any government to stamp its authority on the whole country. So instead of a powerful centre you have regional powers. Warlords. Or these days, drug lords.

'So you should always remember – law is local in Colombia. You may be on territory controlled by the local arm of the military or by the local representative of central government or by some local bigwig or by some guerrilla group – and there are plenty of those – or by one of the drug cartels. If someone offers you any help, try and make sure they can deliver what they say they can.'

'It sounds like a nightmare,' Chris said.

'In some ways it is. It's probably the most lawless country in the world. And yet most people who visit it also think it's one of the friendliest.' Pennington shrugged. He was beginning to enjoy himself.

'That's enough geography,' he went on. 'We don't yet know which group has Carlos Muñoz and Sergeant Anderson, but it's likely to be one of the major drug cartels. I'm using the word "cartels" because they're often called that in the media, but usually they're just phenomenally successful family businesses. And being successful they can each afford an army of hired guns – *sicarios* in local parlance.

'I'm probably telling you things you already know, but . . . cocaine is made from coca leaves. The coca bush doesn't grow in Colombia, only in a few high Andean valleys in Peru and Bolivia. The leaves are picked and reduced to a paste there, and then this is flown north to hundreds of hidden airstrip laboratories in the Colombian backwoods where it is further refined into pure cocaine. From there it's moved by sea and air, mostly across the Caribbean to the States. Over the last few years a growing amount has reached Europe, often via West Indian transit points.

'As you'd expect, the governments of the West are keen to at least reduce the flow, if not stop it. There are several obvious ways of going about this. They can try and stop the Peruvians and Bolivians from growing the leaf, try to intercept the shipments en route, or try to stop our kids wanting to use the stuff. They've tried all three and they're still trying, but the success rate isn't encouraging. The fourth option is to try and help the Colombian Government put its own house in order. Which I assume is why Anderson and Wynwood were out there helping to train an Anti-Narcotics Unit.

'I should add that a lot of people in the Colombian Government and Military have got their own snouts in the trough, and that the anti-cartel noises they make are strictly for show. They need to impress their own people at election time, and the rest of the world whenever there's trade or aid deals in the offing.

'Right. That's the place you're going to. It's a wild place, wild like the Falls Road rather than wild like the Falklands. But then again, it's probably the most beautiful country you'll ever see in your lives. The phrase "a land of contrasts" is pretty much a cliché, but it fits Colombia better than most.'

He sat down.

'Any questions?' Bourne asked.

'What kind of government is it?' the Dame wanted to know.

'What difference does it make?' Eddie muttered.

'There are regular elections, but it would be stretching it more than a little to call Colombia a real democracy,' Pennington said. 'The same groups tend to take turns in power.'

'Sounds like Hackney Council,' Eddie said.

Chris was trying to remember how far north the giant condors lived. He would give a lot to see one of them.

'OK,' Bourne said. 'Since we don't yet know where the prisoners are being held it's more a matter of getting you as near the likely action as possible.' He paused. 'Now this isn't the Falklands, and this isn't a military operation in that sense. You won't be going in armed.'

85

'What?!' Eddie and the Dame said in unison.

Bourne just smiled at them.

'Nothing?'

'You've been trained to look after yourselves without any technological help . . .'

'Yes, boss, but . . .'

'We don't know if you'll be expected. We don't know the connections between the Government, the Military and the cartels. We do know that Englishmen turning up at the Colombian border in the next few days armed to the teeth may make someone suspicious.'

'Border, boss?'

'This one.' Bourne pointed out the border with Ecuador. 'We don't want to fly you into Bogotá for exactly the reasons I've just stated – in the circumstances any English arrivals are liable to be deemed suspicious. So we're going to fly you into Quito, on a regular flight. By the time you get there we may have more information. Either way we'll take a decision about where you should rendezvous with Wynwood inside Colombia. The three of you will then make your way across the border. This is a travellers' trail – lots of Americans, Europeans, Australians, you name it – will be travelling in each direction. You'll just be three more. Your clothing and packs should be chosen accordingly – I don't want three standard-issue bergens in a row. Once you're inside Colombia we can see about getting you properly kitted up.'

'That's a relief.'

'Wynwood will be arranging for a cache.' Bourne looked at them. 'So all you three comics have to do is meet him without drawing attention to yourselves. That's all. Almost a joyride.'

'Thanks, boss,' Chris said with a smile.

'What's the weather like?' Eddie wanted to know. 'Should we take umbrellas?'

It was just past half-past eleven in Bogotá. Wynwood nursed his whisky chaser and stared blankly at the rows of bottles behind the bar of the Intercontinental Hotel. The only other customers were a group of middle-aged Germans in a booth behind him. Every now and then their guttural tones would impinge on Wynwood's consciousness, reminding him how much he disliked them and their nation. When it came down to it, the Germans had all the worst characteristics of the English and none of the latter's few redeeming features. Arrogant, humourless sods!

Wynwood had been propping up the bar since sundown, except for a brief interlude in the adjoining restaurant. He was not particularly drunk – he had been drinking too slowly for that – but neither was he the soberest man in South America.

The same thoughts were circling his brain like Indians round a wagon train. In fact they seemed to be drawing the circle tighter as the evening went on. The sheer absurdity of it was beginning to really piss him off. It all seemed so bloody unreal.

'So make it real,' he murmured to himself. Break the spell, talk to the bitch. Remind yourself why you're better off without her. Call her up.

He called the barman over. The barman told him he could make an international call from reception. Reception told him it would take about ten minutes, if he could wait in the booth. 'Sir does realize it is the middle of the night in England?'

Sir had forgotten that, but what the hell. Wynwood waited by the phone booth, deliberately avoiding any premeditated thought of what he was going to say, until the receptionist indicated he should pick up the phone. It was ringing. Amazing, he thought. All that distance. It was a fucking miracle.

The phone kept ringing. Twenty times, thirty times. It gradually dawned on Wynwood that his wife was not at home.

He could not remember ever feeling so frustrated in his whole life.

He put the phone down with dreadful care and left the booth. The receptionist was saying something, but he ignored him, walking down the three steps and out through the swing doors onto the busy avenue. He stopped for a second, then spun round to the right and broke into a brisk walk. He had no idea where he was going and he didn't much care.

The Colombians filling the crowded pavement – the ones that saw him coming – stepped judiciously out of his way. Some were not so lucky, and simply got shoved aside. Their curses followed him, but he hardly heard them.

The city was like white noise. He went past food stalls doing a brisk trade, cafés with music pouring from their doorways, groups of men gathered round a spinning wheel of faces, coins clattering on a board. He saw none of them.

It was a mile or more before he let the world back in, absent-mindedly agreeing to buy some chewing gum from a child who should have been in bed hours ago. The child's delight was like some sort of switch. Suddenly Wynwood was aware of his surroundings again, and they left something to be desired. The swish shops and elegant squares of the city centre had given way to an altogether harsher environment, full of seedy-looking pool halls, rusty cars and groups of aimless-looking young men.

This was not the safest place in Bogotá, Wynwood realized. Thanks to his dark hair and sun-tanned skin his presence had so far not been noticed. So far. But he had come out without either the Browning or his knife.

'Dumbo,' he muttered to himself, looking round for a taxi to get him the hell out of there.

And then he saw her. She was really something: slimmer than most Colombian women he had seen, with dark hair spilling across brown shoulders, a tight-waisted red cotton dress emphasizing the rounded swell of breasts and hips.

And she was looking at him.

'Would you like some love?' she asked, or at least that was what he thought she said.

And somehow the question made him feel both sorry for himself and angry for feeling it. Yes, he thought, he'd like some love. Who wouldn't? Plus, it would get him off the street. 'What did you have in mind?' he asked.

'Come with me and I'll show you,' she said, offering him her hand. He took it, and she led him away down the side street.

She smelled of soap and water. Christ, he thought, he had not been with a prostitute since he was a teenager. And they didn't look like this round King's Cross. While a voice in his head told him how stupid he was being, his eyes were taking in the smooth brown skin of her shoulders and upper breasts. She stopped at a door and smiled up at him. 'This is my house,' she said.

They went in through an open door and up two flights of stairs to a door with paint peeling off it. She took a key from her purse and opened it. The sound of a crying baby was coming from somewhere inside.

'Go through there,' she said, pointing to another door, 'I will be only a moment.' He did as he was told, and found himself in a surprisingly large room. A large bed took up the far corner, and the only other furniture was a chair and table. On the latter were several books – two of them English primers.

She came in, closing the door behind her. 'You are American, yes,' she said carefully in English.

'British,' Wynwood said. Telling people you were Welsh in Colombia was guaranteed to elicit only puzzlement.

'I learn,' she said.

'So I see,' Wynwood said. This was getting more difficult.

As if sensing this she went to the window and opened the shutters, bathing the far wall with an orange-neon glow from some invisible outside source. Then she turned the room lighting off, removed her belt and, with one simple movement, stepped out of her dress. She was wearing nothing underneath it.

'You like?' she asked.

Wynwood took a deep breath. 'Yep,' he said.

She smiled and walked across to him. She put one hand around his neck, while the other searched for and found the bulge his cock was beginning to make in his jeans. 'Twenty dollars for everything,' she said, her palm lightly stroking him as she waited for his reply.

'Cheap at the price,' Wynwood murmured.

'*Qué?*'

'Sí, twenty dollars.'

Her fingers unfastened his shirt, then his jeans. He stepped out of them, and she pulled down his shorts, took his cock in both hands and began to massage it.

Christ, it felt good.

'I have condom,' she said.

'Great,' Wynwood said. It was a good thing one of them had some sense.

She rummaged in a drawer full of clothes while Wynwood enjoyed the graceful lines of her behind, found the packet of condoms and extracted one for him. Then she lay back across the bed, her legs crossed, with one hand on her stomach, the other holding the condom on the pillow behind her head.

Wynwood lay down beside her and ran his hand down her body.

She handed him the condom and watched while he put it on.

'Would you like me on top?' she asked.

'No,' he said, gently pushing her legs apart and pulling himself on top of her.

She took him in her hand and guided him inside with a practised motion.

He tried to kiss her, and though she didn't refuse it, she didn't take much part in the exercise either. Her body was moving energetically enough. Trying to get it over as quickly as possible, a small voice said in the back of Wynwood's mind. And it worked. His two months of celibacy ended in a satisfying rush.

He lay there on top of her, other thoughts crowding into his mind, hardly noticing as she gently disengaged them and rolled him onto his side.

But he did notice the door slam open.

There were two of them. Both were in their late teens or early twenties, wearing almost identical clothes – T-shirts, tight jeans and trainers. The differences lay in the messages emblazoned on the T-shirts: while one proclaimed the superiority of Pepsi the other endorsed Madonna's claim to be 'Like A Virgin'.

Wynwood swung his legs off the bed and sat on its edge, looking up at them. He made no move to reach for his clothes – that would be seen as a sign of weakness.

'*Buenas noches*,' one of them said with a smile.

Wynwood looked round at the girl to see if she was part of this. Her face betrayed nothing.

'What do you want, *compadres?*' he asked them

The one who had smiled, laughed. The other looked tough. They had seen too many movies. But they were both big for Colombians, Wynwood admitted to himself. And he was not in the best state he had ever been in. He wondered if they were armed.

As if in reply to the unspoken question, Smiler pulled a gun from his jeans pocket, and his partner a flick-knife, pressing the switch as he did so, causing the blade to leap out dramatically.

'I bet you practise that in front of the mirror,' Wynwood said.

The frown deepened. Obviously he did.

'We want everything you have, gringo,' Smiler said. 'It's only fair – you come here and fuck our women and fuck our country. You should pay for all this. It's only fair.'

'And you're Robin Hood and Little John, I suppose?' Wynwood was beginning to realize just how bad this was going to be if he fucked up. Andy was relying on him, and what the fuck was he doing?

'Your money, gringo. And a specimen of your signature with the credit cards of course.'

Wynwood reached for his trousers, pulled out his wallet and handed it up. Frowner stepped forward three paces, taking care not to get between his partner's gun and Wynwood, took the wallet and passed it to his partner.

Smiler's smile widened. With this act of submission Wynwood had removed any anxiety they might have had. Smiler moved the gun from one hand to the other to examine the wallet. Frowner did not bother to retreat the full three paces he had advanced, and his attention was divided between Wynwood and what bounties the wallet might contain.

This was the moment. Wynwood rose and took a step towards Frowner in one swift movement, then continued on, bringing the other foot up in a vicious arc between the man's legs, and the right arm down across the subclavian artery as he buckled.

It took two seconds. Smiler was still trying to juggle the gun from one hand to the other when Wynwood's fist slammed into his throat. He fell back, breath rasping and still clutching the gun. Wynwood trod on his wrist and extricated it from his fingers.

He turned to see the girl looking at him with a mixture of awe and . . . contempt?

He felt suddenly naked.

Frowner was groaning on the floor, Smiler wheezing. Wynwood watched them as he dressed, keeping the gun within easy reach. He handed the girl her twenty dollars, which she took and placed under a pillow without saying a word.

She had made no effort to dress herself. She looked, Wynwood thought, like a fallen madonna, or was he just being sentimental. She also looked about sixteen. Why hadn't she looked that young before?

He turned back to the youths. 'Get up!' he said.

They did so, humiliation and frustration sharing the pain in their expressions.

'Now go away,' Wynwood said. 'And don't bother this girl any more.'

'She is our sister,' Frowner said. It was the first time Wynwood had heard him speak.

He laughed without humour. 'Get lost,' he said.

They went. She looked at him as if she was expecting him to take his money back.

'How do I get back to the centre?' he asked.

'There are taxis,' she said reluctantly.

'Where?'

93

'Round the corner. Everywhere.'

He picked up her dress and threw it to her. 'Show me. And I'll give you another five dollars.'

'Big deal,' she said. But she pulled the dress on.

They went back down to the street. There was no sign of her two 'brothers'. Three taxis were waiting round the first corner, outside what looked, from the tickets littering the pavement, like a betting joint.

Wynwood climbed in, and they drove off. Looking back he could see her standing on the pavement, just staring into space.

Back at his hotel the night clerk gave him his key and a quizzical look. He ignored the man, wearily climbed the stairs and tried to unlock the door of his room. It was already unlocked. He cautiously pushed it open.

'It's only me,' Oliver's voice said from inside.

Wynwood closed the door behind him. The embassy man was sitting in the only chair, an open bottle of aguardiente on his lap. 'Well?' Wynwood asked, sitting on the edge of the bed.

'You look like you've been out on the town,' Oliver commented.

'You could say that.'

Oliver grunted. 'Well, there's no news from London, and in this case no news is good news. It seems to be on.'

Wynwood let his head fall back onto the bed. 'Brilliant,' he said.

'And I think I've located Anderson and Muñoz,' Oliver went on.

Wynwood sat up again. 'Even better. Where are they?'

'Outside Popayán – you know where that is? – about a hundred and thirty kilometres south of Cali. The Amarales family have them. Theirs is probably the third largest of the cartels. Their headquarters is a ranch called Totoro, some

94

thirty kilometres outside Popayán, and that's where my information says they've taken Anderson and Muñoz.'

'This is probably a naive question, but if it's just a ranch not far from a major town, why . . .'

'Why can't the authorities do something?' Oliver smiled. 'It is a naive question. The whole area is in their pocket – police, military, you name it . . . that province belongs to the Amarales.' He poured Wynwood an inch of aguardiente. 'And the ranch itself is like a fortress,' he added cheerfully.

4

It felt strange going off like this, without so much as a knife. It was more like going on holiday, Eddie thought, surveying all the bodies spread around the Gatwick departure lounge who were planning on just that – waiting to be jetted away for a week in the sun. Mind you, he thought, in the old days he usually had taken a knife on holiday.

Their scheduled departure time was still an hour away. Chris had disappeared, the Dame was deep into a Wilbur Smith, and he was bored. Why not ring her, he thought. What harm could it do?

'You're on bag detail,' he told the Dame, and went looking for a phone. It rang just once before she picked up.

'Hi,' he said.

'I knew it was you,' Lisa said.

'No, you didn't,' he retorted. Somehow things like that made him uneasy.

'Yes, I did. Don't be so grumpy. Where are you?'

'At the airport.'

'What airport? Why?'

'I'm going away for a bit. That's why I'm ringing.'

'Oh.'

'I didn't want you to think I'd just disappeared,' he said, surprising himself.

'How long will you be?'

'Don't know. Couple of weeks, maybe a month.'

'Send us a postcard . . .'

'Yeah, look, I haven't got any more money,' he lied. 'I'll be in touch when I get back, OK?'

'OK. I . . .'

The line went dead. 'I' what? Eddie wondered. He stood there for a moment, thinking. She had a nice voice. And she was . . . straight, that was it. She was straight. He liked that. She said what she thought. No bullshit. He liked her. He thought about the time in his back seat and felt something stir in his trousers.

Across the departure lounge he could see Chris and the Dame talking to a young man in a suit. The latter had disappeared by the time he had rejoined them. 'Who was he?' Eddie asked Chris.

'Foreign Office,' Chris said. 'He brought us this.' He handed him a book: *The South American Handbook 1990*.

'In case we get lost?'

'The chaps thought we might find it useful,' Chris said with an upper-class accent. 'Where've you been?' he asked.

'On the phone. I suddenly remembered I hadn't broken a woman's heart yet today.'

'Mission accomplished?'

'I expect she's knee-deep in tears by now.'

'Of gratitude, I expect,' Chris said. He had rung Molly the night before, and she had been downright cool. Still, they hadn't exactly got to know each other yet. 'You got anyone to ring, Dame?' he asked.

'Nope.'

97

'It's all those sisters,' Eddie observed. 'They weaken a man.'

'I thought that was against the law,' Chris observed.

'Not up north – they're used to sleeping four to a bed up there. And you know, one thing leads to another and . . .

'They're sleeping five to a bed.'

'Exactly.'

The Dame observed them tolerantly. 'What you two know about the North could be written on a rabbit turd.'

'I expect everything anyone needs to know about the North could be written on a rabbit turd,' Chris said.

'Maybe it's not the sisters,' Eddie mused. 'Maybe it's not even the pictures of Virginia Bottomley he keeps under his pillow.'

'What then?'

'I think our friend here has made a great discovery. He's realized that there's only one person he really wants to make love to, only one person who won't complain about his appalling technique or embarrass him in the morning by demanding a spoon with the cornflakes . . .'

'Who can this be?' Chris wondered out loud.

'Himself, of course.'

The Dame gave them an ironic round of applause, slammed his Wilbur Smith shut and got to his feet. 'Boarding Gate 22,' he said.

'Sit down, John,' Barney Davies said.

Kilcline obliged.

'I've just been talking to the PM.' He thought about this statement and amended it. 'Listening to her might be a better way of putting it.'

'She's not called it off!?'

'No. It's still on . . .'

'Thank God for that!'

'Yes. There's one fly in the ointment, though. We've had to involve the Americans . . .'

'Why for Christ's sake?'

'Two reasons. One, MI6 insisted they needed CIA help inside Colombia. Two, the Foreign Office insisted that using the Colombian military to pull the lads out was unnecessarily risky. MI6 supported them. So the Americans will do it from Panama.'

'Have they got the range?' Kilcline asked doubtfully.

'They say so. And before you ask, they're restricting it to a Need to Know.'

'Oh good,' Kilcline said sarcastically. 'It won't be in the papers till tomorrow then.'

'I don't think so. They're only helping with a weapons cache for the patrol *in situ* and providing a taxi service. And there's no organizational connection between the two jobs.' He shrugged. 'Anyway, ours not to reason why, etcetera. Let's look on the bright side. It's on. Our man in Bogotá – name of Oliver – will be on a scrambled line to you at 1600 hours our time. He'll be your liaison with Wynwood and the patrol. So set up contact procedures. And make it clear to him that whatever Wynwood wants he should get.' He paused, then smiled. 'I don't need to tell you that, do I? No. OK. How soon can we get our lads away?'

'First thing tomorrow.'

'Good. Let's do it.'

Two hours later Oliver was ushering Wynwood down Carrera 7 towards lunch. Wynwood felt more hung-over than hungry, but Oliver had insisted. They found the restaurant the embassy man was looking for halfway up one of the streets leading down to the Plaza Bolivar.

It was called the Indian Cultural Museum, which did not seem such a strange name for an eating-place once they got inside. The room had more Indian artefacts in it than people, and it was dark, with candles burning brightly on each table. The long wall of windows might have admitted more of the noon sunlight, but the courtyard it overlooked was filled with a dense jungle of foliage, and only the slimmest line of blue sky was visible above the tall plants, creating the momentary impression that they were sitting at the bottom of a well.

There seemed to be only one dish on the menu, so Oliver ordered it for both of them and then disappeared in the direction of the toilets. Wynwood was left to nurse his head. Strangely enough, in every other way he felt better than he had the day before. The events of the previous evening had somehow exorcized something.

Oliver returned to the table. 'Nice, isn't it?' he observed, looking round. 'And quiet. I've just been talking to one of your superiors – a Major Kilcline.'

'Killer.'

Oliver looked at him askance. 'If you say so. I have instructions for you.' He paused while the waiter arrived with a half carafe of Chilean wine, took an appreciative sip, and continued. 'You are to rendezvous with three other men – Martinson, Wilshaw and Robson – tomorrow in the Plaza de Armas in Popayán. At 1900 hours. If either party is late then try again two hours later, then at 0900 hours the next morning and at two hour intervals throughout the day. Is that all clear?'

'Yep.' A good choice of men, Wynwood thought. He had worked with Chris Martinson before, and he had heard good things about both Eddie Wilshaw and Damien Robson.

'Next thing . . . ah, we'll have to wait.'

The food was arriving, but not on plates. Each steak was presented on a wooden board, with a selection of vegetables arranged around it – one potato, one cassava, one dumpling-like object which Oliver said was called an *arepa*. A circular hollow in the board held a small quantity of highly spiced liquid.

Hungry or not Wynwood found it all delicious, and he said so. Oliver gave him a slight bow, as if he was the chef receiving compliments, and refilled their wine glasses. 'Back to business,' he said. 'The four of you are to place Totoro under observation. The cache should be in place soon, and once you have recovered it you will of course be able to talk directly to your people in Belize on the radio. Until then your only link is with me by telephone, and it shouldn't be used by you except in an emergency. I will call you each day with news of your mother. When she comes out of the coma the cache is ready for collection. Understood?'

'What's in the cache?'

Oliver reached into his pocket. 'This is the list I was given by Hereford, with the understanding that I'd ask you if there was anything needed adding.'

Wynwood scanned the list. Everything seemed to be there. Except . . . 'Add a couple of Claymores,' he said, 'with all the usual trimmings.' He read through the list once more, and handed it back. 'Plus I need a car.'

'Here or in Popayán?'

'Here would be better – I'd feel less conspicuous travelling down that way. But I'm really thinking of there – it'll give us some flexibility.'

'I can't see any problem. Any particular make?'

'A Rolls?'

'How about a Fiat?'

'Long as it's not red.'

'I'll see what I can do.' Oliver gestured to the waiter. 'Let's continue this conversation outside,' he suggested to Wynwood.

They left the restaurant and strolled slowly down the bustling Carrera 7 to the Plaza Bolivar.

'This should be safe enough,' Oliver said, taking a seat on a low wall in the centre of the square. 'See that empty space,' he said conversationally, pointing out a large gap in the buildings surrounding the square. 'That's where the Palace of Justice used to stand. Guerrillas occupied it a few years ago, taking about thirty hostages, and the Army decided that the best way to deal with the situation was to level the building. With the guerrillas and the hostages still inside.' He smiled. 'There aren't many races capable of giving lessons in ruthlessness to the Spanish.'

Wynwood could believe it.

'Anyway,' Oliver said, rubbing his hands together, 'two of your troops will be arriving in Belize tomorrow. They'll be ready to drop in on the Amarales family at your invitation.'

'Who's taking us out?' Wynwood wanted to know.

'The Americans.'

Wynwood was not surprised. 'From Panama?'

'Yes. They're also filling your weaponry order and getting satellite shots of Totoro to supplement your work on the ground.'

Wynwood nodded. 'So when can I get the car?'

'You don't need to leave till tomorrow morning.'

'I'd rather get off today.' He looked round to where the twin towers of the cathedral seemed to be almost glowing against the background of dark hills and darkening sky. 'I've had enough of Bogotá,' he said.

'That I can understand,' Oliver said. 'I'll see what I can do.'

Richard Anderson pushed away the lunch tray and went to the window. It was the fourth morning of his captivity, and the lack of information as to his captors' intentions was beginning to get to him. Neither he nor Muñoz had been badly treated – in fact, in many ways, they were almost being pampered. Anderson imagined most prisoners the world over would settle for nicely furnished single rooms with a shared bathroom, three good meals and two hours of outside exercise a day. One of the guards had even lent him one of the pornographic comics which Colombian men loved so much: '"*Would she do that for him?" the handsome Rodrigo asked.*' You bet she would.

No, there was no material discomfort – it was just not knowing what was happening. Not knowing when or whether he would ever see Beth and the kids again.

The view from the window certainly did not tell him much. It faced slightly north of east – that much he knew from the sun – but all he could see was the small yard where they took their exercise, the wall which bounded it and forested slopes rising in the distance beyond it. He could have been in Wales if it was not for the heat.

He wondered where Wynwood was now. Either dead or back in England, he supposed.

A key sounded in the lock. Thinking it was the guard come to get the breakfast tray, Anderson did not bother to turn round.

'Señor,' said a voice he had not heard before. It belonged to a young man with blue eyes and a scar that split his left cheek. 'Come with me, please,' he said. The voice seemed almost liquid, Anderson thought irrelevantly. But polite, he added to himself. If he was being invited to his execution at least he was being invited politely. He walked past the pale blue eyes and out through the door.

'This way,' Chirlo said, leading him down a corridor, past what looked like a security centre, and up a flight of stairs to the first floor. Another short corridor led out onto a wide upper verandah where a man was pouring coffee into three cups from a silver jug. Beyond him lay a panoramic view of the valley leading down to the river.

'*Buenos dias*, Señor Anderson – that is your name, yes?' the man said in Spanish. 'Please have a seat. I am Ramón Amarales and this,' he added, indicating Anderson's escort, 'is Chirlo.'

Anderson sat down. Perhaps at last he was going to be told something of his future.

He accepted the proffered cup of coffee and suddenly noticed the book on the table. It was a Spanish translation of a well-known British book on the SAS.

Amarales noticed his look of surprise. 'I am a great fan of the SAS,' he said, stirring his own coffee. Chirlo, as usual, had taken a seat in the shadows. 'Did you not notice anything familiar about our operation in Malverdes?'

'The SAS doesn't usually attack political rallies,' Anderson said.

'But the method – it was borrowed from your own attack on the Embassy of Iran in London in 1980.'

Anderson smiled. 'We didn't leave an escape route open at the back.'

'Of course not. I am not claiming our men are trained to anything like the SAS's level of efficiency. Yet. But I would like them to be. This is why we are having this talk. I would like you to help train my men.'

'You must . . .'

'Before you say anything, Señor Anderson, let me finish. I have made some enquiries as to how much you are being paid in the SAS – very little, it seems to me, for all that you are prepared to do and risk. I will give you five times your annual salary for a mere ten weeks of your time as an adviser.'

'I . . .'

'One more thing. You will doubtless have one of two major objections to this. If you are a typical honest Englishman you will not want to work for a "drug baron", is that not so? Well, I think once you know more about the realities of our situation here in Colombia you may find it hard to see any great moral difference between working for the Amarales family and working for the families who run the Government in Bogotá. At one level we are all what you would call crooks, at another we are all just trying to make our way in a jungle that is not of our making.

'If, on the other hand, you are not so "honest", then you may be wondering how you will explain deserting your unit for ten weeks to earn a fortune. But you need not worry about that. It can be easily worked out, believe me. For all anyone knows, you are our prisoner. And there are many ways to arrange payment.'

Anderson smiled. 'You have not reminded me of the great objection to refusing you – what will happen to me if I do refuse.'

'Nothing. At present your embassy in Bogotá is considering a demand for half a million US dollars as the price of your return. I expect you have more idea than me whether they will agree to this . . .'

'No,' Anderson said. He did not have a clue.

'Well,' Amarales continued, 'if they are prepared to spend billions on recovering the Malvinas for a thousand shepherds, then it would seem sensible to pay half a million for a highly trained officer like yourself. But . . .' He shrugged. 'I am offering no threats. As you can imagine, money like that is always welcome, but I would rather have your services for those ten weeks if possible.'

Anderson was not sure how to respond. 'Can I think it over?' he asked.

'Of course.'

'And what about Señor Muñoz?'

'I don't think there's much *he* can teach us . . .' Amarales said.

Chirlo laughed, making his presence felt for the first time since the conversation began.

'So it's just a matter of ransom,' Amarales continued. 'A million dollars in his case. He comes from a very wealthy family,' he added. 'The ones who care so much about the poor usually do.' He looked at Anderson. 'Were you in the Malvinas, by the way?'

'Yes,' Anderson said, seeing no reason to deny it.

'Excellent,' Amarales said. 'I would like to talk to you about the reconquest some evening. I have read many accounts of the battles, but there are several questions which never seem to be answered.'

Anderson said nothing.

'Very well then,' Amarales said in dismissal. Chirlo rose from his seat and accompanied the SAS man back downstairs, not saying a word. The key turned in the lock once more, leaving Anderson feeling the need for someone to talk to.

He walked through to the adjoining room, where Muñoz was lying on his bed gazing at another pornographic comic. 'They want a million dollars for you,' he told the Colombian. 'The man himself just told me.'

'Amarales?' Muñoz pulled himself up to lean against the headboard. 'I expect my father will pay,' he said. 'What about you?'

'He only wants half as much for me. But he'd rather pay me to stay on voluntarily to train his goons.'

'I shouldn't put too much store by any promises he makes,' Muñoz said. 'And don't make the mistake of thinking that because he's a well-spoken Spaniard he won't just have you killed. These people only understand the law of the jungle, my friend.'

That's what he said about you, Anderson thought. Jesus, what a country. He would swap all these fucking mountains for one square foot of Morecambe Bay mud. If he ever got the chance.

It was soon after five when their plane completed its descent into the mountain bowl which housed the capital of Ecuador.

The first flight, across the Atlantic, had been uneventful. Chris had drunk, slept and browsed through *The South American Handbook*; Eddie had drunk, slept and watched the movie; the Dame had drunk and read Wilbur Smith. Shortly after noon US Eastern Time they had landed in a grey-skied Miami, and spent another two hours in a departure lounge.

The AeroPeru flight to Ecuador was notable only for the identical gorgeousness of two of the hostesses. They had eaten their third major meal in nine hours and watched an American movie with Spanish subtitles that featured an English torturer working for a corrupt Latino crime syndicate. It had not seemed like a particularly good omen, but the twins had smiled at them as they left the plane.

Customs and Immigration took an irritating amount of time, but otherwise there were no problems. It was almost dark by the time they had found a taxi for the ride into the city.

London had booked three rooms for them at the Hotel Valencia. The receptionist seemed blissfully unaware of this, and after fifteen minutes of argument tiredness was turning irritation into anger. Fortunately, at this moment someone arrived from the embassy, a few notes changed hands, and the reservation was discovered. They went up to their rooms, which were in a line on the second floor front, overlooking the park.

They all trooped into Chris's room. The man from the embassy – 'just call me Stephen' – underlined what the briefers at Hereford had told them, that they would need a couple of hours' rest before their bodies were ready to cope properly with 2700 metres of altitude.

'No problem,' they all agreed.

Stephen arranged to come back at nine that evening, and the three SAS men went to their rooms and laid themselves out.

Eddie could not rest. And he felt fine. He decided that as long as he did nothing too strenuous he would not have any problems. They would probably be heading north in the morning, and who knew when he would ever get to see Quito again. It was not exactly next door to Hackney.

He pushed a note under Chris's door and went out. The streets seemed fuller than when they had driven in, as if everyone had suddenly come out for an evening stroll. There were eating-places everywhere, and walking along the pavements of the old city was like moving through a long line of delicious smells. It was almost enough to make him feel hungry.

He reached a square where a small band was playing, surrounded by a large circle of onlookers. In a farther corner of the same square three jugglers were practising, throwing tenpins between them. It all seemed extraordinarily alive.

Down a narrow side street he got a surprise – pride of place on a stall selling posters belonged to a large picture of a topless Samantha Fox. 'And they say our exports are shrinking,' Eddie murmured to himself. Almost as incomprehensibly, most of the other posters seemed to be of Swiss scenery. He had been under the impression that Ecuador had mountains of its own.

It was gone eight now, yet the shops were all still open. A bookshop had a window display devoted to the Galápagos Islands, which made him think of Chris and his wildlife fetish. Chris had been moaning all day that he had not had time to get a book about South American birds.

They had one inside. It was heavy, would cost most of his cash, but looked good. He bought it and started back for the hotel.

Chris was waiting for him. 'If you collapse from altitude sickness don't expect me to carry you,' he said angrily.

'You'll be too busy carrying this,' Eddie said handing him the book.

Chris looked at it. 'Oh you bastard,' he said. 'You beautiful bastard.' He grabbed Eddie and kissed him on the forehead.

'I thought you two were only into women,' the Dame said from the doorway.

'And goats,' Eddie corrected him.

'Gentlemen,' Stephen said from over the Dame's shoulder.

He shut the door behind him, paused theatrically, and gave them the same time and place Oliver had given Wynwood.

'How long will it take us?' Chris wanted to know.

Stephen considered. 'Four hours to the border, two to get across, five or six more to Popayán.'

'Looks like an early start,' Eddie said.

Wynwood had been woken from his siesta that afternoon by the phone. 'Your car's in the hotel parking lot,' Oliver told him. 'A green Fiat Uno, registration 6785 B 34. It's on hire from Hertz. There are some maps in the glove compartment which I thought you'd find useful. The keys are at the desk.'

'Is the hotel bill paid?' Wynwood asked.

'Until tomorrow lunchtime.'

'OK . . .'

'Only call me if you have to,' Oliver reiterated. 'I'll be in touch.'

'Over and out,' Wynwood said and hung up. He sat on the side of the bed for a moment. 'No time like the present,' he murmured to himself. He gathered up his belongings, packed them into the blue holdall he had brought from England, and left the hotel by the back exit. He found the car, threw the holdall in the back seat, re-entered the hotel by the back door, picked up the key and left again through the front.

In the car he spent several minutes examining a large-scale road map of the country, and made a snap decision. The quickest route to Popayán was via Ibagué and Cali, but he did not fancy retracing his route of three days before. The route via Neiva had dubious roads and would probably be an even longer drive than it looked, but he had plenty of time and it felt safer. It was the way to go.

He pulled the Fiat out into the afternoon traffic. Twenty minutes later he was skirting the ridge of the bowl which contained the city, and heading south on the aptly named Carretera del Sur.

At what seemed the last major intersection before the city fell away he found what he was looking for – a fellow-Caucasian hitchhiker. And a female one to boot.

She had to be crazy, he thought as he pulled over, a single woman hitching in a country as macho as it was lawless. And she was certainly not unattractive, he discovered as she climbed gratefully into the front seat. Her hair was long and blonde, framing a face that seemed instantly welcoming. 'Hi,' she said in the American accent he had expected, stretching long legs to hoist her rucksack into the back seat.

'Hi,' he said.

'Where you headed?' she asked.

'Neiva,' he said. 'That do you?'

'It's great. I've been standing there nearly an hour – anywhere's great. But Neiva's on my way.'

'To where?' Wynwood asked. He could hardly credit she had been there that long. Maybe it was National Celibacy Week in Colombia.

'San Agustín, you know?'

'No, what's there?'

'Wow, don't you know?' she said, unable to believe his ignorance. 'It's like the biggest tourist attraction in Colombia almost. After Cartagena, maybe. There's lots of old statues – really old statues, from before Columbus, you know – and they're spread out on green hills in this gorgeous valley. But that's not all – it's like a kind of place where there's a lot of, you know, travelling people living there. Some have been there for twenty years, ever since the hippie trail started down to Peru in the sixties. It's a really peaceful place.'

'You've been there before?'

'No, but I know people who have. Everyone says it's the one place in Colombia you have to see.'

'Maybe I'll get there,' Wynwood said.

'Where do you come from?' she asked. 'Are you English?'

'Welsh,' he said. 'My name's Joss.'

'I'm Bobbie,' she said. 'From San Diego. How far is it to Neiva?'

'Just over three hundred kilometres.'

She absorbed the information. 'I'll have to stay the night there,' she thought out loud. 'Do you know anywhere good to stay?'

'No,' Wynwood said absent-mindedly. The black Merc two cars behind him seemed to have been there as long as he could remember. Or was he just getting paranoid? He would find out when they stopped for a drink.

'Shall we have some music?' Bobbie was asking.

'I don't have any,' Wynwood said.

'I do,' she said, leaning back over the seat again and rummaging in her rucksack.

He had been afraid of that. A few seconds later Mick Hucknall's voice was echoing round the car. It could have been worse, Wynwood thought. At least it wasn't grunge or Barry Manilow. And it might stop her talking. It didn't, but he didn't really mind.

She was quite entertaining, brighter than she was knowledgeable, and older than she looked. Closer to thirty than twenty, a lot closer. As they swapped tales of their countries and families and travels he began to get the sense that she had been pretty bruised by something or someone, and for some reason that made him like her the more. He had always been a sucker for wounded birds.

Through Fusagasuga he drove, and down from the mountains and into the Magdalena valley, the heat rising to meet them like a damp mist. They crossed the river at Girardot and headed south up its valley, passing the turn-off to Ibagué and Cali as the sun disappeared beyond the western crest. Behind them the black Merc kept its hundred-metre distance, only passing them when Wynwood stopped at a small and grubby roadside stall for two bottles of coke. Three kilometres farther on it pulled back onto the road behind them.

So who was it, Wynwood wondered. Amarales family goons? That seemed the best bet, but how the hell had they traced him? It did not say much for Oliver's security, or for any hopes of achieving surprise in any action against the drug lords. For all he knew the men in the Merc – he assumed there was more than one – were Colombian police or security people in the pay of one of the drug cartels.

Either way, he had to shake them off. His thoughts turned to when, where and how. If it had not been for Bobbie he would have opted for somewhere near and soon. Picking her up to give him protective colouring might have been a good idea, but it looked like he had picked up the tail before her. Now the protective colouring was more like a millstone. He could always just dump her somewhere, but he would have found it hard to dump his worst enemy by a Colombian highway at nightfall, let alone a pretty American blonde with a faith in humanity that verged on the suicidal.

But once in Neiva both he and the car would be more exposed and more vulnerable. And whatever happened he did not want it to happen in front of witnesses. He needed to stay as invisible as a Welshman could in Colombia; he needed to reach Popayán with no one in pursuit.

And even if he had been willing to let his presence be known there was no way he could trust the local authorities. God only knew whose side those in Neiva were on – he might find himself arrested on some trumped-up charge that night and handed over to the Amarales tomorrow.

It had to be before Neiva. And he had to get Bobbie out of the way. A good-sized roadside restaurant, he thought. He had not given his pursuers much warning of his departure from Bogotá, so unless they kept a picnic hamper permanently stashed in their back seat they were probably as hungry as he was. He started watching out for one.

Bobbie, he discovered, had fallen asleep to her Joan Armatrading tape, her mouth slightly open, revealing a pink tongue and perfect American teeth.

He found the restaurant half an hour later, and pulled in to the large parking lot. He nudged her awake. 'Dinner time,' he said. 'My treat.'

'That's very nice of you,' she said, eyes shining.

'Can you go in and get us a table?' he said. 'I'll be with you in a few minutes.'

She looked surprised but said OK.

Once she was gone he recovered the cross-draw holster from the holdall and put it on. He slipped the Browning in, and pulled the windcheater on over his shirt.

Outside the car the air was hot and sticky. The restaurant was perched between the highway and the Magdalena, whose wide dark waters rolled majestically along fifty metres to his right. Wynwood walked across to the front door, brushing insects from his face.

At the door he turned to see the Merc pulling up on the other side of the lot, close to the river. Inside, Bobbie had chosen an ideal table, close enough to the door that he would get a good view of the enemy when they came in. If they came in.

They did. There were three of them, two fairly young and one who looked around forty. The two young ones were both wearing tight-fitting suits which had not been tailored to take account of the shoulder holsters they were wearing. If the older one was carrying a gun it was at his waist. As the three of them walked across to a table on the far side of the restaurant, none of them cast so much as a glance in Wynwood's direction.

He and Bobbie both chose steak and eggs. The waiter delivered their order at the serving hatch, then went to take the threesome's. The older man asked him something, and the waiter cast a quick glance back at Wynwood's table. He had been asked what the gringos had ordered, Wynwood guessed – they did not want to order a good meal themselves and then have to abandon it half-eaten.

He smiled to himself.

'Aren't you hot in that jacket?' Bobbie asked.

'No,' he lied.

They chatted about Bogotá until the food arrived. It was good, and there was lots of it. Bobbie cleared her plate with relish. No fears of anorexia for this one, Wynwood thought.

The threesome across the room were still in mid-meal. Wynwood loudly ordered coffees, and just as vociferously asked where the men's toilet might be. Out the back, he was told, as expected.

He went through the doorway indicated, and found himself in a corridor leading to a back entrance. Once outside he broke into a run, reaching the Merc in a few seconds. He had been intending to shoot out its tyres, but the door was open and it took only a second to take off the handbrake, get round the front and start pushing the car towards the river. As he strained to push it across the slightly raised area of ground by the river bank he wondered if he was doing the right thing. His pursuers would just steal another car . . .

What the hell, he thought, and with one last heave tipped the £20,000 car over the rim of the bank and down into the water. The car slid in up to its roof before the current started to tug it away.

He turned away to find the three men walking towards him, all with guns in hand.

'Gringo!' the older one shouted.

Wynwood remembered Andy's question: 'Do you ever feel like you're in a Western?'

'I think we will have to use your car now,' one of the younger ones said.

There seemed to be no grounds for compromise, Wynwood thought. And they had made a stupid mistake – he would be almost invisible against the darkness of the far bank, while they were silhouetted against the light from the restaurant.

He pulled the Browning from its holster, raised it with both arms and aimed at the younger man on the right. Not at the head, his training told him – it's too dark. He put a double tap through the upper torso, another through the same portion of the older man in the centre, then sank to one knee as the third man fired wildly over his head. Wynwood fired again and the third man went down.

He walked carefully across to the three prone figures. They were all dead. He took a deep breath and started pulling them one by one to the edge of the river. Once he had done that he tipped each one in beside the rapidly disappearing Merc, then walked back towards the restaurant, wondering how much had been heard.

His Browning was silenced, but they would have had to be deaf to miss the shot fired by the Colombian.

Maybe they were, maybe they weren't. No one seemed to be calling the police or cowering behind the hatch.

'You've been a long time,' Bobbie said as he rejoined her. 'I was beginning to get worried. And I thought I heard a shot.'

'They say gunfire is the national music of Colombia,' Wynwood said. 'Shall we go?'

They reached Neiva two hours later. Bobbie asked him if he wanted to share a hotel room. 'Just friends,' she added hastily, in case he had misunderstood. Why not, he thought. He found her about as sexually stimulating as a teddy bear, and he had kind of grown to like her over the last eight hours.

5

Troopers Sam 'Blackie' Blackman and Charles 'Bonnie' McCall sat side by side in the belly of the Hercules C-130. Somewhere beneath them was the Gulf of Mexico. They seemed to have been flying for ever, but according to Bonnie's watch it was only thirteen hours.

'We must be running out of fuel,' Blackie said, running a hand through what the barber had left of his hair. He was a tall Liverpudlian, with a body that looked more gangling than it actually was.

'No such luck.' Bonnie tried to make himself more comfortable for the umpteenth time. He was slightly smaller than Blackie, a ginger-haired Scot with an abundance of freckles. 'I joined the Army to see inside exotic women's blouses,' he complained, 'not the inside of some ugly transport plane.'

'You'd enjoy Oman,' Blackie said. 'The women are exotic and they don't even wear blouses. It's the Arab tradition – they wear veils across their faces and nothing else.'

'Bollocks!'

'It's true. You ask the boss here.'

Mike Bannister was just making his way past them en route for the forward section. 'Ask me what?'

'Is it true that the women in Oman wear nothing but veils, boss?' Bonnie asked.

'Absolutely,' Bannister said with a straight face, winking at Blackie as he moved on.

'Told yer,' Blackie said, rubbing it in.

'Still sounds like bollocks to me. The place would be knee-deep in tourists.'

'It is.'

'I never knew anyone who went there.'

'Majorca – that's in Oman.'

'No, it fucking isn't.'

One of the older troopers across the plane opened his eyes. 'Will you two stop filling the air with bullshit!' he half roared.

Bonnie and Blackie looked at each other and burst out laughing.

'Kids!' the older trooper said vehemently, and closed his eyes once more.

'Sorry, grandad,' Blackie muttered under his breath. Both he and Bonnie were only twenty-two, which might well have made them the youngest men on the plane. They had only returned from jungle training in Brunei a few days before Christmas, and had been expecting a couple of weeks' leave before resuming normal duties in Hereford. Neither of them had seen active service since winning their SAS badges the previous summer. And their nervousness at the prospect, as both were more than half aware, was what was making them behave even more like idiots than usual.

'How much longer?' Blackie asked Bannister, who was passing them again, this time in the opposite direction.

'About an hour,' he told them. 'But it'll seem like three,' he added cheerfully. He had been on enough flights like this to know how long they seemed to the uninitiated.

'One hour,' Bonnie repeated, after Bannister had moved on. 'Thank Christ for that. Do you have any idea where this place is that we're going?' he asked Blackie.

'Belize?'

'No, the place in Colombia.'

Blackie shook his head. 'We'll get briefed soon enough.'

'It's a nice feeling, though, knowing that if you get taken by the enemy, the Regiment'll come and get you back. Makes you feel wanted, don't you think.'

'I doubt if the Regiment would come looking for you plonkers,' observed the veteran with closed eyes.

'I don't think he likes us,' Blackie said.

'He's just a bit nervous,' Bonnie suggested. 'He doesn't want to let us down when the time comes.'

'Your time'll come sooner than you expect if you don't shut the fuck up!'

'See, I told you. He's all heart really.'

'Who did you ring from Heathrow?' Chris asked Eddie. They were only an hour out of Quito, but it felt like a world away as their bus ground its way up the road towards the distant mountain pass. To their left the land dropped away like a stone, down to where a toy river flashed silver in the morning sun.

'Her name's Lisa,' Eddie admitted. 'I only met her this week,' he added, as if that absolved him from further questioning.

'Where?' Chris asked.

'In a wine bar. She's a student, but she waitresses to help pay the bills.'

'Uh-huh. What's she look like?'

'Er, lovely body, dark hair – long, nice smile.'

'Well that narrows it down.'

119

'Christ, I don't know. How do you describe someone? I guess her face is a bit cat-like, if you know what I mean.'

'Yeah. What colour eyes?'

'Dunno.'

'Don't know!?'

'Brown, probably. I never notice the colour of people's eyes.'

'Bet you noticed how big her tits were.'

'Yep.' He smiled at the memory. 'Perfect,' he added.

'You sound . . .' Chris hesitated. 'How can I put this without you feeling insulted . . . You sound *interested* in this one.'

'Could be.'

Chris laughed. 'Mr Commitment.'

Eddie grinned. 'You know what it's like in this job. You never get the time.'

'I know. I sometimes think that's why some of us do it.'

'You?'

'I sometimes wonder. You gonna see her again?'

'Hope so. We gotta get home first.'

'Yeah,' Chris agreed.

They sat in silence for a minute or so. 'But look at it,' Chris said eventually, staring out at the vista of mountains receding into mountains beneath a pure blue sky. 'Fucking beautiful. It just makes me want to get out. Moments like this I love the SAS and I hate it. Love it for bringing me out here and hate it for rushing me through it at a hundred miles an hour.'

Eddie followed his gaze. 'It's an improvement on the Falls Road,' he said.

Four seats back the Dame was staring out at the same scenery. Before leaving Quito they had agreed not to travel as a three-some, even on the Ecuadorian leg of the journey, and it had not been hard deciding who would be the odd man out. All of them knew that in any group of three loners the Dame would out-loner the other two. So, unless there was some sort of emergency, he would not be communicating with Chris and Eddie until they all 'accidentally' checked into the same hotel in Popayán. Which suited him fine. He liked the two of them, but he liked his own company better.

Wilbur Smith's was not bad either, but the suspension on the bus was so bad that reading was impossible. He supposed the landscape was beautiful, but he was bored with looking at it. Trying to traverse it on foot would be something; cruising through it on a bus, no matter how uncomfortable the seats, was no challenge to anyone.

But the Dame had to admit there was something else too. He had always found landscapes like this – gargantuan bloody landscapes – made him feel a bit uneasy. He remembered feeling that way, feeling vaguely threatened by it all, when he was about ten and the family had gone to Scotland for their summer holiday. Maybe that was why he wanted to get out and show it who was boss, he thought suddenly. Yeah, maybe that was it.

He had a sudden mental picture of the two Provo bodies lying in Kenneally Street, the blood and the rain. He had done that. Shown them who was boss. He had had no choice. But was that all it meant? Could you just walk away? Or did it leave some invisible mark on you? Some patch of darkness somewhere.

His dad had always laughed at religion, even though his mother had always gone to church on Sundays. 'She only goes for the singing,' his dad used to tell them, but she didn't. 'Somebody must have dreamt all this up,' she would say, and it was hard to imagine anyone other than God dreaming up the Garth flats in Sunderland.

His dad had been unimpressed by the logic. He had 'better things to do than pray to some bearded old fart the rich had invented to make the poor feel better'. Like drinking himself into his usual Sunday stupor with his mates.

'You'll roast,' his mother used to say, and maybe that was what his dad was doing. But the Dame could not really believe it – just about everybody who knew the man had loved him, and that had to count for something.

His mother and his sisters loved the Dame, but would that go on one side of some balance sheet, the bodies in the rain on the other? Was that how it worked? If so, how did they measure it all, the good and the evil? It all seemed crazy.

But he had killed eight people now, and though every one of them had been trying to kill him, it still seemed a lot. Maybe that was how you measured it, by how it felt. In which case Hitler must have gone to heaven. Which was nuts.

There was no way of knowing. Maybe you did just walk away.

'The British Ambassador,' the President's personal secretary announced from the door. The President rose somewhat reluctantly to his feet and ushered the Queen's representative in Bogotá into the ornate Spanish chair which faced his desk. He checked the office door was properly closed and reseated himself in the rather more comfortable product of a modern Swedish manufacturer.

'Good morning, Mr President,' the Ambassador began. 'I have some good news.'

'Yes?' Estrada said, his palms together in front of his chin.

'The operation will soon be under way.'

Estrada lifted his eyebrows. 'How soon?'

'I'm afraid I don't have that information as yet. But of course as soon as I do, you will be informed.'

Before or after it's all over, Estrada asked himself. 'Thank you, Mr Ambassador,' he said.

'I have also been advised that the United States Government has been apprised of the situation to date, and that it is possible there may be limited United States participation in the operation,' the Ambassador went on. 'But,' he added, 'I am asked to convey to you personally the assurance of both my Government and the United States Government that no United States troops will set foot on Colombian soil.'

Estrada grunted. 'Is that all?' he asked.

'That is all,' the Ambassador agreed, getting to his feet.

'I would appreciate as much notice as possible of the actual operation,' Estrada said, his hand on the doorknob.

'Of course.' The Ambassador bowed and left.

'Get me Señior Quintana,' Estrada told his secretary. 'I'll be upstairs.'

They reached the border town of Tulcan soon after eleven. From there it was a taxi ride to the border itself, which was marked by a river at the bottom of a small valley. Border posts had been set up on either end of the river bridge. The Ecuadorians just waved them through, and they walked across to where the Colombian border guards, all toting sub-machine-guns, were waiting to herd them into a long, low building. Inside an officer was waiting to examine their passports. He had a sub-machine-gun lying carelessly on the desk beside him.

Chris and Eddie were behind an American couple in the queue, and this turned out to be good news. After aggressively asking the two Americans a string of questions in staccato Spanish, and nearly reducing the woman to tears before finally letting them through with ill-concealed reluctance to the paradise that was Colombia, the officer greeted the two SAS men with a wide smile and enquiries about the health of Mrs Thatcher and Gary Lineker.

Eddie told him how much he admired the Colombian player Carlos Valderama, which made the officer's day. 'Enjoy your stay in Colombia!' he said, waving them through with a flourish.

They watched from a distance as the Dame came through, hoping he didn't think he had time to convince the Colombian that Sunderland were a football team.

Another fleet of taxis carried everyone on into the town of Ipiales, where they climbed reluctantly into another bus for the six-hour trip to Popayán. So far so good, Eddie thought, as they started off on the first leg to Pasto, climbing a valley that seemed large and deep enough to lose the Grand Canyon in. He could see what Chris meant, sort of. He almost felt like getting out himself. Almost.

Luis Quintana was shown into the President's private quarters, and was pleased to find that just for once no American soap opera was flooding the room with 'sound and fury signifying nothing'. Where did that line come from? he wondered. He couldn't remember.

The TV was on, but with the sound turned down, and the obvious delight of the local game-show contestants was mercifully muted. The President was staring into space, a look of frozen anxiety on his face. Looking at him, Quintana wondered if his own ambitions for the presidency were at all sensible. He did not want to end up like Juan Estrada, perpetually unsure of himself, a virtual prisoner in his own palace, only ever at ease in front of televised fantasies from North America.

'*Buenas tardes*, Juan,' he said, lowering himself onto the other sofa without waiting to be asked.

Estrada grunted and bit his thumb. 'The English are on their way,' he said unhappily.

'I thought that was what you wanted.'

'I'm not so sure any more. In fact I'm beginning to regret letting you talk me into it.'

Quintana smiled thinly, but did not bother trying to correct this minor revision of history. 'It was a good idea last Monday, why is it not a good idea today?'

'Perhaps it was not a good idea on Monday.'

Quintana tried a change of tack. 'What do you mean – they are on the way? When? How many of them?'

'Oh, they don't tell me that. You know what the English are like – they tell you nothing very politely and at great length. "Soon" – that's what it comes down to. "Soon". A few days? A week? They say they will give me exact times and dates when they have them, but I wouldn't put it past them to tell me after it's all over.'

Quintana could not help thinking that if he was in the English commander's shoes he would do just that. He went back to the first problem. 'I still do not understand why it is a bad idea,' he said calmly.

'What if it *fails?*' Estrada said. 'I know these SAS men are supposed to be supermen, but they must fuck up sometimes. What if they fuck up here? We'll have a pile of English bodies that we can't explain away. Everyone will know that the Government must have been involved, and the cartels will be screaming that I am just a foreign stooge and they are the only true Colombians.' He looked coldly at Quintana, unaware that the opening credits for *Knot's Landing* were rolling silently across the screen behind him.

Quintana repressed a smile. 'If by any chance it should fail – I still think the odds must be heavily on success, but just

125

supposing it does fail – things will not be that bad. Muñoz will presumably be dead, which would be a plus, particularly since it would be obvious to everyone what lengths you were prepared to go to try and save him.'

Estrada was impressed despite himself. 'Perhaps,' he admitted. 'In any case it's too late to change our plans now.' He turned to glance at the screen, and turned back to Quintana. 'Just one more thing. The negotiations for the ransom – how are they proceeding?'

'They have given us until Wednesday to agree the terms.' He shrugged. 'If the English mean what they say it will probably be all over by then.'

'Good. Thank you, Luis.'

It was a dismissal. Quintana was only halfway to the door when the TV sound boomed back on.

He walked down the stairs which led from Estrada's private quarters to the Presidential offices, going back over what he had just said to reassure Estrada. It had been half true, he thought, but only half. Certainly Muñoz would be gone, but would Estrada receive the benefit? The President was probably right in thinking he would be damaged by the revelation of British involvement – after all, the Malvinas War was still fresh in many minds, and gringos were gringos.

Reaching his own office, Quintana sat thinking by his window for several minutes. With both Muñoz and Estrada out of the running he could not think of anyone with a better prospect of succeeding the latter than himself.

Somewhere in the distance a bell chimed nine o'clock. Eddie and Chris were slowly working their way round Popayán's Plaza de Armas, looking out for a large tousle-headed Welshman. It was their second circuit; on the first they had

126

passed the Dame sitting on one of the benches, deep in conversation with two young women whose rucksacks bore Australian flag badges.

'Finds sisters wherever he goes,' Chris observed.

'It's obscene,' Eddie agreed.

The three of them had arrived in the Popayán bus station soon after dark, found a middling hotel courtesy of the handbook, and had found time to shower and change before coming out to keep their appointment with Wynwood. Popayán itself, insofar as they could tell by night, was exactly what the handbook said it was: an attractive old colonial town full of narrow streets, white buildings and university students.

'Here comes Ivor the Engine,' Eddie murmured.

Wynwood was strolling across the square towards them. 'Eddie, Chris!' he almost shouted in his sing-song voice.

'Hello b . . .' Chris bit off the word 'boss'.

'Hiya, Taff,' Eddie said brazenly, offering Wynwood a hand to shake. 'And what brings you to sunny Popayán?'

Wynwood grinned. 'Same as you, I expect – the peaceful climate. Have you two eaten?' he asked. 'I'm starving, and there's a place just down there . . .' He pointed across the square. 'Where's your friend, by the way?' he asked Chris.

'He's watching us now,' Chris said quietly. 'Just lead off and he'll follow.'

'Right.' Wynwood led them across the square and a few yards up Calle 5 to a restaurant named La Plazuela.

The Dame arrived at their table a few moments later.

Wynwood examined his three new partners. With his own mass of dark curls, Eddie's unruly blonde mop, Chris's shock of spikes and the Dame's near-skinhead cut, the four of them did not stand out as an obvious team. Which was not only good, but a marked improvement on the early eighties, when so many SAS men had adopted unruly long hair for under-cover work that it had become like a new uniform.

Clothes-wise the differences were few. Chris was wearing a shirt and jeans, the rest of them T-shirts and jeans. All wore some sort of windcheater and boots. Too bad, Wynwood thought – travellers were not known for their originality of dress.

They ordered food and kept the conversation to impressions of Colombia and what was going on back home. After paying the bill they found a store selling beer and took the bottles back to Wynwood's room at the nearby Hotel Acapulco. It was somewhat swisher than their own hotel.

'I thought it was important that we weren't all staying in the same squalor,' Wynwood explained.

'It's being so old,' Eddie explained to the Dame. 'He needs his comforts more.'

The Dame smiled and opened a bottle of beer. 'Not bad,' he reckoned, after a first taste. 'Not Newcastle Brown, but not bad.'

'OK,' Wynwood said, sitting himself down on the floor with his back to the wall. 'To business. How did Man U do on Boxing Day?'

'Lost 7-0 to City,' Eddie offered.

'Uh-huh.'

'They drew 1-1 with Everton,' the Dame said.

'That sounds better. You lot didn't have any trouble getting here?' he asked Chris.

'Nope.'

'There were the twins on the plane,' the Dame suggested. 'We had to hose Eddie down after the flight.'

'And then we had to spend a week in Quito looking for some bird-watching book,' Eddie added.

'Well, I did have a minor problem or two,' Wynwood said, and told them the story of the car that had trailed him from Bogotá.

They listened in silence, jokes forgotten.

'So who knows?' Wynwood concluded. 'The operation may be blown. I'll call Bogotá tonight, pass on the information, then wait and see if Hereford or London have any news or suggestions.'

'OK, boss,' Chris agreed. Each SAS patrol tended to operate much of the time as a group of equals regardless of rank, but in this case there was no doubt in anyone's mind who was boss. Apart from anything else, Wynwood knew the territory.

'What do we do in the meantime?' Eddie asked.

'Tomorrow I want to get a look at Totoro – that's the name of the estate or ranch or whatever it is where we think Andy and Muñoz are being held. Chris can drop me off a few kilometres out and pick me up later. You two can just amuse yourselves. Separately would be best. Get rested up, get used to the altitude. I have the distinct feeling this one is not going to be a picnic.'

'There's just one other thing, boss,' Eddie asked deadpan.

'What?'

'Did you give Bobbie one?'

Wynwood eyed him tolerantly. 'Let's just say she's been given a standard by which to judge other men.'

'Maybe she wanted more than an evening paper, boss.'

6

'Are there any *people* in Belize?' Blackie asked.

'Doesn't look like it, does it?' Bonnie agreed. They were walking across the strip of tarmac which separated the barrack from the HQ building. To their right two Hercules C-130 transport planes were being busied over by ground staff, and beyond them a quartet of Harriers were parked in line. And that was about it. In every direction the airfield seemed to end in a wall of jungle. The sky was a uniform blue-white, the air thick and humid. They were in the tropics all right, but if they had not been told where they would have had no way of knowing. It didn't *feel* any different to Brunei.

They were on their way to the morning briefing, along with the other thirty members of C Squadron's Mountain and Air Troops. Judging by the eyes turned their way as they entered the briefing room they were the last ones there.

'Sorry to drag you away from your pleasures,' Major Bourne greeted them sarcastically. 'I'll try and make sure this doesn't take too long.'

'They were only tossing each other off,' a voice said.

'Some of us have heard of women,' Blackie said.

Bourne waited as the laughter subsided. Sometimes he wished that he could get through just one briefing, just one, without a parallel seminar in sexual innuendo. But when all was said and done, it was just a way of releasing tension. As the actress said to the bishop, he thought to himself.

Thirty pairs of eyes were watching him.

'I thought you might all like some clear idea of what you're doing here,' he began. 'As things stand at the moment, one of our number – Sergeant Anderson of the Training Wing staff – I'm sure you all remember him from Basic Training . . .'

There were several groans.

'Sergeant Anderson is being held for ransom by a Colombian criminal organization – one of the cocaine cartels. A well-known Colombian politician is being held with him, for the same reason . . .'

'I bet they want more for him than Andy Anderson,' someone remarked.

'Twice as much,' Bourne replied. 'The villains in question are the Amarales family. They have a fortified estate just outside Popayán, which, for all you geographic illiterates' – he turned to the large-scale map of Colombia behind him – 'is here in the southern mountains.' He turned back to face them. 'Negotiations are under way,' he went on, 'between the two Governments and the villains, but that needn't concern us. We're going in to get Andy back. And the local politician too while we're at it.'

'Boss, what happens if our politicians pull the plug on us at the last moment?'

'I don't think there's much chance of that. Of course, if it happens, it happens. No matter what you and I might think of our politicians, we're here to carry out their decisions, not question them.'

There were more groans, this time of resignation.

131

Bourne smiled. 'Stop getting your knickers in a twist,' he advised them. 'I think this is a Go, and you might as well believe likewise until you hear otherwise. Now' – he took hold of the map and flipped it over to reveal a blown-up satellite photograph of Totoro – 'you've each got a copy of this in front of you as part of the briefing pack. I want you to take it away and memorize the layout. And of course everything else in the pack. Someone's working on a model as I speak, and tomorrow we should be able to start some detailed planning. By then we may have additional information from our surveillance patrol. Most of you probably know the men concerned – Joss Wynwood from Training Wing and Chris Martinson, Eddie Wilshaw and Damien Robson from B Squadron's Mountain Troop.'

'Not B Squadron, boss!'

'I'm afraid it was the best we could come up with at short notice, Trooper. The four of them should be *in situ* sometime tonight.'

'Do we have a date yet, boss?'

'If today is D1, we want to be ready to go by the evening of D3. That's all I can tell you, at present. And we haven't yet decided between HAHO and HALO for insertion. Nor has it been decided whether we need to send in two Troops or just the one.'

Some heartfelt groans were heard.

'I know you'd all love to go,' Bourne said. 'We'll see. For the moment, go through the briefing packs, and spend some time considering the advantages and disadvantages of each insertion method in these circumstances. Right, any questions?'

'How are we getting home, boss?'

'That's a remarkably pertinent question, Trooper. Since it's only approximately two hundred kilometres across this

132

4000-metre mountain range to the Ecuadorian border we considered turning the whole business into an endurance exercise. However, it was felt that that would be unfair to the Colombian politician. So you're being lifted out by our allies.'

'Not the Yanks, boss? They couldn't even lift their own men out of Iran.'

'This is a rather easier proposition for them, Trooper. This time we have the cooperation of the local Government.'

'But do the local military always listen to their Government?' someone wanted to know.

It was an intelligent question, and Bourne could not help feeling a little proud of the questioner, even though he had been put on the spot. 'No, not always,' he admitted. He would not insult the men in front of him by telling them anything less than the truth as he understood it. 'We're not expecting any trouble from that direction,' he went on, 'and we'll take all steps to make it even more unlikely, but we won't be ignoring the possibility either.' He waited for a follow-up but none came. 'Any more?' he asked.

There were no more questions.

'OK, get all the information we have packed in among your brain cells – I'm sure there's plenty of spare space. And I know it's New Year's Eve, but try not to wash away everything you've learned on a tide of beer tonight. Enjoy yourselves, but remember, we may be in action the day after tomorrow. If any of you have ever tried free-falling with a hang-over you'll know what I mean.'

There were a couple of assenting murmurs.

Bourne left the room. In the back row Blackie and Bonnie looked at each other. 'Hey-ho,' Blackie sighed.

'Or hey-lo,' Bonnie said. 'I don't know which is worse – floating around next to the moon getting frostbite, or plummeting down at about a hundred miles an hour hoping the bastard who made your parachute had his mind on the job that day.'

'You're an inspiration, you are,' Blackie said.

'I always thought Colombia was a record label,' Bonnie said sourly.

Wynwood and Chris got an early start, driving out of the city soon after eight. It was a beautiful day, the sun rising through an almost clear blue sky. In the far distance mere wisps of cloud sat on the shoulders of the mountains. They followed the main highway to Cali for the first few kilometres, then turned off onto the lesser road Wynwood had traversed from Neiva the previous morning. Chris was driving, Wynwood examining Oliver's large-scale maps as he applied camouflage cream to his face and neck.

After another few kilometres they crossed a bridge over the energetic waters of the upper Cauca, and turned right again, up the river valley. The road was paved, but seemed little used. Cocaine money, Wynwood guessed.

Ten minutes later he told Chris to pull over. They were in a relatively narrow section of the valley, where the Cauca and the road shared most of the flat ground and forested slopes rose quite steeply on either side towards invisible heights.

'Totoro is about two kilometres further up the valley,' Wynwood said, 'and since this road doesn't seem quite as busy as the M25, I think it would be better if you went back the way we came rather than drive past the entrance.' He looked at his watch. 'Eight forty-seven,' he said. Chris checked his and nodded. 'Eight hours should do it,' Wynwood reckoned. 'So let's say here at 17.00. If I don't show, two-hour intervals until I do. Or until Man U win the League.'

'Christ, we're not hanging around that long.'

Wynwood smiled, checked the binoculars and the Browning in his cross-draw.

'Do you want to take this?' Chris asked, offering him the bird book.

'The book to spot 'em, the Browning to shoot 'em? I don't think so, Chris. You go and sit on a mountain with it.' He reached for the door. 'I'll see you at two.'

The sound of the car receded as he started climbing the eastern slope of the valley. There was little undergrowth beneath the trees, so the going was not particularly hard, and he had to remind himself to stop every few minutes because of the altitude. After about half an hour he found himself on a kind of shelf and, reckoning he was now high enough, started following it southwards. So far he had seen no sign of human life – no path, cigarette ends, litter, traps. The forest seemed as virgin as the day it was born.

He climbed in and out of two valleys cut by streams running down to join the Cauca. It was in the third such valley, he judged from his map, that he would find Totoro. He consciously slowed his pace, eyes and ears straining for any sign of danger.

Another kilometre went by. He was too far east, he judged. He would have to do some tree-climbing, which was not an activity he took much pleasure in. It was worth it though. Swaying in the top of a thirty-metre tree he could see a thin line of smoke rising into the western sky. He was too far to the east.

He took a compass bearing, clambered down and started off again. Twenty minutes later he found himself about to emerge from the trees at the head of a broad valley. The source of the smoke was laid out below him, no more than a kilometre away. Totoro.

It took him almost half an hour to find a good viewing position where an old landslide had created a gap in the screen of trees. Laid out behind tufts of grass he could bring his binoculars to bear on the whole complex.

The valley below was almost rectangular, only narrowing to a sudden point just beneath his position. The stream which had made it clung to the foot of the eastern slope – to the left as Wynwood looked. Both slopes were steep, rearing up at something close to forty-five degrees. They were tree-covered, with the notable exception of the lowest hundred metres or so, which had been stripped, presumably for security reasons.

The two lines of trees faced each other across a valley floor some five hundred metres wide. From where Wynwood lay to the confluence of the stream with the north-south-flowing Cauca it was about three times as far. Beyond the Cauca another steep, tree-covered slope blocked the natural horizon.

Man's work in the valley was not quite so tidy. The road ran alongside the river, crossing it just before disappearing away to the north. A paved entrance road left it amid a copse of trees and curved up towards the ranch, passing between gates set in a high wire fence after a hundred metres, and more gates set in a high stone wall four hundred metres farther on, before ending in a wide circular parking space at the heart of the inner compound.

The outer compound, that area surrounded by the high wire fence, took up more than half the valley floor, ending at the tree-line to the right and just beyond the stream to the left. It had been largely denuded of trees. Wynwood could see two horses standing together away near the main gate.

The inner compound, surrounded by a stone wall some three metres high, was almost square, with each side about two hundred metres long. The main house – a two-storey villa with flat roof and first-floor verandah – was at Wynwood's end. It had two single-storey wings that had obviously been added at a later date. Three more buildings – one of two storeys, the others of one – stretched along the inside of the northern wall. Beyond them there was a helipad, but no helicopter. The south-western corner was mostly lawn, and boasted a couple of canopied tables.

There were several armed guards in evidence, some stationary and some moving. Wynwood watched one of the latter slowly walking the southern fence. When he reached the far corner he took something from his pocket and seemed to speak into it. There was obviously a security centre somewhere in the complex.

Wynwood got out a pencil and began sketching the layout as accurately as he could. He worked quickly, knowing that the squadron in Belize would be getting satellite blow-ups, and that his main job that day was to find the surveillance patrol an observation post and a hide location. He found them both within the next two hours.

Retreating uphill from his vantage point, he had drawn a wide circle round to the south and west before cresting the ridge of the slope that rose up from the stream due south of the compound. About a third of the way down the slope he found a climbable tree that offered an almost uninterrupted view of the estate. There was a swimming pool behind the eastern wall which had not been visible from his previous position.

On the other side of the ridge, one valley away from Totoro, he found the ideal spot for their hide: a wide gully in the valley side which boasted the extra protection of a large uprooted tree.

He could see no disadvantages to this site, but it was not yet two o'clock, and he might still have time to look for something better once he had found somewhere for the helicopters to land.

Eddie walked across the arched bridge, then down some steps to the park which stretched out alongside the river. There were lots of students sitting on the grass and under the palms, while others paced up and down murmuring to themselves. Maybe here they had exams at Christmas, he thought.

A couple of hundred metres on he came across a huge open-air blackboard, with a dozen or so students busy drawing equations on it. The whole thing made him smile, though he was not sure why.

There were lots of trees, though few of them seemed particularly tropical; in fact most seemed not that different from the sort you would find in Epping Forest. He stopped to watch two art students having their photographs taken with their paintings, huge canvases covered in abstract designs which, like the trees, seemed just a little strange. It occurred to him that this was a difficult place for Europeans to understand; it was different but not really different enough. You felt like a foreigner but at the same time you didn't.

Still, none of the locals had any trouble identifying him as one. As he walked through the park the word 'gringo' came at him in a bewildering mixture of mutters, growls and simple observations. The park ended, and away across two blocks he could see a statue on a hill. He walked up the road, and found a path which spiralled up towards the summit.

The statue turned out to be a large and suitably aggressive-looking conquistador. From its base Eddie could see the town spread out below him – a grid pattern of mostly white buildings in a wide plain bounded by distant mountains. It didn't look like Hackney. In fact it looked damn peaceful.

Appearances could be deceptive, of course. Two teenagers were coming up the path he had climbed, carrying a ghetto-blaster between them. Loud and distorted heavy metal blared from its speakers. They took one look at Eddie and disappeared from sight round the other side of the statue. Not out of earshot, however. Their ghetto-blaster, apparently aimed at Ecuador and Peru, still strained at its speakers like a wooden boat in a thunderstorm.

Home sweet home, Eddie thought. He wondered what Lisa was doing. 'Happy New Year,' he murmured.

On the other side of the town the Dame was walking round the block which contained the Cathedral. It looked like a fortress, with its high walls and corner tower, but the Dame didn't think that was why he found it forbidding. B Squadron could be over those walls in fifteen seconds.

He stopped at the front entrance and stared up at the sun-shadowed stonework and the dome floating in the blue sky. There seemed to be a stork or something like it nesting under the eaves. Chris would know.

He crossed the road and entered through the small door which had been made in the larger ones. After the bright sunlight it seemed almost lightless inside, but after a while his eyes began to adjust and he started walking slowly down a side aisle, watching those sitting in the pews, their pleading faces turned upwards towards the stricken Christ.

He looked away, and tried to make out details of the dimly lit paintings on the walls. Surely the men who had painted them would have wanted them seen more clearly than this. A sign caught his eye, telling visitors, in English, not to use flash.

Dull gold gleamed everywhere; it was like being swallowed by a huge golden whale. And yet . . . his eyes were drawn back unwillingly to the upturned faces. So much need. And he knew what for. He could not put words to it, but he knew what for.

He got to his feet, aware again of the church around him. The thought crossed his mind that death would be like this golden darkness. He shook his head and started back down the aisle, towards where a thin wash of light was seeping in from the invisible doorway.

Chris did what Wynwood had told him to do – went and sat on a mountain. Once back on the main road he simply turned the car uphill, and watched as the view through the windscreen grew ever more spectacular. After an hour or so he emerged onto a vast, rolling plateau. For what seemed like thirty kilometres in every direction palm-studded fields and hills stretched away towards purple mountains. Above it all myriad banks of cloud rolled across an enormous sky. It seemed like a land custom-made for giants.

He parked the car and walked up to the crest of a nearby knoll, book in hand, and had no sooner sat down than a hawk-like bird appeared almost directly above him, drawing lazy circles in the air. It was white with prominent black markings either side of the neck. A black-shouldered kite, the book told him.

The next few hours went by like minutes, and it was with some reluctance that Chris abandoned his perch to collect Wynwood.

The upper slopes of the Cauca valley were still bathed in sunshine, but the light had already deserted the road in its bottom, and Wynwood seemed to almost leap from the shadows at the arranged spot.

'Well?' Chris asked as they drove back down.

Wynwood told him about the layout of the estate and the potential hide. 'There's a pretty wide flat clearing about a kilometre to the northeast which should do for the pick-up,' he added.

'Great.'

'Yeah, but dropping in isn't going to be so easy. It's all forest.'

'What about the front garden?'

'It may come to that.'

His New Year soirée was going well, Luis Quintana thought. A fair slice of the cream of Colombian society was there, which not only reflected well on the respect in which he was held, but also on the wealth of the coffers which would be available to him for financing a presidential campaign.

Noticing his wife across the room he thought she looked almost desirable. Perhaps, he thought sourly, the two of them could start speaking to each other again in the coming year.

At that moment he noticed Rafael Lamizares standing alone, and took the opportunity he had been waiting for all evening.

'Could I have a word, Rafael?' he asked.

'Of course, Luis. A private word?'

Quintana nodded. 'The garden, perhaps?'

Lamizares followed Quintana out onto the terrace and down into the shadows of the path which circled the lawn. The two men had known each other for twenty years, ever since they had attended the same college in the United States, and both had risen high in the Party. Quintana was an important minister, and though Lamizares had no official Government post, those well versed in Colombian politics considered him one of the most powerful men in the country. He was the Liberal Party's kingmaker. Or, more accurately, its President-maker.

'I have a question for you, Rafael,' Quintana began, once they had moved far enough away from the house. 'A hypothetical question, of course.'

'Of course,' Lamizares said, smiling. Over the distant centre of Bogotá a firework flashed red stars into the sky.

'If Estrada was not to stand or not to be selected by the Party, do you think I would stand a chance of the nomination?' Quintana asked.

'Is he thinking of not standing?'

'Not that I know of.'

'Then he will be selected.' Another rocket showered stars into the sky, this time green ones.

'It looks that way. But six months is a long time – something might happen to undermine his popularity. Who can tell?'

Lamizares stopped and looked at him closely. 'Who indeed?' he said sardonically. 'Well, in this highly hypothetical situation, and assuming that whatever it is that undermines Estrada's popularity does not also undermine your own, then . . . well, I would make you second favourite to Muñoz. Always assuming his family agrees to pay the ransom, of course. A long way second though, Luis, I'm afraid to say. This is not my personal preference, you understand. It's what I suspect would be the Party's preference.'

Quintana said nothing, savouring the possibility.

'Of course,' Lamizares went on, 'if Muñoz didn't come back, I suspect the radicals would find it hard to agree on his successor. In which case I don't think there's much doubt you would be the favourite.'

It was what Quintana had wanted to hear. 'Thank you, Rafael,' he said with more than his usual sincerity, 'for indulging a few New Year daydreams. Let's go back in.'

The phone rang in Wynwood's room. 'There's a long-distance call for you, Señior Wynwood,' the receptionist told him.

'Fine,' Wynwood said.

Oliver's voice came down the line, but there was no click to suggest the receptionist had hung up.

'Hi, Joss,' Oliver said. 'I just called to tell you I can't make it. Would you believe five of our people are down with colds, which only leaves two to man the phones.'

'I'm sorry to hear that, Jim.'

'Yeah, well, can't be helped. I'd still like to see you on the sixteenth if that's possible?'

'Sure. What number's your apartment again?'

'Seventy-three.'

'I remember now. OK, see you then. Bye Jim.'

Wynwood hung up, picked up the list of numbers he had just made, and went out to use one of the public phones in the Plaza de Armas. He chose one as far from prying ears as possible, punched out the code for Bogotá and the numbers Oliver had just given him – 521673.

The embassy man answered immediately. 'Hi,' he said, 'everything OK?'

'No,' Wynwood said. He told Oliver about the men in the Merc.

'Oh hell' was the first response; 'I'd better get on to London' the second.

Wynwood waited for more.

'Did you check them for ID?' Oliver asked.

'There wasn't time.' Had there been? he wondered.

'No matter, it probably wouldn't have told us anything.'

'Seems to me,' Wynwood said, 'the best place to find out whether it's blown is Totoro. I think we should establish the surveillance operation right now.' He told Oliver about the recon that day. 'It didn't look like they were preparing a reception committee. And if they do, then if we're *in situ* we'll know about it.'

'There's a problem with that – your cache. We were going to deliver to certain map coordinates and let you collect, but it's been decided that such an operation would be unnecessarily complicated. Instead, we intend to deliver direct.'

'To the hotel room?'

'No, of course not. But the delivery is tonight, which is why I say there's a problem with establishing the surveillance immediately.'

'Where?'

'A lay-by off the Cali-Popayán highway, three kilometres north of the turn-off to Silvio, about ten kilometres south of Pescador. On the west side of the road. A blue and cream coffee truck, bearing the name Café Liberador. You got that?'

'Yeah, we stop for coffee.'

'The driver's name is Manolo Ochoa.'

'When?'

'Ten this evening.'

'We could pick up the stuff and then establish surveillance.'

'If you say so. I thought . . .'

'Always assuming the night vision equipment is on board.'

'It is.'

'And everything else?' Wynwood was thinking how good it was going to feel to be a soldier again.

'Even the Claymores.'

'Great. Thanks, Oliver. Hope to see you in some other life.'

'Good luck.'

Wynwood put the phone down and walked back across the square and up Calle 6 to the others' hotel. He found the Dame reading, took him down to where Chris and Eddie were playing cards, told them what he had just discussed with Oliver, and asked them what they thought.

The decision was unanimous.

'What are we going to do with the car, boss?' Chris asked.

'It's either hide it close by or one of us has got to hide it some way off and walk all the way back in.'

They thought about it for a moment. 'What are the chances of hiding it close by?' Eddie asked.

'I don't really know,' Wynwood admitted. 'I didn't see any obvious places.'

'Neither did I,' Chris said.

'Then I vote for a long way off,' Eddie said. 'If it's found close by then the thing's blown, it's as simple as that.'

'He's right,' the Dame agreed.

'OK, who's going to take the long walk?' Wynwood wanted to know.

'I will,' Chris said. 'Anyone else is liable to get lost.'

Eddie sprayed him with the pack of cards.

'What about the hotel?' the Dame asked.

'We'll check out. Tell 'em we're taking the night bus,' Chris suggested.

'Where to?'

'Wherever it's going.'

Wynwood looked at his watch. 'We've got an hour and a half. I'll pick you up out front in half an hour, OK?'

'Yes, boss.'

Thirty-two minutes later Wynwood was piloting the car past the bus station and onto the Cali road. Chris was sitting beside him in the front, examining a photocopy of the large-scale map which Wynwood had just made in one of the town's numerous student shops. Eddie and the Dame sat behind, each keeping an eye on the view from his window. As far as they could tell the town was indifferent to their departure – no suspicious eyes seemed to be following the Fiat.

Wynwood was pleased. Male gringo foursomes in cars were not unknown, but they were not exactly common either. Now all they had to worry about was running into a military checkpoint.

They drove north along the dark highway, mostly in silence, as each man subconsciously prepared himself for action.

Wynwood almost missed the lay-by specified by Oliver: in the moonless dark it seemed to jump in and out of his head-lights in an instant. He pulled over, and all four men got out.

The road was deep in a wooded valley, and the only illumination came from the stars and their own sidelights. 'I'll wait by the car,' Wynwood said. 'I think two of you should stay in the trees here, one across the road, yes?'

They all agreed.

'Chris, you take the Browning,' Wynwood said. He looked at his watch. 'Twelve minutes. Let's go.'

The delivery was early. Chris and Eddie had only just taken up position in the trees, and the Dame was barely across the highway, when headlights breasted the hill to the north and a truck rumbled down the incline and pulled across into the lay-by.

The legend 'Café de Liberador' adorned the sides.

There were two men in the cab. The driver climbed down and walked towards their car, leaving his mate behind. '*Buenas noches*,' he said. 'You are American?'

'No, British.'

146

'Good, good. I am Ochoa.' He raised a hand to his comrade, who also got down, gun in hand.

'What's the gun for?' Wynwood asked urgently.

'*De nada*', Ochoa said. 'Manuel,' he shouted, '*el fusil!*'

The other man laughed and put the gun back up on the seat. Wynwood wondered if he would have found being shot amusing. It must have been a pretty close thing.

'Come,' Ochoa said. He led Wynwood round to the back of the truck, into which his mate had disappeared. Behind the sacks of coffee beans they could hear him. A moment later his head emerged and then the rest of him, humping a large canvas bag out across the pungent cargo. 'There are two,' he said, dumping the first on the tailgate. Wynwood looked inside and found gleaming metal.

Two minutes later the truck was pulling out onto the highway and disappearing in the direction of Popayán. The four SAS men reconvened by their car.

'This doesn't seem like a very good place to check the contents,' Wynwood observed.

'Let's do it on the move,' Eddie suggested.

'Yeah,' Wynwood agreed.

They piled back into the car. Wynwood turned it round and headed back towards Popayán as Eddie and the Dame, more than half-hidden by the bags on their laps, went through the contents.

'What should there be in here, boss?' Eddie asked.

'Four MP5SDs, three Browning High Powers, one L96A1 sniper rifle with a nightscope, two Claymores, four sets of night-vision goggles, a PRC 319 radio and two spades. Food supplies for a week.'

'It looks OK, but it's hard to tell without unpacking everything.'

147

'If it's not all there, there's not much we can do about it anyway,' Chris said. 'The turn-off's coming up,' he added.

'I know.' Wynwood said curtly. He was feeling the adrenalin beginning to flow. They were no longer just four tourists – they were four heavily armed soldiers behind enemy lines. Always assuming you could find a line in Colombia.

He turned off the main road, and it was like leaving the world behind. There seemed to be no traffic on the mountain road to Neiva, and there was likely to be even less on the Cauca valley road. For the next fifteen minutes they would be somewhat conspicuous. And there was nothing, Wynwood thought, that the SAS hated more than that.

The fifteen minutes dragged slowly by, Wynwood driving, the others just sitting, in a tense silence.

'This is it,' Chris said softly.

Wynwood pulled the car over and killed the lights. They all got out, ears and eyes straining for danger.

The only sounds came from the rushing river, the only light, and a ghostly one at that, from the crescent moon rising above the hills ahead and the sparks of silver it struck on the water.

Eddie and the Dame pulled the canvas bags from the back seat and boot. 'I'll take one of the Brownings,' Chris said, and did so, with a spare magazine of ammunition. He looked at his watch. 'Twenty-two forty-eight,' he said. 'I'll try and dump this at least ten kilometres away, so' – he did a rough mental calculation – 'you should see me before dawn.' He climbed back into the driving seat. 'Enjoy your digging, lads,' he added, and started the engine.

As he turned the car the other three shifted the canvas bags off the road and into the trees. By the time the noise of its engine had faded into nothing they were about thirty metres up the slope. A convenient area of nearly flat ground offered a chance to rationalize the baggage.

First they picked out the night goggles and put them on. The world was suddenly a stranger, greener and more visible place. Next they emptied out the canvas bags, and while the Dame went to work burying one of them in the roots of a tree Wynwood and Eddie divided its contents into roughly equal weights for their rucksacks and bodies. Everything Wynwood had asked for was there. He offered Oliver a silent vote of thanks.

The three of them applied camouflage cream to their faces and wrists, checked each other's artwork, and started off, Wynwood picking out the trail, Eddie and the Dame carrying the large bag between them. At first they seemed to be making an incredible amount of noise, but as they climbed a breeze blew up, rustling the trees and helping to hide the sounds of their passage. The ambient light also increased, and they were able to dispense with the night goggles.

With the compass and his experience earlier in the day Wynwood had no trouble finding the way, and it was only the weight and awkwardness of what they were carrying which prevented a really brisk pace. As it was, they covered the three kilometres to Wynwood's first observation post in just over an hour, and the other two got their first sighting of Totoro.

By night it looked more like a prison, Wynwood thought. Arc lights covered both the outer fence and inner wall; floodlights bathed the buildings. There seemed to be more guards than there had been by day, but it might well have been that they had been less visible in mere daylight. Wynwood hoped to God they had no thermal imaging devices. It did not seem likely, but then not much about the cocaine cartels did.

The last lap, circling round to the hide position Wynwood had found beyond the ridge of the valley's southern slope, took another hour, mostly because they were sacrificing speed in the interests of silence.

It was now 01.15, and their work was far from over. Eddie and the Dame went immediately to work with their spades, digging out a hide-cum-sleeping area in the form of a cross some five metres wide. Each arm had space for one of them to lie down, leaving the central hub for their equipment.

While the troopers dug, Wynwood took out the PRC 319 and set up the two tuning antennae. Once he had the right frequency he typed out the call-sign on the small keypad, checked it through, and sent: 'Condor calling Hummingbird.'

The magic message came back: 'Hummingbird receiving.'

Wynwood passed on the information that they were in the process of establishing the observation post outside Totoro. 'Hummingbird' told him that they had good daytime satellite photographs of the area, and that, based on these, they had a list of queries needing answers. The words 'Do you have a pencil?' appeared on Wynwood's display.

He smiled to himself in the darkness and took down the list, half wondering why he was bothering, since everything on it – details of the defensive structures, security guard patterns, lighting, power sources – would have occurred to him in any case.

After arranging to call at 22.00 the next day he signed off.

'Watch out for tarantulas – over and out' was the last incoming message.

Bastard, Wynwood thought. He packed away the PRC 319 and went across to where the other two were still digging. 'Looks soft enough,' he observed.

'It's so easy I'm reluctant to give up my spade,' Eddie said.

'Good,' Wynwood agreed. 'I'll go over the ridge and cut some wood for the roof. And I'll take those.' He indicated the two rucksacks already filled with earth for dumping at a reasonable distance from the hide.

It had been a long day. It was going to be a long night.

'Hey, boss,' Eddie said quietly, 'before you go. It's New Year. How about a silent rendition of "Auld Lang Syne"?'

Wynwood grinned. 'Why not,' he said, linking up arms. The Dame looked at them as if they were both mad, sighed, and walked over to complete the circle. And for a minute or more the three men gently raised and lowered their arms on the dark Andean hillside, miming the words in silent harmony.

7

The small amount of dawn light filtering through the roof of their star-shaped hide was a good sign, Wynwood thought, as he lay on his back in one of its arms. Above him rows of cut branches supported the waterproof sheeting they had brought with them, and above that a thin layer of turf with vegetation cover had been added. An unsuspecting stranger might fall in, but someone looking out for it would have to search the small dip in the slope with a very suspicious eye to spot anything.

Raising his head, Wynwood could see Eddie's feet just protruding from one of the arms at right angles to his. A low snoring could be heard, which was not so good. He looked at his watch. It was 06.15. Time to get moving. He crawled towards the centre of the star, and raised his head up through the hollow ball of vegetation they had placed there.

'Morning, boss.' The Dame's voice was so low he only just heard it. Looking up he could see him perched astride the split trunk of a tree.

Wynwood scrambled out and walked across, taking care to vary the route. 'No sign of Chris?' he asked.

'He arrived about twenty minutes ago. He's gone down to wash.'

'I'll do the same when he comes back.' It was important to keep clean – the less they smelled, the more chance they had of remaining undetected, particularly by dogs.

Chris appeared, so silently that he almost made Wynwood jump. Another good sign, he thought. This had the makings of an excellent patrol. The two men smiled at each other. 'Wake Eddie up,' Wynwood told the Dame. 'We'd better have a meeting. Oh, and tell him to bring the make-up.'

'A pleasure,' the Dame said.

'No problems?' Wynwood asked, squatting down next to Chris.

'Nope. The car's in a bush about twelve kilometres away. It's about fifty metres from the road, and I did my best to cover up the tracks. It's hard to tell in the dark . . .' He looked around. 'Shouldn't we have someone on lookout?'

'We will soon. As far as I can tell, no human has set foot in this valley for months. Or on any of the slopes overlooking Totoro. They may be armed to the teeth down there, but the notion of active defence seems to have passed them by, thank Christ. So I think we can do without a lookout for ten minutes. We need to talk about the day's work.'

Chris nodded his agreement. 'I could do with a few hours' sleep.'

'You're first in the queue. Ah, here comes Sleeping Beauty.'

Eddie and the Dame made a circle with the other two. 'Where's breakfast?' Eddie asked.

Everyone ignored him.

'This is the plan for the day,' Wynwood said. 'We'll do four-hour shifts in the observation post, starting with Eddie, then me, then Chris. By then it'll be dark again and we'll re-evaluate. After Eddie's done his shift and the Dame has had some sleep the two of you can go up the mountain and look for a decent landing zone.' He looked round at them all. 'How's that sound?'

'Sounds good, boss.'

'Right, you two get some sleep. Next shift is 10.30 hours.'

Chris and the Dame disappeared into the hide. Wynwood and Eddie took out the tubes of camouflage cream and started work. First they applied a light base coat to dull the shine on all exposed areas of skin, then a second coat of darker streaks in random patterns. Each checked the other to make sure neither had missed anywhere.

Then they turned to the MP5s, swathing them in strips of green and brown cloth that Wynwood had torn from a shirt bought for that purpose on his arrival in Popayán. More strips were tied round the binoculars.

'You've got the veil?' Wynwood checked.

Eddie pulled the sheet from a pocket. Using the binoculars behind it would have a minimal influence on vision, but would eliminate any chance of tell-tale reflective flash.

Lastly the two men each walked a few paces to check for sound. Neither rustled, jingled or clattered.

'Let's go,' Wynwood said, and led off up the slope. At the top of the ridge they approached with caution, advancing on their stomachs, but beyond the crest was nothing more than empty forest and the distant roofs of Totoro in the valley below. They crossed over and worked their way down-hill, constantly alert and as silent as they could make them-selves, careful to leave no trace of their presence, and on the lookout for traces of anyone else's.

They found none. At the observation tree Wynwood waited while Eddie climbed up, returned his eventual thumbs up and then climbed back over the ridge to their camp, where he took his place in the tree some thirty metres from the

154

hide, and spent much of the next four hours considering their options for rescuing Anderson.

Kilcline leant back in his chair and grimaced at the taste of the tea in his mug. How many times did he have to tell the stupid bastard that stewing the stuff didn't improve its taste?

He put the mug down with a thump that sent tea slopping over the side, and with reflexes that did credit to a man of his years managed to yank the report from Bogotá out of the way in time. He read it through again, then gazed gloomily out of the window at the dull grey winter day.

If he was reading between the lines correctly, then Joss Wynwood seemed to be using up his lives rather fast at the moment. Not to mention the lives of others.

The men who had followed the big Welshman southwards from Bogotá worried Kilcline. They could have been under orders from any number of authorities, legal or otherwise – always assuming you could tell the difference in Colombia – and there was no way of finding out which. If they had been working for the Government, that was probably OK. If the cartels, then it might be, or might not be. It depended on which cartel. It might even have been some damn-fool game of the Americans.

The bottom line, Kilcline thought to himself, was simple enough. Had the operation been blown? Did the Amarales family know they were coming? And the answer to that could only be discovered by surveillance. If this Totoro ranch was being made ready to face a major attack it should be obvious enough. And if that was what Wynwood's patrol reported back then they would have to abort and think again.

He tried another sip of the tea. It was colder.

155

There was another way of improving the odds. Assuming that any leaker would have to be high in Colombian Government circles, then some judicious misinformation might be in order. The place was a given, so it could only be the time.

A day later, Kilcline thought. If they told the Colombian Government the operation was set for a day later than it actually was, and that information was leaked, then Totoro might have some forewarning, but there would still be at least some element of surprise. Of course, the British Government might not want to tell porkies to the Colombian Government. He had better find out.

At 10.30 Chris relieved Wynwood, Wynwood went to relieve Eddie, and Eddie came back to check the Dame's make-up. Satisfied, they took the large-scale map and began working their way east up the slope.

According to the map, the road below Totoro ran roughly parallel to the 2000-metre contour, and the slopes above eventually ended in peaks nearly 5000 metres above sea level, but the two SAS troopers were not aiming to climb that far. About three hundred metres above them there seemed to be a wide ledge on the mountainside, almost a plateau, which might offer a suitable LZ. There was no way of knowing without having a look.

At first the going was not particularly difficult, the vegetation not particularly tropical. In fact, Colombia above 2000 metres did not seem that dissimilar to Wales at sea level. Until you looked back, that was, and found yourself watching clouds floating along in the valley beneath you.

After half an hour or so, as the slope steepened into a tumbling mess of broken rock, the vegetation began to thin. Another fifteen minutes and they were over a rise and onto the ledge. Here, on a space about the size of two football fields, small palms that resembled enormous pineapples and the occasional outcrop of stone were all that dotted a grassy heath.

The valleys below, which held Totoro and their hide, were completely invisible from where they stood. The slopes on the far side of the Cauca valley rose up in the distance towards rocky heights and blue sky.

'What do you think?' the Dame asked, squatting on his haunches.

'It'll do,' Eddie said. 'Though I wouldn't fancy landing in one of those pineapples.'

Wynwood started his watch by surveying the entire panorama and noting down the position of every man and vehicle he could see. Then he went through Eddie's notes.

No one had arrived from the outside world during the last four hours, and no one had left the valley either. The movements of the Amarales's security guards – those that could be seen, at least – had all been neatly noted down. It did not look like they operated to any rigid pattern. This, though predictable, was unfortunate.

One man and one woman, the first answering to their description of the elder Amarales brother, Ramón, had sat on the verandah drinking coffee. The woman had been a 'stunner'.

Wynwood smiled to himself and went on reading. There had been no sign of either Anderson or Muñoz.

He went through another survey of the panorama before concentrating on the inner compound. Always assuming Andy and Muñoz were here, and the embassy in Bogotá had not been given the runaround, where would they be? There was no way of guessing, but somehow they had to find out. And not only the building, but also the room. It was going to be hard enough penetrating the inner compound; if they had to conduct a room-by-room search of all the buildings they might as well give up now.

The morning wore on. Wynwood carried on noting the movements in the valley below and scouring the set-up for any other information that might prove relevant. Shortly after midday he was watching the space between the compound wall and the main house when he thought he caught a movement on the wall's white inner face. The shadows of people moving, perhaps.

Taking an instant decision, he clambered down from the tree and made his way two hundred metres or so diagonally up the slope to the east. There he shinned up another suitable tree and aimed his binoculars at the space which had previously been invisible.

'Geronimo!' he murmured. Two men were walking in the space – Andy and Carlos Muñoz. Both looked fit and well.

Seconds later they were being ushered in through a door in the back of the main house. Wynwood had not seen them a moment too soon. Now all he needed to know was which room. There seemed to be a lot to choose from.

Back in the tree close to their hide, Chris was cleaning his weapons, unloading and breaking them down, wiping off any moisture they had acquired from the dew, checking the movement of all the moving parts, finally reloading the magazines bullet by bullet. Every now and then he would stop to listen or watch a bird in a nearby tree, and wish that he could check an unfamiliar plumage or physiognomy with the book he had left in the hide. Books, though, were among the most visible things made by man, and he was too much of a professional to risk shiny white pages in a tree. He would just have to remember the blue-green breast, the badger-like face with its white streaks on black. Anyway, what did it matter what it was called? A name would hardly make it any more beautiful.

'Are you suggesting we deliberately mislead the Colombian President as to the timing of our operation?' Alan Holcroft asked.

'Yes,' Barney Davies said. His heart had sunk when he had discovered Holcroft on the other end of the line, but he supposed he should not have been surprised.

'This operation is being mounted at the President's request,' Holcroft said, as though he was talking to a particularly obtuse schoolboy.

'Then he'll want it to be a success,' Davies came back. 'Come on, you're not telling me that "Need To Know" criteria haven't reached the Foreign Office yet?'

'That's hardly the point . . .'

'I think it's exactly the point,' Davies said, grabbing what looked like an advantage. 'But I'm not sure that's what we're talking about here.'

'I don't follow you,' Holcroft said haughtily

'You were against this operation from the beginning. I can respect your opinion in the matter. But I think you may be in danger of letting your antipathy to the operation seriously undermine its chances of success.'

'Lieutenant-Colonel,' Holcroft said, 'military success can be quickly and easily measured. Diplomatic success is harder to measure and never certain, because the game is never over.'

'I understand that.'

'Good. I in turn can appreciate your concern for your men. I will recommend that the deception you suggest be

159

implemented. With any luck we can explain it away later as the result of someone's incompetence.'

It had been dark for almost half an hour when Chris returned from the observation post. He fed himself while Wynwood read through the notes he had made over the last four hours. Then the two of them joined the Dame in the nearby tree for a conference.

'It seems like we have a reasonably efficient, but not very well armed, outfit to deal with,' Wynwood began. 'There's usually between five and six guards outside, probably another three or four inside. They seem to do an eight-hour shift, which would mean one shift on duty, one in reserve and one sleeping. Thirty men, of whom twenty can be deployed immediately. They're all carrying automatic weapons, mostly M16s, though we've noted at least four Kalashnikovs. We haven't seen any grenade-launcher attachments but that doesn't mean they haven't got any. We haven't seen any heavier guns, which probably does mean they haven't got any. Agreed?'

'Yeah,' Chris said. 'I seem to remember reading something about how much these guys like grenade-launchers – so maybe we should assume they have them.'

'OK. We think Andy and Muñoz are in the main house. But whatever building they're in, the best entry point for a rescue party has to be through the wire on the far side, yes? If we can persuade our incoming lads to make a big noise on this side, that should help. Plus, a sniper on the far side to take out as many guards as possible.' He turned to the Dame. 'I'm told you can shoot.'

'All those hours at the fair on Sunderland beach,' the Dame sighed.

'Well, after we've finished this chatting, you can work your way up and round the head of the valley and onto the far slope. Find a good position. And while you're at it, take the International's nightscope with you. See if you can see anything of our boy through the back windows.'

The Dame nodded.

'Well, that's one rough plan,' Wynwood said. 'Either of you got anything better?'

They hadn't. The Dame collected the nightscope and melted away into the forest.

'If the Ops HQ buy this,' Chris asked, 'how are we going to divide it up? Am I going in with you?'

'No. I'll go in with Eddie.' He saw the signs of mutiny gathering in Chris's eyes. 'You're the only one here I would trust not to get lost in a blackout in a licorice factory. If we don't get the incoming lads down here as fast and as quietly as possible then everything else is down the chute.' He held Chris's eyes. 'Agreed?'

'Agreed.' The word came out reluctantly, but it came out.

'And I want to see if Eddie's as good as he thinks he is.'

'He is.'

They sat in silence for a few moments. Wynwood broke it. 'You get some sleep,' he said. 'When I relieve Eddie at 22.30 he can take you up to the LZ they found.'

'What are you thinking?' Blackie asked. Bonnie was gazing down at his steak and kidney pie, looking unusually serious.

'I don't know really. Thinking about home. My mum and dad. Friends I went to school with. Dunfermline.'

'Any particular reason?'

Bonnie absent-mindedly dragged a chip through the gravy on the end of his fork. 'You'll think it's stupid. I mean, I think it's stupid.' He looked round to make sure no one else was listening. The airbase canteen was almost empty.

161

'What is, for Christ's sake?'

'We're not very old, are we?'

'You noticed.'

'You know what I mean. It sort of gets real when you think about what could happen.'

'Like not beating the clock?'

'Yeah. You know that stupid thing they say in films – "I'm too young to die!" Well, fuck it, Blackie – I *am* too young to die! Know what I mean?'

'Course. But you know, my great-grandad died last year, and he was ninety-four. And I reckon if he'd had the energy he'd have got up and shouted out the same thing: "I'm too young to die!" He wasn't ready, I'll tell you that. Only a couple of months before that, he was still trying to feel up the nurses in the hospital.'

Bonnie grinned. 'Yeah. I know. It's not that I'm scared. At least I don't think that's it. I'd just be really pissed off if I got killed by . . . well, you've seen 'em in *Miami Vice* – all those sleazeball Colombians with fancy earrings and half a ton of gel on their heads. Getting killed by another soldier would be bad enough but . . . You know? There's too much to do. It'd be a waste.'

Blackie leaned across and stole a chip. 'Like they say – Who dares wins.'

Half an hour before relieving Eddie in the observation tree Wynwood set up the PRC 319 and started to transmit. Belize acknowledged. He relayed all the information the patrol had gathered since the last transmission, and then offered them a précis of his proposed plan of attack.

This turned out to be a dead ringer for the provisional plan that the 'green slime' – Intelligence – in Belize had drawn up on the basis of their satellite photographs. Wynwood was somewhat less pleased to be told that the operation would be under way in less than twenty-four hours. He reminded them that they had not yet discovered the exact location of the hostages.

They asked him what he had planned for the following day – a picnic?

8

As on the previous morning, the patrol abandoned their continual surveillance of the valley for a brief dawn meeting. 'I just want to check everyone knows what's going on,' Wynwood said. 'Sometimes in situations like this it's hard to remember who you've told what to.' He looked round. 'You all know when we're expecting company. But we have a lot of jobs to get through before then. First off, we have to try and pinpoint which room or rooms Andy and Muñoz are being held in. Second, I want to check out our approach to the compound from the far side of the valley in daylight. Third, we have to keep a watch on Totoro, particularly for any incoming reinforcements. Fourth, we have to make sure we all get enough sleep during the day to be on top form tonight. Show those goons from C Squadron what real SAS soldiers can do.' He looked round again. 'All right, so far?'

The other three nodded. 'Yes, boss.'

It had been light outside for well over an hour. Luis Quintana knew this because his brain had refused to stop thinking long enough for him to get back to sleep. He checked his watch on the bedside table – it was almost eight. It was time to get up. He got no farther than the edge of the bed, sitting there naked, still thinking.

'Luis,' a small voice said behind him.

Julia's face was mostly hidden by her tumbling hair, but her arms were reaching up to him, her nipples peeking above the top of the sheet.

Quintana was tempted, but . . . He took her hands, kissed them and recrossed her arms across the breasts. 'I have work to do,' he said. Her smile turned into a yawn.

He put on a dressing-gown and walked through into the other room of the apartment he rented for her. As usual it was strewn with the clothes they had discarded with abandon the night before. He placed water and coffee in the filter machine and stood there watching it bubble.

Yes, he decided. Yes.

Two things had kept him awake most of the night – a slightly queasy conscience and a fear of being caught. The former was easier to deal with. Why should he worry about a bunch of gringos, who by all accounts were not much more than highly trained thugs? He would have no compunction about the death of Colombian thugs, so why agonize about a few Englishmen? Soldiers died, it was as simple as that.

The second problem was more acute. For all he knew, he and Estrada were the only two men in Colombia who knew about the operation. If that was the case then it would not be hard to pinpoint the source of a future leak. Still, he could not believe that was the case. Estrada was incapable of keeping his mouth shut, and there would be others in the know – the English and American embassies almost certainly.

He had worked out that the Americans would have to be involved – there was no one else in a position to extract the English soldiers. And if the cartels did not have informants in all the significant American military and police agencies then his name was not Luis Quintana.

Yes, he told himself. Yes.

He took a small book from his pocket and reached for the phone. There was no guarantee that the call could not be traced, but the number was unlisted and would be difficult to trace back to him. He had to take *some* risks, he told himself. He looked up the Popayán number and dialled it. After several rings a male voice answered, its anger tempered by sleepiness.

'Am I speaking to Miguel Amarales?' Quintana asked.

'Yes, who . . .'

'Just listen, please. This is a warning. I know Carlos Muñoz and an English officer are being held at Totoro . . .'

'Who the fuck are you?'

'Just listen. I am a friend. A military operation is being planned against Totoro, by the English and Americans. President Estrada has given them his permission. The attack is scheduled for 1 a.m. on the fourth – that's tomorrow night.'

There was silence at the other end. 'How do you know this?' a calmer voice asked.

'Just believe it,' Quintana said, and put the phone down. He took a sip of coffee and realized he was sweating. Just one more call, he told himself.

This time he called the international operator and asked for a number in Panama City. The saying was that it paid to kill two birds with one stone, but Quintana saw no harm in throwing two stones at the same bird.

Major Bourne brought the briefing room to some semblance of order. 'Gentlemen, the first piece of news is that we have the green light for tonight . . .'

A raucous outburst of cheering followed.

'But I have bad news for half of you. It has been decided that only one Troop will be used – and Air Troop has been chosen . . .'

The room divided into expressions of delight and disgust.

'After our discussions yesterday,' Bourne continued, 'and due consideration of all that was said, it has been decided to use a HAHO drop. Air Troop's much greater experience in using this technique is the reason it has been chosen.'

There were murmurs of grudging comprehension.

'Of course this HAHO drop will mean longer in the air, but the overriding priority with this infiltration is secrecy. Air Troop will leave the aircraft twenty kilometres to the north-west of the target, free-fall for ten seconds, deploy at around 8500 metres and glide' – he smiled at their side of the room – 'gracefully as birds for an anticipated fifty-five minutes before reaching the LZ. You'll need oxygen of course. You'll be taking a couple of CADS with the 81mm mortars.

'The C-130 will depart at 18.30 hours, and will be refuelled en route by a tanker. You will exit the aircraft beginning at 23.05 hours, and will be airborne, as I said, for approximately fifty-five minutes, landing here' – he pointed out the landing zone's location on the large-scale map – 'at approximately 24.00 hours. The LZ itself is basically a bald patch on the mountain, one of the few, I might add, so aim yourselves well. The ground surface is relatively flat but broken, so watch out. One of the surveillance team will be there to meet you, listen to your bullshit about what great parachutists you are, and then guide you down the mountain to the target. It's a two-kilometre walk, all downhill, through medium forest. Not difficult, even for you lot. Any questions so far?'

No one had any. It had suddenly got through to them that it was real, Bourne thought.

He continued. 'The weather forecast is good. At jumping altitude the wind will be around ten knots and the visibility upward of sixteen kilometres.'

'And it'll be bloody cold,' a voice muttered.

'Bloody cold,' Bourne agreed. 'But you can warm up on the ground. It should be around fourteen degrees centigrade when you land. No rain is expected. The moon is only four days old, so the ambient light will be limited. You will in any case all be carrying PNGs.' He looked round inviting questions.

One arrived. 'Are we likely to meet anyone between the LZ and the target, and if we do, what are we supposed to do with them?'

'It'll probably be my mother,' another voice said.

'I wouldn't want to do anything with her,' replied a third.

'It's extremely unlikely you'll meet anyone. Even Trooper Peacock's mother. But if you do, there are no hard and fast rules. Use your discretion. It shouldn't be too hard to tell the difference between a shepherd and a Colombian gunman.'

It was not a very good answer. Bourne knew it, and he suspected quite a few of the men did too. But there was not a better one, and they all knew that as well.

'What about the local authorities?' someone else asked. 'Are there any military bases in the area?'

'I was coming to that. Both the Army and Air Force have bases here in Popayán' – he indicated the place on the map – 'the 17th Brigade and the Juan Pinero Squadron. And no, I don't know who Juan Pinero was. The army brigade is an infantry unit, about six hundred men, armed with automatic weapons but not much else. The Air Force squadron only consists of a few modified UH-1 helicopters. If they're being properly maintained, which is doubtful, they might be effective by day, but their crews have no night-fighting experience.

'Basically, we don't expect any problems from either of these sources. First, someone would have to alert them, and whether the Amarales would even want to is a moot point. Second, the military commanders would have to respond immediately, without obtaining any sanction from higher up. Third, even if the two units' reaction times were a quarter of what we think they are, they'd be hard pushed to bring any force to bear in the two hours you'll be on the ground.

'One thing you won't like, though,' Bourne admitted, 'you'll be wearing helmets throughout this one.'

A chorus of groans erupted. The SAS tradition was never to wear helmets except during parachute drops.

'And American helmets to boot,' Bourne continued, rubbing salt in the wound. 'They've been borrowed from US Special Forces for a trial, and you all look just like guinea pigs, so . . .' He grinned. 'These helmets have built-in radios,' he went on, 'for transmitting and receiving. And they should be ideal for coordinating a night action like this one. Which, by the way, is now officially designated Operation Snowstorm. Snow, for those of you who've been living a truly sheltered life, is slang for cocaine. Right. Any questions at this stage?'

'Who thinks up these names, boss?'

'We get them from TV cartoons, Trooper. And I forgot to say, you will have a test session with the helmets this afternoon. Now, where had we got to . . .'

'We were being led like lambs to the slaughter by some no-hoper from B Squadron,' a voice from the back suggested.

'They've been there for days now,' another voice added. 'They've probably started buggering llamas.'

169

'Your knowledge of the world's fauna does you credit, Trooper,' Bourne said after the groans and laughter had subsided. 'But to continue. Once you reach this area' – Bourne placed a finger on the map – 'the force will be split, with two patrols heading this way . . .'

Miguel Amarales decided against the telephone; he wanted to convey this information to his older brother in person. The arrogant oaf had really landed them in it this time – a visit from the goddamn English Special Forces. What priceless irony. The very people Ramón was always prattling on about! His heroes!

It took him just under the usual half hour to reach Totoro, five minutes to pass on the anonymous warning and express his own anger.

Ramón ignored the latter and derided the former. 'Where would they come from?' he asked incredulously. 'A British aircraft carrier in the Pacific? Ascension Island? Heathrow? This is a fantasy. Someone is trying . . .' Even as he listened to himself speak, Ramón was beginning to wonder. Could they really be coming?

'You are not listening, brother,' Miguel was saying. 'If they have Estrada's approval then why not Air Force transport?'

'We would know,' Ramón said firmly.

'Or they could call on American support,' Miguel persisted. 'The Americans are only four hundred miles away in Panama.'

Ramón could not deny the possibility. 'But for one soldier – it's absurd. Paying the ransom would cost them a tenth as much as mounting such an operation.'

'Whoever said politicians were intelligent?' Miguel wanted to know. Having got his brother on the defensive, he was willing to let his anger abate somewhat. 'Does it matter in

170

any case? Let's assume the information is genuine. Why not just move Muñoz and the Englishman somewhere else, and let the British know we have done so? We can phone their embassy in Bogotá.'

'No.' Ramón was firm. 'If they are coming here, I at least want some bargaining cards.'

'OK,' Miguel agreed. That at least made sense. 'They can't land the whole British Army out there' – a sweep of his arm took in the valley – 'and they will rely on surprise, yes? Well, they won't get that. Jesus, Ramón, if there's anyone in Colombia knows more about these bastards, it's you. How will they come? How do we defend ourselves?'

Ramón looked marginally more cheerful. 'We even have an expert on the premises,' he murmured.

'The Englishman.'

'Of course. We can ask him.'

'You mean Chirlo can ask him.'

'Yes.'

The two men who came for Anderson did not look him in the eye. It was a bad sign, the SAS man thought, though he could not begin to think of any reason.

He was taken out of the main house, along a path in front of the low building adjoining it, and into the next building down. His final destination proved to be a room with no furnishing save an electric socket. The wires which ran through some sort of amplifier to a pair of clip-on electrodes had not yet been plugged in. The man with the scar was standing waiting by the window. Bad news was an understatement.

'Sit down,' Chirlo said in his soft, liquid voice.

Anderson did so. The two men who had brought him stood either side of the closed door, guns in hand.

171

'Do you know what these are?' Chirlo said, walking across and picking up the electrodes, letting the wires slide through his fingers as if they were a girl's hair.

'Yes,' Anderson said.

Chirlo seemed to address the floor. 'Señor Amarales has received news that men from your unit – the SAS, is that right?' – he raised his blue eyes questioningly – 'are planning to attack us here tomorrow night.'

'I don't believe it,' Anderson said.

'I find it hard myself,' Chirlo agreed. 'But it doesn't really matter one way or the other. We are going on the assumption, you and I, that it is true, and we are going to work out exactly how to go about defeating such an attack.'

Anderson struggled with himself to keep calm. 'If I tell you to fuck off,' he said, 'you're going to attach those to my balls, aren't you?'

Chirlo nodded.

'How will you know if I'm telling the truth?' Anderson asked.

Chirlo looked at him for a moment. 'That's not really your worry, is it?'

'It isn't?'

'If you tell me your friends are going to come over the hill in tanks I may find it hard to believe. Then I will fry your balls. Keep making sense and – who knows . . .' He smiled. 'Do you have children?'

'Yes,' Anderson said, knowing what was coming.

'It's as well. There are two other things you should bear in mind, gringo. One, Señor Amarales knows a lot about your methods already – he won't be easy to fool. And two, I have no problem inflicting pain. I don't need to and I don't need not to. Now, before we begin . . .' He gestured to one of the men, who came forward, undid Anderson's trousers and pulled both them and his underpants down to his knees.

Chirlo gazed at Anderson's genitals with admiration. 'You are a lucky man,' he said.

'Size isn't everything,' Anderson murmured in English. He felt the cold metal clips fastened to his scrotal sack. A second later a shaft of agony coursed through him, forcing him to arch his back.

'Just to show you the price of not being frank,' Chirlo said.

Anderson was breathing fast, sweat running into his eyes. 'I'll tell you whatever you want to know,' he said through gritted teeth. An inner voice was telling him: keep lucid, keep calm. Tell them as much as you can of what they could work out or find out for themselves.

'Good. How many men do you think your people might send. Ten, twenty, forty?'

'A squadron,' Anderson said. 'Sixty-four.'

'How will they get here?'

'By plane. They will parachute in.'

'Where to?'

'I couldn't say . . .' He saw Chirlo's hand move towards the switch. 'I couldn't . . .' he insisted quickly, starting to take in fast and shallow breaths again. One of the tricks taught at Hereford was to pretend to hyperventilate in these situations. 'I have seen nothing of the area. If everywhere else is steep and forested they could choose to land in front of the house.'

Chirlo walked away from the switch, running both hands through his hair. 'So how will they get away again?' he asked.

'There will have to be a helicopter pick-up,' Anderson said. Even a child could work that out, he thought.

'From where?'

'That would depend on what they intend and how confident they are. If they don't intend leaving anyone alive here then the pick-up could be from your helipad. If they're just coming for me, then it could be any flat space big enough and secluded enough. Maybe somewhere down that road I could see from the verandah.'

Chirlo looked at him thoughtfully. 'You have not told me anything I could not guess,' he said.

'That's true,' Anderson admitted, 'but I have answered all your questions.'

The Colombian thought some more, then suddenly signalled the guard to remove the clips. Anderson tried not to look too relieved.

'I will pass on your answers to Señor Amarales,' Chirlo said. 'Tomorrow there will be new questions. More precise questions.' He opened the door, told the guards to take Anderson back to the main house, and disappeared.

Anderson walked back across the tarmac trying hard not search the forested slopes too obviously. Chirlo had not asked him the key question – would there be a patrol already keeping the estate under surveillance? If they really were coming to get him – and he still found it hard to believe – then there would be. Somewhere up on those slopes a fellow SAS soldier would be watching him at this very minute.

What would they need to know, Anderson wondered as he was led through the house and back to his room. Of course! His and Muñoz's whereabouts. Which building, which room. Well, they should know which building by now. He would have to think of some way to let them know which room.

High in the observation tree Eddie watched Anderson being led back across the tarmac and into the main house. There was something about the way the SAS man was walking – he seemed to be dragging his feet slightly – which made Eddie uneasy. Maybe Anderson had been walking the same way half an hour earlier, and he just had not noticed it. Maybe the man was ill. Or maybe something had been done to him in the other building.

Why would they want to torture Anderson? For fun? Or because he could tell them something? What could he tell them? It seemed doubtful that Anderson knew Terry Wogan's personal number, or that the Amarales family would want it. No, much as he disliked the thought, Eddie could only think of one thing the Amarales would want from Anderson – help in planning a defence against the Englishman's comrades. Which meant the operation was blown.

As he considered this, Eddie saw the long-haired brother, Miguel, leave the house, almost leap into his red sports car and roar off towards the inner gate. It swung open to let him out, as did the gate in the outer fence.

Eddie noted the departure in his log. Miguel had been at the house for an hour and forty minutes. Could his arrival have had anything to do with Anderson's trip across the yard? There was no way of knowing. Certainly, if the Amarales were now expecting an imminent attack they were not showing any urgency in preparing to meet it. Perhaps he was jumping to the wrong conclusions.

He hoped he was. If half the Colombian Army suddenly showed up down below then the operation would be called off, and they would have to slink back out of Colombia the way they had come in. Which might be a lot less risky than going in for Anderson and Muñoz, but who the hell joined the SAS for a less risky life.

Eddie shifted his cramped limbs and carefully examined the watch beneath his sleeve. Another forty minutes. He sighed and lifted the binoculars again. Having come this far, he thought, it would be a real pain in the arse not to get a crack at entering the evil coke barons' lair.

'He seemed as surprised by the idea as you were,' Chirlo told Ramón, his eyes straying across the room to where Victoria was half sitting, half lying on the leather couch. She had arrived alone the previous day, but had so far made no attempt to communicate with him; or anyone else, for that matter. She had spent most of the last twenty-four hours sitting on the verandah and staring into space. At that moment she caught his eye and smiled. It was with some difficulty that he brought his mind back to the business in hand.

'If it's true we'll get confirmation from someone,' Ramón was saying. 'In the meantime . . .' His voice trailed off, and he stood there, massaging his chin between thumb and forefinger.

Chirlo waited, stealing another glance at Victoria.

'How many men did he think?' Ramón asked him.

'He said sixty-four, but he would be bound to exaggerate. It doesn't really matter, does it? – they are coming for him and Muñoz, and presumably they want them alive. We have all the cards.'

Ramón grunted. 'That's what the terrorists at the London embassy thought,' he said. 'I want some men on the roof,' he added suddenly, 'Permanently. And I'm going to call your husband,' he said to Victoria, 'I think it's time he fulfilled some of his family obligations.'

'Just don't bring him up here unless there's a good chance of getting him killed,' she said coldly.

Chirlo felt a warm glow of anticipation in his heart.

'I think this might be a good time for us to exhibit some

solidarity,' Ramón said curtly, dialling a Popayán number.

Victoria did not bother to reply.

'Armando,' Ramón said into the phone, 'we may have a problem here . . .'

Raul Meneres wiped his brow with his handkerchief and put the results of his handiwork carefully to one side. A beer, he thought, and headed for the fridge. The cold Budweiser was on the way down his throat when the telephone rang.

It was Alfonsín, who worked in the fuel depot at the airbase, asking him if he would fancy a ride down to Balboa, in Panama, the following evening. There was a good dogfight on at the Boneyard.

Meneres wondered why Alfonsín would not be working on the special op. 'I thought you were working tomorrow night,' he said casually.

'No . . .'

'That idiot Corles told me there was some special op.'

'That's tonight . . . and anyway Corles should try learning to keep his mouth shut.'

'Be like you trying to stop screwing women.'

'Yeah, maybe,' Alfonsín agreed, obviously pleased with this comment on his sexual profligacy.

'Yeah, Balboa is good,' Meneres said. 'But I'll probably see you this evening anyway . . . I've got some work to catch up on . . .'

He hung up and took another swig of the Bud. The *sicario* had told him the wrong day, he thought. He had said it was Wednesday night. Well, maybe technically it was, but five past midnight was still Tuesday night as far as anyone with any common sense was concerned. It would serve the fuckers right if he pretended he had never heard otherwise.

But then they would not pay him.

Out on the slopes the day wore slowly on. Chris stood lookout over the hide as Eddie and Wynwood slept, then took his own turn in the hide as the Dame took over at the observation post and Wynwood went to reconnoitre the north slope.

By dusk Wynwood had satisfied himself as to where he and Eddie would sit out the waiting hours, and how they would approach the compound. He started working his way back round the head of the valley to where he could get the clearest sight of the back windows of the main house.

Reaching the point where he had first put Totoro under observation, Wynwood settled back into the undergrowth just beneath the ridge. In the valley below he could see the now familiar outlines of the floodlit compound, the fleeting shadows of the guards, the empty helipad. There were now two guards on the roof. Wynwood had listened to Eddie's suspicions and guesswork, and hoped the former were ill-founded, the latter simply wrong. These two guards were the first evidence he had been right.

Wynwood methodically scanned the inner and outer compound for corroboration. He could not find any. Perhaps the guards on the roof were just a whim. He went back to the job he had come for – looking for Anderson.

The main house was a patchwork of lit and darkened windows, but all were covered by either blinds or curtains. Wynwood took out the nightscope and started examining them one by one. The lit squares were almost blinding, the dark ones just that.

'You beautiful bastard!' Wynwood murmured to himself. Through the fourth window from the right, but only with the aid of the nightscope, he could make out a light flashing

178

on and off. A message in the SAS's favourite Morse code:
N-E-R-O-O-M-N-O-R-T-H-C-O-M-E-A-N-D-G-E-T-M-E-M-
U-N-O-Z-O-N . . .

'I'll buy you a pint in the Slug,' Wynwood murmured. Feeling
like a load had been lifted from his mind he resumed his return
journey. In half an hour he would be back at the hide.

In the observation post Chris had watched the sun sink
behind the western mountains, the light swiftly fade in the
valley below. Then the switches had been pulled, flooding
the compound with artificial light.

Beyond the reach of the floodlights and arc lights it was
now fully dark, and darker than it would be for most of the
coming night, since the crescent moon would be making its
appearance in a hour or so.

He had now been perched in the tree for over three and
half hours, but he was not bored. He rarely was these days.
One of the great things he had learnt in the SAS, and particularly in situations like this, was to make every moment count.
Every sight, sound, smell, touch and taste could be experi-
enced, enjoyed, even relished. In the civvy world everyone
was too hooked on motion, speed and cheap sensation. His
old friends from school, they only seemed happy when they
were either pissed out of their skulls or being entertained by
something or someone. None of them could sit still for more
than a moment. It was really sad.

The wind seemed to be getting up. No, it was not the wind
– it was the sound of a vehicle. A heavy one. With a sinking
sensation in his stomach, Chris trained his binoculars on the
point where the Amarales entry road reached the valley
highway. An armoured car swam into focus, and behind it
another one. They rumbled in through the two pairs of gates

and pulled up on either side of the parking space at the heart of the inner compound. Both were armed with M60 machine-guns. A man emerged from the main house to greet the two crews and escort them across and into one of the side buildings. He came out again almost immediately and went back into the main house. Silence reasserted itself.

Strange, Chris thought. The arrival of the armoured cars suggested real concern, but there was still no sign of any real urgency. It was as if the men in the house were expecting trouble, but only at some later date. Chris wondered if the green slime had been dabbling in misinformation.

It was two minutes to seven. His relief should arrive at any moment. He strained his ears, but could hear nothing before Eddie's face appeared in the tree below him.

'Problems,' Chris said, handing him the binoculars.

Eddie looked and grunted. 'I thought I heard something as I came over the hill,' he said. 'There's not much action down there though.'

'That's what I thought,' Chris confirmed. 'I'll get back and report.'

'You think they'll call it off?' Eddie asked.

'They'd better not.'

Wynwood agreed. His euphoria at finding Anderson was somewhat dented by news of the armoured cars, but not totally diminished. 'I think you could well be right,' he said, when Chris offered his theory of an attack expected at a later date. 'And we'll soon know,' he added, as he set up the PRC 319 for transmission.

The Ops HQ was apologetic. The patrol should have been told before of the decision to mislead the Colombian Government over the date of Operation Snowstorm.

'Bloody typical,' Chris muttered, when Wynwood told him. 'But good news, I take it. They must have taken the odd reinforcement into account?'

'It's still on. They'll be leaving Punta Gordas' – he looked at his watch – 'in twenty-seven minutes. But there's one change to the plan. They've borrowed a job lot of Yank helmets for the op, with state-of-the-art radio fitted. And they want us to be wearing them too, so Eddie will have to be at the LZ with you, and bring ours over to the north slope while you lead the troop down the other side.'

'Makes sense,' Chris observed. 'You three being out of communication for over two hours before the balloon went up always did seem a touch on the risky side.'

'A touch,' Wynwood conceded. 'Though from what we've seen the last couple of nights there's not a lot going on around here between one and three in the morning.'

Captain Mike Bannister watched the second hand of his watch move its way round to the appointed moment. 'Gentlemen,' he said loudly, as it reached it.

The other fourteen men sitting on either side of the C-130's swaying belly turned their faces in his direction. Each of them was wearing an unzipped one-piece thermal suit over the usual jungle-camouflaged fatigues. Elasticated straps held the Passive Night Goggles (PNGs) around the communication helmets, ready for lowering over the visors when the time came.

'Time to get rigged up,' Bannister said.

The Hercules, which until then had resembled a hall full of thoughtful statues, became a writhing mass of activity, as the 'chutes, primary and reserve, were passed along the two rows. The fourteen men zipped up their thermal suits and split into seven pairs for rigging the 'chutes, checking each strap on their partner's rig as if his life depended on it – which it did.

Blackie and Bonnie were one of the pairs. They counted off and checked each other's connectors, rigged each other's reserve 'chutes in front, with each man's MP5 tucked in behind it. The bergens were then hooked underneath the back-mounted main parachutes, making each man look rather like an oversized child whose trousers had fallen down.

'You're done,' Blackie told Bonnie.

'So are you.'

Bannister started working his way down the plane, testing each and every strap with a hefty tug, and giving each man the thumbs up when he had finished with him. Once he had passed everyone fit to jump, he submitted to being rigged by one of the NCOs.

'How long now?' Bonnie asked.

'Another half an hour.'

Wynwood lay just behind a slight lip in the north slope, his head masked by ground foliage. The crescent moon, now high in the sky above and behind him, cast a thin wash of light into the surrounding forest, but nothing like enough to render the PNGs redundant once the time came to move.

It was now nearly one o'clock and while one piece of Wynwood's brain would have rather liked the reassurance of hearing a distant C-130 and catching a glimpse of far-off parachutists, the sensible side was hoping that his first news of their arrival would come from the returning Eddie. And soon.

Below him the guards went about their random pacings and the house lights were mostly out. For the first time in days the thought of Susan crossed his mind. To his surprise it did not come accompanied with the usual empty feeling in the pit of his stomach. Instead he found himself remembering some of the good times they had shared together. That hurt too, but in a different way. Regret, he guessed, was the price of just about everything which could be won and lost. Anger was just denial; regret was about accepting that something was gone.

A couple of hundred metres to his right, perched in a tree which almost overhung the outer fence, the Dame scanned the compound through the Schmidt & Bender telescopic sight. The adjustable rubber butt pad of the L96A1 sniper rifle rested comfortably against his shoulder. The subsonic 7.62-calibre ammunition rested in a convenient niche of the tree.

He aligned the crossed hairs of the sight on the head of the taller roof guard and gently squeezed the trigger. 'Pooff,' he said to himself. If there had been a bullet in the chamber the man would have been dead.

In a couple of hours' time there would be a bullet in the chamber. The man's life depended on what time they changed shifts, and that did not seem much in the way of life insurance. The Dame wondered why these thoughts never worried him when the time came for action.

Blackie and Bonnie watched as the two of the air crew manoeuvred the Controlled Air Delivery System (CADS) chutes into position. These, which would carry the 81mm mortars, were radio-controlled 'chutes. Two of the troop would have the task of guiding them down through the Colombian night by hand-held transmitters. Blackie was glad he was not one of them – he had the feeling his hands were full enough already.

Three metres away Bannister's watch reached another deadline. 'Gentlemen,' he said loudly. 'Time to hook up.'

Each man leant forward and attached the plastic hose from his mask to one of the two oxygen consoles in the centre of the gangway. 'This is the bit I hate,' Bonnie murmured to himself a few seconds later as the pilot began depressurizing the plane and his ears popped. It slowly grew colder.

Bannister's eyes were almost continuously on his watch now. Blackie stared at him, wondering what would happen if the watch suddenly stopped. He was beginning to feel the adrenalin flow. Though he had made only a dozen or so jumps he was not afraid – far from it. In fact he found it hard to think of anything that for sheer thrills could begin to compete. And yet he wondered if you ever got used to these last minutes of waiting or that moment on the ramp with the whole bloody world waiting to watch you drop. He doubted it.

'Time to switch to personal,' Bannister's voice came in loud and clear through the helmet. Each man shifted the hose connector from the console to the bottle at his belt. There was about thirty minutes of oxygen in each bottle, more than enough to reach breathable air, barring some catastrophe like landing on a giant condor's back.

The Hercules was slowing down. 'On your feet,' Bannister told them. There was a low rumble and the night sky suddenly appeared in the widening gap as the back of the plane divided to make the jumping ramp.

'We'll check the helmets,' Bannister said.

'One,' said the first voice. The numbers two to fourteen followed. 'Fifteen,' Bannister finished off. 'Break your partner's light.'

Each of the American helmets had a chemical light set in its upper rear face which was activated by cracking its shell. As seen through the PNGs, they would help guide the troop down in a tight formation.

The ramp was fully down now, the lead jumper waiting beneath the glowing red light. Behind him thirteen other troopers, two CADS and, bringing up the rear, Mike Bannister.

The light turned green.

As usual the last few seconds waiting his turn to jump seemed eternal to Blackie, but once he was out on the ramp there was no time for thought. He followed Bonnie into space, straight into the free-falling position, facing down but with the body arched back, arms and legs stretching out. Meanwhile the eyes were homing in on Bonnie's light below, and the body was struggling to stabilize itself before the brain finished counting to ten and the hand pulled the ripcord.

The 'chute's release jerked him upright. So far so good. Blackie grasped hold of the control toggles and started to turn a fall into a glide. Beneath him, ahead and slightly to the right, the red chemical light on the back of Bonnie's helmet was clearly visible through the PNGs. Blackie manoeuvred himself into line and, for the first time in a crowded half minute, had time to think.

'I'm going to South America,' were the words that came into his mind. He would have laughed out loud if the oxygen mask had not made it impossible.

For the next few minutes Blackie concentrated on breathing and flying his 'chute, watching Bonnie below and taking glances at the altimeter built into his reserve 'chute. The land below was still an undifferentiated black mass, showing no shadows from the moon he knew was behind him. Despite the thermal suit he felt bitterly cold.

It could only get warmer, he reminded himself. They were below 8000 metres already, and for the first time things were beginning to take on shape below. The circular horizon was slowly rising towards them, the air *was* getting warmer.

Flying the 'chute became a pleasure only alloyed by the slight anxiety which went with any imminent landing. Ahead of him the team was descending in a long graceful curve to the left as Number 1 corrected their course to compensate for either an error of navigation or an unexpected wind strength. They were heading due south down towards and along the spine of a mountain range. If Blackie's memory served him well the dropzone was a meadow somewhere on the western side of these mountains at around 2300 metres. So far he could see nothing but sheer faces and steep slopes. But his altimeter had only just gone through 5500 metres, and the highest peaks were still rushing up to meet them.

The line swayed again, this time to the right, passing the peaks on its left, gliding diagonally down across the upper western slopes.

A kilometre and a half from Totoro, and at least three hundred metres closer to God, Chris and Eddie were huddled together beneath a slight hillock on the edge of the landing zone. In front of them half the world seemed to be silhouetted against a violet sky. Above them the moon shone white and razor-edged, and the stars seemed closer and clearer than they ever did in England.

'Visibility is approximately ten light-years, Captain,' Eddie murmured.

'Thank you, Mr Spock,' Chris said. Even with a view like the one in front of him, the adrenalin was beginning to pump through his veins.

He looked at his watch again. It was forty-nine minutes since Belize had told them over the PRC 319 that the jump was in progress. Any minute now.

But it was Eddie who saw them first. 'Here they come!' he said, a sense of excitement seeping out through the laconic Cockney accent.

And there they were, looking like a string of widely spaced pearls in the northern sky, slowly growing into a long line

186

of Tinkerbells floating down towards Never-Never Land, and finally revealing themselves as fully equipped SAS soldiers swinging down towards the plateau.

Blackie could see the meadow now – a large light patch on the dark slopes – and gingerly applied his air brakes as he began swinging out slightly to the left of the direction Bonnie was taking below him. The one great peril of landings like this was landing on top of the man in front, so even numbers had been assigned the right-hand approach, odd numbers the left. This effectively doubled the time between landings.

Blackie corrected his course slightly, moving himself farther away from the forested slope to his left, then released the air brakes and slid down towards the meadow, aiming for a straight run of grass between darker growths of vegetation. He hit the ground running, almost tripped, but managed to stay upright.

He got out of his harness, folded the canopy and packed it into his bergen, and looked up just in time to see Captain Bannister cover the last few feet to earth.

They were down.

9

In the bathroom attached to his private rooms Chirlo lay half-submerged, thinking about Victoria Amarales. All evening, while Ramón had quizzed him on the state of their defences, and how they could be improved the next day, she had been destroying his concentration by giving him the eye. And when she had finally announced to Ramón that she was staying the night she had given Chirlo a look which could hardly be misinterpreted.

They had never slept together here at Totoro; all their past assignations had been in hotels in Popayán or Bogotá or Cartagena. Either she was tired of subterfuge or so bored that she hoped to precipitate a family crisis. It did not make much difference either way. She knew he would go along, and she was right.

He was probably not being very wise, but so what? She was ten years older than him, probably cleverer than him, and certainly boasted a finer lineage. The Amarales were as near pure Spaniard as you could get, whereas he could trace Spanish, German and Indian blood in his own veins. He thought Ramón and Miguel would probably be outraged by his sleeping with their sister. Miguel would, certainly. Ramón might be more amused. But her husband would not care. Armando Noguera was not interested in anything over the age of fourteen.

Not that Noguera caring would matter anyway – like Chirlo, he was just an employee of the Amarales. But he supposed Ramón and Miguel did matter. He had done well out of working for them – half a million dollars in the Bogotá branch of the Bank of Venezuela. He could probably double that in the next two years and retire a millionaire at the age of twenty-six.

On the other hand, he thought, he was pretty sure he could find similar employment elsewhere, if he wanted it. He didn't, but he could. He didn't need the Amarales any more than they needed him – it was a relationship of equals, regardless of whose blood was the purest. And it was not as if he would be raping their sister; she enjoyed it every bit as much as he did. He stood up and reached for the towel.

Five minutes later he was in the security room, making sure that everything was running smoothly. 'I don't want to be interrupted for an hour unless it's absolutely necessary,' he told the duty officer.

'Sí, boss,' the man said, and went to answer one of the routine call-ins from the guards outside.

Chirlo walked upstairs, past the guard at the head of the stairs, and checked that the two guards outside the prisoners' rooms were awake. Satisfied, he turned and walked back along the long corridor, passing Ramón's rooms and the ones Miguel used when he was staying. The light was still on under the door of Victoria's suite, which did not surprise him.

He stood there a second, wondering if love and lust was driving him into a major mistake, and decided they were not. He knocked softly.

'Come in,' she said.

He closed the door behind him. The room in front of him was lit but empty; her voice came from the one beyond. 'You took your time,' she said.

'I had duties to finish,' he replied stiffly, walking through. She was lying on the bed, a book lying open and face down across her breasts, but otherwise completely naked.

Her body was everything he remembered it was.

She put the book aside, exposing her beautifully formed breasts. 'Take your clothes off,' she said.

He did so, pleasantly conscious of her eyes on him, then came across and leant over her, kissing her on the lips. She responded for a second, then gently pushed his mouth down till he was sucking on her nipple.

He tried to shift his body astride hers, but with a smooth shift of her legs she trapped him between them, and in almost the same motion started pushing his head further down, running his tongue across her stomach and down. With one final push and a tightening of her legs around his back she had him where she wanted him. 'Now you can start kissing me,' she said.

Chris and Mike Bannister had known each other for years, and they greeted each other warmly. The two of them might have just run into each other in a Hereford pub, Eddie thought watching them, rather than halfway up a Colombian mountain, still with a house-call to make on a drug baron. He only hoped Bannister did not ask Chris about the bird-life, or they would be stuck up in the meadow till dawn.

C Squadron's Air Troop were packing away their 'chutes and oxygen equipment, helping to unload the two remote-controlled CADS, and generally preparing themselves to march. Eddie exchanged silent smiles with those men he had run into before, some in his training intake, others in the Stirling Lines canteen or the pubs of Hereford.

Chris and Bannister talked for only a couple of minutes. Eddie was given a bergen containing radio helmets for himself, Wynwood and the Dame. They synchronized watches, checked that everyone was ready and started off down the mountain.

Seventeen Brits, Eddie thought. The Stray Cats' 'Sexy and 17' started playing in the back of his brain. The silvery light of the crescent moon danced on the single file of helmeted heads below him. It was on nights like this that a man felt really alive.

With silence more important than speed, Chris did not try to force the pace. In addition he was mindful that the line of troops behind him were carrying a lot more than he was, had just spent almost an hour engaged in the exhausting business of guiding a parachute down from 10,000 metres, and had not walked this route before in daylight, let alone by the feeble light of a ten-per-cent moon.

In London it was shortly after six in the morning. The Prime Minister was working her way through one of several waiting red boxes in her private office when the telephone rang.

'It's Lieutenant-Colonel Davies, Prime Minister,' the secretary told her.

'Put him through.'

'I thought you'd like to know,' Barney Davies said, after they had exchanged good mornings, 'our troops are on the ground in Colombia.'

'That's splendid. How long will they be . . . on the ground?'

'Four hours is the period we've allowed for.'

'I'd like to be kept informed, Colonel.'

'Of course, Ma'am.'

She thoughtfully replaced the receiver and went to look out of the small window. At that moment a ray of sunlight seemed to alight on the roof opposite. It seemed like a good sign.

It took them a little over an hour to reach the head of Totoro's valley. Here Eddie's path diverged from the Troop's, and he could afford to speed up his progress. Another twenty minutes brought him to the Dame's tree. The Wearsider received the news of the Air Troop's successful arrival in his usual phlegmatic way. He had no news – the valley below had apparently gone to sleep.

Wynwood was more obviously relieved by Eddie's tidings. He put on the helmet and listened to the younger man's explanation of how it operated. 'Bannister will call you up when he's in position,' Eddie concluded.

On the other side of the valley Chris led the Air Troop along an imaginary contour line about a hundred metres up from the edge of the forest. Dropping off Puma patrol with the first mortar due south of the inner compound, the remaining eleven men walked on another four hundred metres to a position near the edge of the trees level with the outer gate. Jaguar, comprising Bannister and seven other men, were to remain here. Bannister would coordinate the entire diversionary action, using the seven men under his command to intervene if and when it seemed useful.

This left Ocelot, comprising Chris, Bonnie, Blackie and a South Londoner who bore the endearing nickname of Dopey, to continue on to the road. They emerged from the trees a few minutes later and there it was, skirting the feet of the hill. By Chris's reckoning the intersection with Totoro's entry road was out of sight round the next bend, about four hundred metres to their right. 'Ocelot to Jaguar,' he said quietly into the helmet mike, 'road clear.'

They waited for a full minute, listening to the light breeze in the foliage above them and the steady chatter of the river that lay just beyond the road. Then Chris led them down, moving slightly to the left to take advantage of the cover offered by a lone copse of trees.

They crossed the road and reached the river's edge. The water ran fast, but not deep. It looked cold. It was cold. The patrol carried the mortar across and advanced down the left bank, all wearing their PNGs.

The outer gate came into sight through another line of trees. Two men were standing chatting just beyond it by an unlit gatehouse. They did not look like they were expecting anything other than boredom.

Invisible against the dark slope and inaudible against the rushing water, the patrol moved forward until it found a sighting of the gates that was uninterrupted by trees. Chris hand-signalled for them to set up the mortar. When Blackie's thumbs up announced completion of this task he spoke softly into the helmet mike once more: 'Ocelot to Jaguar: ready to go.'

Crouched on his haunches about four hundred metres to the east, looking down along the front line of fence which contained the main gate, Bannister acknowledged the message. He had already received the same message from Puma patrol. He looked at his watch. It was 01.55 hours. Ten minutes behind schedule, so far. 'Jaguar to Condor,' he said, 'are you ready to go?'

'Condor to Jaguar,' Wynwood said, 'we're ready.'

Bannister took a deep breath, thinking for a second how silent it all was. 'Jaguar to all units,' he said succinctly. 'Time to party. You have two minutes, Condor. Ocelot, prepare to fire at the end of those two minutes.'

'We're on our way,' Wynwood replied. He and Eddie raised themselves from their prone position and began to edge their way down through the trees. At the forest's edge, thirty metres of bare ground away from the high wire fence, they stopped and waited and watched. Neither had their PNGs down over their eyes: the lights were far too bright.

About now, Eddie thought to himself.

On the other side of the river Bonnie dropped the shell into the mortar tube and covered his ears. The explosion shook the valley. As it died away another followed echo-like on its heels, and the fence below them seemed to shiver with fright. Wire-cutters at the ready, Wynwood ran down the bare slope, Eddie right behind him.

Wynwood set to work cutting a flap in the de-electrified fence, while Eddie kept watch. Several bursts of gunfire reverberated in the distance, then all was silent again.

No more than five seconds after the first mortar had landed, the Dame took out the farther of the two guards on the roof with the silenced sniper rifle. The guard had been standing right on the edge, and the bullet through his brain knocked him off the roof and out of sight behind the building. His partner must have heard him hit the ground because he turned, saw no one there, and looked wildly round before the Dame's second shot brought his life to a sudden, anticlimactic end.

Having removed these four eyes from the roof, the Dame started scanning the outer compound, ready to take out anyone who threatened to interrupt Wynwood and Eddie's forced entry.

A guard was walking their way, more to get a view of what had caused the explosions by the gate than because he had seen any intruders. The Dame aligned the cross-hairs in the scope and squeezed the trigger.

In Victoria Amarales's bedroom the light of the explosions flashed across the sky just as she and Chirlo were blissfully skirting round the edges of a mutual orgasm.

'What the fuck?' he asked breathlessly, as the booms rattled the window panes.

'Oh no,' she groaned, as he slid himself out of her and scrambled naked to the window in time to see the second mortar round land close to the guardpost by the outer gate. 'We're being attacked,' he said, as much to himself as to her. He grabbed his trousers and pulled them on, snatched the automatic from the bedside table and started for the door. As he went through it he shouted 'Stay there!' over his shoulder.

'Enemy on your left down,' the Dame's calm voice said in their helmets as Wynwood and Eddie raced across open ground towards the stone wall which enclosed the inner compound.

Wynwood made a stirrup for Eddie, boosted him up onto the top of the wall, and then waited while the younger man assessed the situation. It was not easy to assess. Since they were behind the main building, Eddie's only view of the inner compound was through a narrow gap between it and one of the barracks-like buildings on his right. The only certainty was that the place was in a slowly growing uproar. Lights were going on, people shouting, feet running.

Of more immediate import, he could see no one in a position to stop them penetrating the main house.

At the other end of the corridor from his lover's bedroom, Chirlo found the faces of the hostages' guards brimming with questions.

'I don't know what's happening,' Chirlo snapped. 'Just stay at your posts. And keep alert if you want to see the morning.' He headed for the stairs, descended them three at a time and turned left into the security centre.

Fernández was at the microphone, with two other *sicarios* standing behind him on either side of his chair, like courtiers behind a throne. They all looked up with relief when Chirlo appeared.

'Are we being attacked?' one of the men asked.

'Yes,' Chirlo said curtly, biting back the more sarcastic reply that came to mind. 'What the fuck's happening?' he calmly asked Fernández.

'I don't know, chief. Pérez came on, but then he disappeared again . . .'

'Try the gatehouse.'

Fernández did so. 'Nothing,' he said.

'Chief?' a voice came in. Chirlo recognized Pérez's voice.

'What's happening, Manuel?' he asked, leaning across Fernández.

'Christ knows. Mario is dead, and Cayano is wounded. Not seriously. Some sort of bomb, mortar maybe? There were two of them.'

'What's happening now?'

'Nothing, that's what crazy. We can't see anything or anybody. If there's anyone out there they're not moving . . . It could have been dropped from a plane, I suppose, but I didn't hear one . . .'

Was that possible, Chirlo asked himself. Could the British be dropping bombs on them? Or some other cartel? What for? No, it was a crazy idea.

Another thought crossed his mind. 'Start calling round,' he told Fernández. 'You,' he told one of the others, 'wake up

196

the sleeping shift. No,' he corrected himself, 'first get the Army guys up and in their armoured car – that's what they're supposed to be here for. Then wake the others. Move!'

Eddie was just reaching an arm down to Wynwood when a guard came running round the corner of the building. Eddie twisted onto his side, bringing up the MP5, but it was not necessary. Before the man had even seen the figure on the wall a bullet took half of his head away.

'You're clear,' the Dame was saying in his helmet. Eddie gave him a wry wave of the hand and turned once more to help Wynwood up onto the wall.

'You're still clear,' the Dame's voice said.

They both dropped down to the ground, waited a few seconds, and headed out across the inner yard to the side wall of the main building's north wing.

'Good luck, lads,' the Dame said.

They had some immediately. The side door opened, admitting them into a long dimly lit corridor. Doors stood open on either side with darkened rooms behind them. They each took a doorway and waited for any sound nearby. There was none. The corridor was still empty. About forty metres down there was a pool of brighter light surrounding what looked like the bottom of a staircase. As Wynwood examined it a figure appeared and disappeared. Now they could hear the low buzz of conversation.

Wynwood gave Eddie the hand signal to advance, and the two of them inched their way forward along the corridor.

On the edge of the trees to the south Mike Bannister checked his watch and spoke into the radio mike: 'Jaguar to Puma: your turn.' Ten seconds later a mortar bomb landed twenty metres away from the inner gate. Another twenty seconds and the second bomb straddled it.

'Someone tell me where that landed,' Chirlo said into the mike. Why the fuck had Ramón insisted on putting the security centre in the bowels of the house?

Two voices began answering him together.

'Pérez,' Chirlo insisted.

'A bomb on the inner gate. It is a mortar – somewhere in the trees, I think.'

'Are the armoured cars moving?'

'Not yet.'

Chirlo stood there for a moment, thinking furiously.

The *sicario* returned with four soldiers, the two armoured car teams. Chirlo grabbed the front one and almost pulled him towards the front door. 'There's a mortar up on that hillside,' he said. 'Go and get it.' The officer seemed about to argue, but the Walther PPK in Chirlo's hand seemed to convince him. The four men hurried across the yard towards their vehicles.

The Dame had been waiting for them. The problem was they only had fifty metres to run, and once the first of the four went down they ran extremely fast. Two made it into the shelter of their car, engaged the engine, and started rolling it down the drive towards the inner gate.

Ramón's wife always said he slept the sleep of the dead, and it was true that the combination of wine and barbiturates did not make him the lightest sleeper in the world. That was the idea. There was not much point in hiring an army to defend yourself if you were going to be woken up by any little problem.

The four bombs which landed on and around the inner and outer gates were neatly absorbed into a recurring dream he had of arriving with the conquistadors five hundred years earlier, with Hereford's 81mm mortars standing in for Balboa's cannon. It was only his sister shaking him violently by the shoulders which brought him back to the twentieth century.

Where the hell was Ramón? Chirlo thought.

'There's no answer from Ruiz, or either of the Romales brothers,' Fernández said.

'Where were they on duty?'

'The Romales brothers were on the roof.'

Chirlo had another thought. 'Get me Pérez again.'

'Yes, chief.' Fernández made the connection.

'Is the fence still switched on?' Chirlo asked Pérez.

'No, the first bomb blew a hole in it – the power's down.'

'Shit.' Chirlo brought his fist down towards the table, then aborted the motion in mid-air. At least it was beginning to make sense. 'Fall back to the inner gate,' he told Pérez. 'You,' he told the remaining *sicario*, 'come with me.'

He moved cautiously out of the security centre and towards the bottom of the stairs. If he knew anything at all about military tactics they would be somewhere in the house by now.

Eddie and Wynwood had passed within five metres of the security centre's open door two minutes earlier. Now upstairs, Eddie placed a single eye round the corner of the corridor, saw the two guards and was seen by them. He stepped out and fired the silenced MP5 from the hip, cutting them both down. 'OK, boss,' he said softly.

The pair of them moved down the corridor, checking each room was empty of possible opposition, until they stood over the two dead guards. Each had a pair of keys in his pocket. Eddie opened the first door, and the two of them went in commando-style.

Muñoz was sitting beneath the window, looking none too happy. Seeing Wynwood's familiar figure, he sighed.

'Your partner is next door,' he said in Spanish.

Wynwood edged back into the corridor, found it was still clear, and unlocked the final door.

Anderson was behind it, holding a torn length of sheet. 'I expected you to abseil in through the window,' he said disappointedly.

'There are bars across it.'

'I know.'

Wynwood handed the other man his Browning and smiled. 'Just shut up and follow me,' he said. 'Condor to Jaguar,' he told the helmet, 'we're on our way out with Tom and Jerry.'

'All clear, boss,' Eddie's voice came from outside. He fell in behind the two sergeants as they started back down the corridor.

Chirlo hurled himself up the stairs, his bare feet making next to no noise on the carpeted stairs. The men in the corridor above did not hear him coming, but it was someone else who paid for their mistake. Chirlo's brain took in the four men, the guns, reckoned the odds and crashed his body through the door opposite, all in a tenth of a second.

The bursts from Eddie's and Wynwood's MP5s would have encountered only empty air if Victoria Amarales had not chosen that instant to emerge from her brother's room further down the corridor. Wynwood's took her in the upper torso, Eddie's in the head. She was dead before she hit the door-frame.

Ramón slammed the door shut on her lifeless body.

The three SAS men and Muñoz were left in command of an empty corridor. Somewhere ahead of them was the enemy. It seemed sensible to find another way out.

'You two, check in there,' Wynwood told Eddie and Anderson, pointing out the room opposite the one in which Anderson had been held. 'I'll hold the fort.'

The two men went in one after the other, slamming their backs against the wall. The room was empty save for an array of body-building equipment. French windows led out onto the verandah.

Outside they could see an armoured car which was a dark shape in the outer compound, sending sparks into the night as it fired blindly at the southern slope. An essay in utter futility, Eddie thought.

The inner compound, by contrast, seemed empty. He hand-signalled Wynwood the all-clear.

The Welshman fired one last burst at a door down the corridor which was inching open, then walked swiftly through to the verandah, and headed down towards its far end behind the others. No one seemed to be looking their way. The plan was working perfectly, Wynwood thought. They know there are soldiers out there, but they can't see them, and they can't stop trying to see them.

Eddie clambered down to the ground and Muñoz was lowered to join him. Wynwood and Anderson followed with rather more agility. In spaced single file they rounded the building where Anderson had been tied to the chair. The inner wall was twenty metres away.

'All clear,' the Dame told them.

For Bonnie and Blackie down on the road it had all seemed a bit of a doddle. Once their patrol had fired its planned mortar rounds they had been reduced to keeping watch for any sign of unexpected arrivals on the valley road.

The news of the prisoners' release had come over the radio helmets a few minutes earlier. The next message would be the order for withdrawal to the pick-up zone. It looked all over bar the drinking, Bonnie thought; he would have to fail to beat the clock some other time.

And then he saw the lights, or rather their glow beyond the bend down the valley. 'Incoming,' he said.

'Lights on the road to the north,' Chris was telling Bannister. 'No visual sighting as yet.'

Blackie was recalibrating the mortar to the prearranged setting for the bridge across the river, some four hundred metres away to the north.

One headlight, two headlights, appeared round the distant shoulder of the hill. A rumbling sound added confirmation that the lights were not tricks of the imagination.

'Ocelot to Jaguar: these are not friendlies,' Chris was telling Bannister, though how he could see anything through the nightscope against the brightness of the headlights Bonnie had no idea. Nor did he much care. 'Prepare to fire,' Chris told him and Blackie.

The lead lorry was fifty metres from the bridge, twenty-five . . .

'Fire.'

The mortar went off with a whoosh, the bomb landing almost under the front wheels of the truck, filling the cab with flames.

Bonnie dropped another bomb into the tube. Another whoosh, and he thought he could see shadowy figures breaking out in both directions from behind the burning truck.

'Jaguar to Ocelot: what strength?' Bannister was asking.

Chris examined the scene through his PNGs. 'Ocelot to Jaguar. As far as I can tell, just two truckloads of men. They're carrying automatic weapons, but I can't see anything heavier.'

'Jaguar to Ocelot: disengage,' Bannister said. 'Start making your way home.'

'Roger. Let's move,' Chris told the others.

They collapsed the mortar, and started working their way back along the river bank. Behind them the new arrivals were still lying low, waiting for more incoming fire, oblivious of their retreat up the river bank. Somewhere further up the valley a heavy machine-gun was firing.

They recrossed the river, which seemed even colder the second time round, and slipping across the empty road, moved up the slope into the dark and welcoming embrace of the forest.

Chirlo looked down at the bloody, broken body. 'What is happening?' Ramón was asking him, but Chirlo ignored him.

'She is dead,' Ramón said. 'We cannot help her now. We must help ourselves.'

Chirlo went down on one knee, swept her up in his arms, and carried her off down the corridor, back to her room. There he lay her on the bed, careless of the robe falling open to reveal the bullet-raddled body to which he had been making love only an hour before. He leaned down and placed his cheek against the stomach, his tears coursing down to mingle with the still-slippery blood.

After a few minutes he slowly raised his head, pulled the robe closed and stared down at the ruined face. The men who did this will die, he said to himself. If he had to travel the length and breadth of the earth they would die. And not easily.

Familiarity with the ground ensured that Wynwood, Eddie, the Dame and the two ex-prisoners arrived at the landing zone well ahead of the others. Bannister's last contact with the incoming helicopters suggested they were on schedule, and confirmation of their 0400 hours Estimated Time of Arrival came through as the three of them set out the four infrared landing lights.

A couple of minutes later they could hear the faint scraping rhythms of the blades. Another minute and first one, then a second dark shape appeared round the shoulder of the mountain slope, dim silhouettes against the night sky.

'Condor to Jaguar,' Wynwood asked. 'Our transport is in sight. Where are you?'

Chris's voice replied. 'Ten minutes away. Tell them to wait.'

Wynwood was halfway into a smile when the leading helicopter exploded in a ball of flame.

10

The second Blackhawk seemed to fly straight through the destruction of the first, but touched down apparently unscathed just a few seconds later. Everyone in the valley was aware of the explosion. Even inside the main house at Totoro they were aware of a momentary flash, like distant sheet lightning or the flicker of a fluorescent bulb. Chirlo looked up, sudden hope in his eyes.

The units still climbing towards the landing zone had a closer view – one moment the hills above them were dark against the stars, the next a blaze of orange fire.

'What was it?' Bannister asked, more calmly than he felt.

'One of the choppers has gone,' Wynwood answered in the same tone.

'Crashed?'

'Exploded.'

'What about the other one?'

'We're checking it out now.'

Or rather the Dame was. As the patrol's explosives specialist he had not even bothered to volunteer, but just shouted to the others to stay back and got on with it. He was underneath it now, inching along on his back examining its belly with his torch.

He did not know how long he had, but it could not be that long. While his eyes scanned every likely hiding place and the sweat gathered on his chest, his mind seemed to stand apart, utterly detached. He had the strange feeling that the men he had killed that evening were there rooting for him.

Maybe the fear of death made brothers of everyone, he thought.

And there was the bomb, taped almost directly beneath the cockpit. It seemed to be ticking up a storm – just like Captain Hook's crocodile, the Dame thought. Probably a cheap alarm clock.

It looked like a parcel wrapped tightly in plastic sheeting, with nothing other than the noise to indicate that it was a bomb, let alone what type. There was no sense in trying to unwrap it. The light was too poor, and time was doubtless on the bomb's side.

He gingerly pulled at the tape holding it to the helicopter's skin, which came off with more ease than he had expected. He let the bomb down onto his stomach, then wriggled his way out from under the helicopter, clutching it with one hand, and slowly got to his feet.

The temptation to throw it was almost irresistible, but such violent motion might well set it off. Breathing deeply he started walking towards the trees. The tick seemed to be growing louder by the moment, but he knew that was just a trick of the mind. Some twenty metres into the shelter of the trees he stopped and lowered the bomb gently to the ground behind a large trunk. And then, finally giving way to normal human fear, he ran like the blazes back the way he had come.

'The second bomb has been removed,' Wynwood was saying into his mike. 'Brilliant,' he told the Dame. 'I . . .'

The bomb exploded before he could finish the sentence, leaving an impression of bars across purple light on the retina, the sound of trees collapsing into one another, and a blazing fire in the overhead foliage.

'That was the second bomb,' Wynwood told Bannister via the helmet. 'No one was hurt.'

'Shee-it,' one of the American crew said under his breath.

The Dame looked at the burning trees, and said nothing.

Eddie and Anderson were coming back from their examination of the first chopper's remains. 'Both pilots are dead,' Anderson confirmed.

The two Americans seemed to wake up to the fact that the bodies had not been brought down. 'Hey, we can't leave them here,' the senior man said aggressively.

'Were they friends?' Anderson asked.

'That's not what I'm saying . . .'

'It would take all night and most of the day to find all the pieces,' Anderson said.

'The bombs were under the cockpit,' the Dame added.

'But . . .'

'How many men can you carry?' Wynwood interrupted.

The pilot gulped and took a second to compose himself. 'OK,' he said, 'sorry. These birds can take two crew plus eleven fully loaded troops.'

'How many without loads?'

'The official weight limit is 1200 kilos, so sixteen, maybe even seventeen . . .' He shrugged. 'With the external tanks fitted we can't afford to push it. The fuel situation's tight enough as it is . . .'

'Twenty-one's out of the question?'

The pilot looked at him. 'I'd love to. But no way. Even if we got the damn thing over the mountains, we'd never make the border.'

It was what Wynwood had expected. He turned to Anderson.

'I think you and Muñoz should go with the guys who just came in. The four of us got here without any help. We can get out the same way.'

'Forget it,' Anderson said. 'I'm not getting on that helicopter with fifteen overfed gorillas from C Squadron. If they don't bring the thing down they'll fart each other to death in the confined space. I'm coming with you.'

'Andy, we're here to rescue you. Maggie's orders.'

'Tough. I know this country, Joss. Fifteen will have a better chance than sixteen in the chopper, and five of us will have a better chance than four on the ground. Especially if I'm one of the five. OK?'

Wynwood sighed. 'OK, but Bannister will have to go along.'

'Let's just tell him.'

'Lack of rank has its privileges?'

'Something like that.'

'You two'd like to see some more of Colombia, wouldn't you?' Wynwood asked Eddie and the Dame.

'Sure,' the Dame said casually.

'I was wondering how I was going to tear myself away,' Eddie said. 'Here come the unlucky ones.'

The fifteen men of C Squadron's Air Troop were filing into the clearing behind Chris. Wynwood waited for Bannister, then took him aside and explained the situation. 'Haven't you contacted Belize?' the Captain wanted to know.

'What for? We're in the best position to make the judgements that need making.' It was a typical SAS answer – rank was all very well in its place, but it should not be allowed to get in the way of correct decisions. 'And there's no time for fucking around,' Wynwood added, pushing his advantage. 'They'll have seen the fireball down in the valley, there's less than two hours till dawn, and Christ knows who or what's been alerted. Just take Muñoz and your lads and get the fuck out of here. Personally,' he added with a grim smile, 'I'd rather take my chances with the Amarales than have to tell the Yanks two of their pilots have been spread all over the landscape.'

'It's their security that was blown . . . but yeah, OK, it makes sense . . . Do you want anything left?'

'You'll have to leave it all behind anyway for weight reasons. We'll take what we need. Let's go.'

Bannister went off to organize his troops. Wynwood sent Eddie and Chris back down the path to keep a lookout for possible pursuit, and set the Dame to work putting together the travelling kits they had not been expecting to need. Anderson went to explain the situation to Muñoz, who had sat out the entire episode of the bomb in a kind of suspended disbelief on a rock at the edge of the landing zone.

Leaving the Colombian with the American pilot, Anderson rejoined Wynwood over a map. 'Which way?' he asked.

'Good question. I'm not even sure it matters. As long as we can put a decent distance between ourselves and here tonight, we can get the Yanks to pick us up tomorrow night.'

Anderson laughed. 'You reckon? I wouldn't like to count on it. Do you think the Americans are going to send another helicopter just like that? I mean, how are they going to explain the loss of this one? They can hardly deny it was in Colombian airspace illegally – not with the pieces all over a Colombian mountain.'

'What are you saying?' Wynwood wanted to know.

'That we may well be on our own. That we have to assume we are. That we have to get the hell out of this country without any help. That it matters which way we walk.'

Wynwood grunted his assent. 'So which way?' he wanted to know.

'From here? Over the mountains to San Agustin.'

'Why not head for the coast?' Wynwood wanted to know. He wondered if Bobbie would still be in San Agustin.

'Because, like they say in the best movies – that's the way they'll expect us to go.'

'If they think we're still here.'

'We have to assume they can recognize a disaster when they see one.'

'Yeah, all right . . .'

'And San Agustin is in a different province – the local law and order may not be so hostile. There's lots of tourists, which means that there's less chance of being noticed. And there'll be lots of buses to Bogotá. Everything'll be hunky-dory.'

'Right,' Wynwood agreed sardonically, looking at the map. 'And how far is it to this place of sanctuary?'

'Only a hundred and thirty kilometres or so.'

'Across a 6000-metre mountain range!'

'It's just two long walks across the Brecon Beacons in a row.'

'Jesus!'

Barney Davies was picking up the phone before the first ring had died away.

'Boss?' Kilcline asked.

The intonation of the voice instantly told Davies it was bad news. 'What's happened?' he asked.

'One of the helicopters exploded at the landing zone. It was sabotaged. They both were – but they managed to disarm the bomb on the other one.'

'Casualties?'

'Just the pilot and co-pilot. Dead. But they had to leave the surveillance team behind. And all their equipment.'

The unwelcome thought crossed Davies's mind that British forces these days were in no financial position to leave their equipment behind.

'Anderson insisted on staying with the surveillance team,' Kilcline was saying.

'Christ, what for?' Davies asked, suspecting personal heroics.

'It was either him or someone else. He knows the country, he knows Wynwood.'

Davies offered Anderson a silent apology. 'But we got Muñoz out?'

'Yes, we've done our bit for Colombian democracy.'

Well, at least it had not been a complete waste of time. 'And we've got five men on the ground in Colombia.'

'They got themselves there. Who says they can't get themselves back? I wouldn't bet against Joss Wynwood walking to Panama.'

'Yeah. What about the Americans?'

'I think you'll have to take that up with the Prime Minister.'

'Oh Christ,' Davies said. 'I'd forgotten about her.'

An hour after dawn an Amarales helicopter arrived from one of their laboratory complexes on the Amazonian slopes of the Andes. Meeting it on the helipad, Chirlo and Carlos Fernández joined the pilot and his Indian passenger in the cockpit.

'Up the mountain,' Chirlo told the pilot, pointing towards the slope silhouetted against the early morning sky. 'It's not far. Carlos here will tell you exactly where.'

The *sicario* directed the pilot to the clearing. They flew in past the slope bearing the remnants of the American helicopter and touched down in almost the same spot the other American had used the night before. Chirlo jumped out and prowled round the site. Everything was exactly as Fernández, the leader of the pre-dawn search party, had told him it was. Only one helicopter had landed here, and it was obviously not the one now scattered across the landscape. So two had come for the enemy, and only one had left. Unable to take all their equipment with them they had made a pile of it and then exploded some device to render it unusable.

Which left one important question unanswered: had there been room for all of the attackers in the one helicopter? A soldier usually weighs considerably more than his equipment, Chirlo told himself. It all depended on how much leeway they had given themselves.

He waited for the Indian, Manomi, to return with the answer, wondering what Ramón's reaction would be to his sister's death once the shock had worn off. Would he just want to wash his hands of the matter, see the loss of the hostages as a lost business opportunity, Victoria's murder as just an unfortunate tragedy? Or would he want to fight back?

He stared at the panorama of mountains all around him, a feeling of great emptiness in his heart.

Twenty minutes later Manomi emerged from the trees and walked towards him, his face expressionless.

'Well?' Chirlo asked.

'There are recent tracks heading up the mountain,' the Indian said. 'Boot tracks.'

'How many?'

'It is hard to say. Four or five, no more. They are either very big men or carrying heavy loads.'

Chirlo looked at his watch. It was 7.45 – the enemy had about three hours' start. 'You can track them?'

Manomi looked surprised. 'Of course.'

'Good. I will send up ten men to accompany you. Yes?'

'They will have to be good walkers.'

Chirlo grimaced. 'I'll do my best. The helicopter can ferry the men up here and then start an aerial search for them. If we get a sighting we can move you up by air.'

The Indian just nodded and sat himself down. 'Send some food,' he added as Chirlo turned to leave him. 'One day's worth. A few gringos should not be hard to catch in these mountains.'

'These are not ordinary gringos,' Chirlo said. 'They have been trained for circumstances like this.'

Manomi looked vaguely interested for the first time. 'Good,' he said. 'Then send two days' food.'

Barney Davies finished talking to Jimbo Bourne in Belize and wondered how to prepare himself for the ordeal ahead. A glass of whisky would not go amiss, he decided. And make it a double, he told himself. This, he decided, was exactly what the American who had organized the Tehran hostage raid must have felt like before picking up the phone to call Jimmy Carter.

Oh well, he had better phone her before the Americans did. Or the Colombians. Davies took a stiff gulp of whisky. At least she would not be able to smell his breath down the telephone line.

She was either addressing the Cabinet or on the toilet: it was several minutes before he heard the familiar voice.

'Prime Minister . . .' he began.

'Lieutenant-Colonel Davies,' she almost gushed. 'Have we counted them all back?'

It was a joke, he decided. And not in very good taste considering the circumstances. 'I'm afraid the news is not all good, Prime Minister,' he said.

A cold wind seemed to blow down the line. 'Why, what has happened?'

He told her.

'Let me get this straight. Your troops carried out their mission successfully, and would all be back in Panama by now if the American helicopter had not exploded.'

'That is correct, Prime Minister.'

'Forgive me for asking this,' she continued, 'but will President Bush be telling me the same story when I talk to him?'

Davies decided he would lose nothing by being blunt. 'If his people tell him the truth, and if he tells it to you, then yes, Ma'am.'

Her answering grunt could have meant many things. 'And we have five men still on the ground in Colombia?' she asked after a moment.

'Yes, Ma'am.'

'And what are you doing about getting them out?'

'At present, nothing.'

'Nothing!?'

'With all respect, Ma'am, there's nothing we can do. If we'd had the capacity to airlift our men out of Colombia then we wouldn't have needed help from the Americans in the first place. A request for further help would require a decision from you. From the Government, that is.'

The distinction did not interest her. 'I will talk to the President,' she said.

'But at the moment we don't even know if the enemy realizes that some men were left behind. I would advise that we don't draw attention to the fact . . .'

'Not even the attention of the Colombian Government?'

'With respect, Prime Minister, the details of the operation must have leaked from somewhere, and the Colombian Government seems the most likely source.'

There was silence on the other end.

'I think I should add,' Davies said, 'that even if their presence on the ground is known, these men have a fair chance of extricating themselves from the situation.' He had thought long and hard about saying this, hoping it would not weaken any resolve there might be in the way of providing the five men with outside help, but had decided he had no real choice. At present only five lives were at stake: sending in more to rescue them would raise the ante. And if all the Americans had to offer was exploding helicopters then maybe his men would be better off on their own.

'What are they going to do – walk out of Colombia?'

'If necessary, Prime Minister.'

'I will have to think this over,' she said. 'I will call you back later this morning.'

Thank you, Prime . . .' he started to say, but she had hung up. He took another gulp of whisky and stared angrily at the wall.

There was hardly any sign that it had happened, Chirlo thought, looking out across the verandah towards the gates. The gatehouse looked undamaged from this distance, the fence whole. The armoured car was still sitting in the middle of the outer compound; presumably its crew was still trying to recover from their failed attempt to shoot the forest. What a farce!

He heard the arrival of Miguel behind him and turned to join the meeting. Victoria's husband Noguera had arrived an hour earlier and had seemed, to no one's great surprise, not exactly devastated by his wife's death. Much the same could be said for her brothers. Ramón still looked pale, but that had more to do with his own brush with death; he had shown no sign of regretting Victoria's. The arriving Miguel seemed equally unmoved, offering his condolences to Noguera with all the emotion of a weather report. Basically, neither brother had ever forgiven Victoria for being the intelligent one of the three.

There was a silence lasting about half a minute, like those they hold at the beginning of football matches to honour someone recently dead. In the Amarales living-room there was no whistle to signal its end, but the participants all came out kicking anyway.

'Well, now we know where your stupidity has taken us, Ramón,' Miguel began. 'Our sister is dead, your hostages are gone, and our family will be a laughing stock throughout the nation.'

'Do you think so little of your sister that you can use her death to score points against me?' Ramón asked angrily. 'Where were you last night while the rest of us were fighting off the gringo soldiers? Not with your family. You have no right to accuse me.'

'Ramón, Miguel,' Noguera said. 'This is no time for blaming each other. What has happened, has happened. We must decide what to do now.'

'What is there to do?' Miguel asked with a cold laugh. 'We cannot bring Victoria back. Or the hostages, come to that. All we can do is learn from our mistakes,' he added, looking straight at Ramón. 'And cut our losses.'

'Our losses are seven men and a sister,' Ramón said quietly. 'How do you *cut* them?'

'Friends . . .' Noguera implored.

'Señores,' Chirlo said. 'I have some new information. Some of the gringo soldiers did not manage to escape in the helicopter.'

Both brothers looked at him as if he had taken leave of his senses.

216

'It is true. There must have been inadequate space for them all. Four, perhaps five of them, headed into the mountains on foot. Manomi is tracking them.' He looked at the three of them coldly, waiting for their response.

Miguel was the first to react. 'They will have a long walk home. It is of no concern to us . . .'

'No concern?' Chirlo asked, barely managing to keep his anger under control. 'These are the men who murdered your sister, Señor.'

'He is right,' Ramón said. 'We have a family obligation. And' – he insisted, ignoring Miguel's obvious disagreement – 'we can repair the lost prestige you're so concerned about.'

'You're a complete hypocrite,' Miguel told him. 'Victoria may have been our sister and Armando's wife, but none of us will grieve for her and we all know it . . .'

'Miguel!' Noguera said, but he did not deny it.

Chirlo felt Ramón's glance resting on him – the elder brother had obviously not missed the depth of his reaction to Victoria's death the night before. I loved her, Chirlo wanted to say. And she was worth a dozen of you.

'I will see to it that they do not escape,' he said instead.

'Good,' Ramón agreed. 'Armando, we will need your help.'

Noguera seemed less than enthusiastic. 'There are problems,' he said quickly. 'Bogotá will ask questions. I already have two men dead from last night.'

'Exercises,' Ramón said succinctly. 'You will mount exercises.'

'It is not so easy . . .'

'Armando,' Ramón said, 'we have always thought of you as one of the family, and this is a matter of family honour. Do you understand what I'm saying?'

Noguera swallowed. 'Yes, Ramón.' And he did. Victoria was no longer around to protect him from her brothers.

About twenty kilometres from Totoro, and almost a thousand metres higher, the five SAS men were toiling up what might have been a shepherd's path if there had been any sign of sheep. Someone had made it anyway, and Wynwood doubted if it was hikers. The higher they got the more the feeling grew that man had never set foot in these mountains before. Maybe there was an Andean yeti. Or Bigfoot. *Pie grande*. Or something like that.

Wynwood checked the map again. Another couple of kilometres and they should come to a small pass. From there they would descend into another valley and then start climbing again.

The mountain slopes were still covered with vegetation, though the type of tree had changed from mostly deciduous to mostly coniferous. The important thing was that they had cover if they needed it. Which was one of the reasons for their dawn decision to keep walking, rather than hole up for the day.

'If they're following us and we stop, they'll catch us,' Chris had argued.

'They may not be following us,' Wynwood had countered, mostly from a desire to play the devil's advocate. 'They may just mount a helicopter search, in which case we'd be better off out of sight.'

Both arguments had had something going for them. Wynwood hoped they had guessed right. All of them were very tired, particularly Anderson, who had not slept for almost thirty-six hours. He claimed to have suffered no ill effects from his period of imprisonment but Wynwood was not convinced, for his old partner seemed strangely subdued in those moments when he thought no one was looking.

Walking ahead of Wynwood, lead scout Eddie seemed the most alert of them all, his Cockney swagger somewhat muted but far from suppressed. Wynwood had been impressed by the Londoner's efficiency over the last few days, but he did not have a clue what made him tick. He seemed too cynical even for the SAS. At least he looked better in his jungle hat than he had in the ridiculous helmet.

Eddie himself was enjoying the morning. Ever since infant-school days – covering every square foot of the pitch Steve Perryman-style for the school team – he had been known for his incredible physical stamina. He could walk another twenty kilometres yet without really feeling the pace. Only his eyes felt really tired, and that was a consequence of wearing the PNGs for an extended period.

For a while he had wondered why this latest disaster had not fazed him more. But it just had not – that was all there was to it. In this world you took what was coming and you made the best of it. He disliked riding in helicopters anyway. And it really was a beautiful morning. He smiled to himself as he thought of all the millions of men trapped in offices and factories and tube trains and high-rise flats who would never know what this life was like. And he thought about Lisa and wondered if he could ever learn to live without it.

Two men behind Eddie, Anderson alternated his gaze between Wynwood's back and the patrol's left flank, for which he was responsible. At the moment it consisted of the small and beautiful valley out of which they were slowly climbing. It looked like a Western setting, needing only a cabin with smoke rising from its chimney and a lone rider's horse picking its way across the shallow mountain stream.

This morning he would have been back in the chair with the cold electrodes fastened to his balls. Would he have told the man with the scar what he wanted to know? No, because the man would not have known the truth from the lies. But if he had known . . . He could still feel the moment the pain hit him. Like every other SAS soldier, Anderson had been through the sensory-deprivation and interrogation training sessions, and he had found them as harrowing as anyone else. But what had happened the day before was something else altogether. He had just had the one shock, but still he felt as if his life had been changed, perhaps even fundamentally. How it would affect him in the long run he did not know. But he wanted to, and as soon as possible. This was one reason, he now realized, why he had been loath to get aboard the helicopter. There was no exorcism available in Hereford, only in real action.

Behind Anderson, Chris was responsible for the patrol's right flank. This consisted of an overhanging slope rising to invisible heights above their line of march. He scanned what he could of it, despite the near-certainty that the enemy was extremely unlikely to be above them. Amarales men – or Colombian Army men come to that – could only have got ahead of them by air, and only once that morning had they caught the distant sound of a helicopter, and that far away to their rear.

Chris did have another reason for scanning the heights to their right. If he remembered correctly what he had read in his book there were Andean Condors in these mountains. Not many of them, but some. He would happily give a month's pay to see one on the wing.

Behind Chris, officially designated 'Tail-end Charlie', the Dame regularly swung round on his heel to check that there was no danger to the patrol from the rear. There was almost a hundred metres between him and Eddie, and the spaces between each man and his neighbours were deliberately irregular. They were a professional outfit, the Dame thought proudly. They did things *well*. And when they got home they would have some story to tell.

Yet he wondered why he never told his sisters anything of his experiences as an SAS soldier. It was not security – they would never breathe a word if he told them not to. And it was not that he felt ashamed of anything, or that they needed protecting from the real world. If you lived in the Garth flats you knew about the real world, all right.

No, it was just that they were women, and women were not interested in the same things as men. His sisters would be interested in his experiences because they were his, not because of the experiences themselves. They would want to know what señoritas he had met. He would tell them about Barbara on the bus and the two Australian girls in the square at Popayán, and they would tease him about them for months. He smiled to himself and turned round on his heel. Behind him there was only Colombia, spread out like a huge geography lesson.

The pilot returned for fuel and lunch. Chirlo gave him the former, and told him to get back in the air.

'If they are in the area you described they are hiding, Chief.'

'Look again, then widen the area,' Chirlo told him.

'What do you think?' Wynwood asked Anderson. Ahead of them the pass stretched at least a kilometre and a half into the distance, before disappearing over its rim and into the wide blue sky. A small stream bubbled its way down between long slopes of mixed grass and scree. Cover was non-existent.

'What's the choice?' Anderson asked.

'Dig in here until dark.'

'There's not much more cover here.'

That was true enough, Wynwood thought. 'OK, let's go on.'

Luis Quintana waited for the President to stop preening himself in front of the window and tell him the detail he had just received from the military in Popayán.

'There are several Englishmen somewhere in the mountains,' Estrada said with a faint smile on his face. He suddenly laughed. 'You have to hand it to the Americans,' he said. 'They take the minimum number of helicopters and then crash one. What morons! If I was Mrs Thatcher I think I'd bomb Washington.'

Quintana smiled too. At least no one seemed to be publicly raising the question of sabotage. The Americans must know, but that did not matter. 'What are you going to do about these Englishmen?' he asked.

'Me? Nothing. The Amarales are looking for them, and since the Military Commander in Popayán is their brother-in-law I expect they're getting some unofficial help. Officially, I don't even know these Englishmen exist. When I talked to London and Washington this morning no mention was made of them.'

'What did London and Washington tell you?'

'That they'd rescued Muñoz and lost a helicopter and its pilot in the process.'

'Yes, we will soon have Muñoz back,' Quintana agreed. He could not understand why Estrada was in such a good mood.

'He's finished,' Estrada asserted blandly. 'I shall talk to the nation tonight,' he added, passing across a rough draft of what he intended to say.

Quintana read it through, and realized what was plastering the smile across Estrada's face. The whole business had played right into the President's hands. On the one hand he would welcome Muñoz's release on humanitarian grounds, while on the other he would condemn the foreign incursion as a violation of Colombia's sovereignty, an insult to the nation. Without even mentioning the two in the same breath, Muñoz would be tarred with the American brush and Estrada's place would be secure in the coming nomination fight.

'It reads well,' Quintana said mildly, handing the draft back. Why, he thought to himself, did political luck always seem to bless those who deserved it least?

They were more than halfway up the pass now, though whether the far side would offer more cover was a moot point. Chris had said it would – west-facing slopes got more rain, and therefore had more vegetation – but Wynwood tended to put more faith in Sod's Law than in geography textbooks.

He really was beginning to feel tired now. Even Eddie's legs were showing some signs of strain. Another few kilometres and they would get under cover, sleep a few hours and then push on after dark.

There was even a buzzing in his ears.

'Chopper,' Eddie shouted, and there it was, appearing in the V of the pass ahead.

'Spread out,' he yelled, but he need not have bothered. The members of the patrol split off to the right and left like a well-oiled machine, searching for whatever cover they could find.

Wynwood threw himself 'behind' a shelf of rock which only protruded about three inches above the grass and searched the sky for the helicopter. For a few seconds he could hear it but not see it, and then it emerged from over the ridge behind him, swooping down across the shallow valley. A man in the passenger seat was half leaning out, sub-machine-gun at the ready, and as the craft swooped above Wynwood, its rotors sweeping the grass into his face, the crack of automatic fire resounded above the engine.

Answering fire came from across the valley. Andy and Eddie had opened up with their MP5s.

The helicopter swooped round in a wide arc and then slowed to a virtual hover above the valley a couple of hundred metres ahead of them, as if uncertain what to do. And then the pilot's head suddenly jerked away, the helicopter reared up like a bucking bronco, seemed to hover again for a moment, and then dropped like a stone to the ground. The explosion seemed to wash around the valley like water trapped in a maelstrom. Flames and black smoke gushed into the blue sky.

Looking round, Wynwood saw the Dame still holding the sniper rifle cradled against his shoulder.

'The boy can shoot,' Wynwood murmured to himself. He lay still for a few seconds, straining his ears for the sound of another helicopter, then got slowly to his feet.

All five men walked forward towards the burning helicopter. In the cockpit two Colombians had lost their chance to choose between burial and cremation.

'The pilot was talking into his mike,' the Dame said.

'So they'll probably know how many of us there are,' Chris observed.

'With any luck they won't have any more helicopters to spare,' Anderson said.

Wynwood grunted. 'With any luck they'll think twice about risking another one.'

'Why are they bothering?' the Dame wanted to know. 'What good will it do them?'

'I think they've taken it personally,' Wynwood said. 'We killed a woman back at the house,' he went on, turning to the three who did not know. 'She just stepped out of a doorway into the line of fire,' he added, and shrugged. 'So they may not be worrying too much about risk-evaluation. This may be a matter of family honour. Or something like that.'

'Great,' Anderson murmured. 'We come all this way, and you start a family feud. Just like the bloody Welsh!'

Wynwood gave him a cold stare. He did not feel guilty about the woman's death, any more than he would have done if she had stepped out in front of his car on the M4. But he did not like the fact that it had happened, and he did not feel like making a joke of it.

'Let's get on,' Chris said, trying to fill the breach. 'I need some sleep, and I'd like some sort of roof over my head, even if it's only a tree.'

Wynwood, though, was extricating the PRC 319 from his pack. 'I think we ought to let Belize know we've been spotted,' he said.

Estrada and Quintana had just finished working their way through the latest American extradition requests when they were informed of the British Ambassador's request for an audience.

They grinned at one another. 'Bring him up,' Estrada said. 'Guess what he wants to talk about,' he said wryly to Quintana. 'You stay,' he added, as the other man got up to leave.

The Ambassador was shown in. After exchanging greetings with the President and being introduced to his Minister for the Interior, he was ushered into the usual ornate and uncomfortable chair.

'Before you begin,' Estrada said, 'I should tell you Señor Quintana is fully cognisant of last night's events.'

The Ambassador nodded. 'I have just received some additional information in that regard,' he said. 'I regret to tell you this, but five of our soldiers were left behind at the scene.' If he was expecting a shocked reaction he was disappointed.

'That is unfortunate,' Estrada agreed. 'Do you know where they are now?'

'Somewhere in the mountains. I am sure you will not take offence if I say that they are probably reluctant to approach the local authorities.'

'Of course not. I would be reluctant to approach them myself,' Estrada said with a broad smile.

The Ambassador sighed inwardly, smiled outwardly. 'The British Government would like to request your help in finding and escorting these men to safety,' he said formally.

'Of course, of course. We will do everything we can,' Estrada said, turning to Quintana for confirmation. The Minister nodded his agreement. With about as much sincerity as a tea-drinking chimpanzee, the Ambassador thought.

'But, as you know, our powers are somewhat limited,' Estrada went on. 'If they had not been, there would have been no need for your soldiers to be there in the first place, yes? But we will try. Of course we will.'

'There are several guerrilla groups active in those mountains,' Quintana added helpfully.

Just before dusk Chris woke Wynwood for his shift on lookout. 'Come and have a look at this,' he said, leading the Welshman back to the position they were using on a sheltered ledge above the camp. The sun had set beneath the western mountains, leaving the vast expanse beneath them bathed in shadow. 'Down there,' Chris said, handing him the sniper rifle's nightscope and pointing.

Wynwood could see nothing with the naked eye. With the scope he could just pick out a line of figures ascending a slope far below. 'Huh,' he said.

'Who *are* those guys?' Chris murmured.

'How far away do you think they are?' Wynwood asked, ignoring the *Butch Cassidy* reference.

'In distance, about three kilometres. In time, several hours. And it'll be too dark to track soon. I don't think we've got anything to worry about.'

'Yeah?' Wynwood asked, one eyebrow raised.

Chris grinned at the absurdity of what he had just said, and made the necessary correction. 'From them, that is.'

'OK,' Wynwood said, 'I'll keep an eye on 'em. Get some sleep.'

'Yes, boss.'

The news of the helicopter's destruction brought Chirlo a savage satisfaction. All day a little voice in his head had been telling him that Manomi was just an Indian who had seen a chance to make some money, that the tracks he was following were either non-existent or made by someone else entirely at some distant time in the past, and that all the Englishmen were back in Panama or wherever it was they had come from.

The little voice had been wrong. They really were out there in the mountains. Five of them, according to the pilot's last report, including the one who had been a prisoner.

Where the fuck did they think they were going?

He had thought they were just keeping themselves out of harm's way until someone friendly came to collect them, but it was beginning to look like no one was coming.

The way these gringos were going they were either lost or intending to walk right across the mountains. The first possibility did not seem very likely. But if they were trying the second then what was their intended destination? It had to be somewhere in the Magdalena valley.

He left the security centre and walked upstairs to the library, pulled out a map of the area and examined it. They could be aiming for San Agustin, or the airport at Pitalito . . .

Either way they would be making themselves vulnerable again.

Walking back down the corridor, he passed one of the TV lounges. As usual, and despite the circumstances, Ramón was spending the afternoon in front of a Hollywood movie.

Chirlo walked down the stairs, letting his anger cool into something closer to sadness. I was the only one who cared for you, he told the woman who was still living in his head.

11

By 22.00 hours all five men had had at least four hours' sleep. It was not exactly enough, but it would have to do. Far beneath them the pursuit had camped for the night, the distant glow of their fire like a flare in the nightscope.

'Look on the bright side, lads,' Anderson said, eliciting groans from Eddie and the Dame. 'If this was the "Long Drag" over the Beacons you'd be having to contend with rain, snow and sadistic bastards from Training Wing like Joss here. And here we are on a beautiful night, sky full of stars, not too hot, not too cold. Perfect walking weather.'

'And *two* sadistic bastards from Training Wing for company,' Eddie observed.

'Let's get started,' Wynwood said.

The first hour was the worst, as the muscles stiffened by the previous day's exercise wreaked their revenge. After that it was just a matter of putting one foot in front of the other. This, they all knew, was exactly what their training had been for, and each man called on those inner reserves he had not known he had before the SAS forced him to find them. It was hard, it hurt, but there was no denying it also brought a deep sense of satisfaction.

It was not a night for talking, and even on their rare rest stops barely a word was exchanged. Each man was too busy inside himself, cajoling himself, getting the best out of himself. The surroundings helped. Walking through this land of lofty peaks, cavernous valleys and endless sky was like walking through a dream, taking each man back to the lost fantasies of childhood, to the roots of his own being.

By the time the first glimmer of dawn appeared over the eastern horizon they were starting their descent into the upper reaches of the Magdalena valley, more than half the journey done. At the foot of a high pass, just below the tree line, they made camp for the day. A mist was rising from the valley below, and for a moment they could all have been in Wales again, waiting for the lorries from Hereford to take them home.

'Your call to the State Department,' his secretary informed Alan Holcroft. He grimaced and picked up the receiver.

'John!' he said jovially. He had always found that false bonhomie seemed to put Americans at a disadvantage. It was as if one part of them knew it was false, while another part could not bear to believe it.

'Alan,' John Stokes, his American opposite number, responded with rather less enthusiasm.

Already Holcroft knew he was going to get nowhere. Not that he particularly wanted to, or thought he deserved to, but the Prime Minister had other ideas. They had used our air bases to attack Libya, and the least they could do was let us use theirs to . . . well, 'attack Colombia' were the words she had used, but Holcroft had presumed this was only a figure of speech, and that her actual intentions did not go beyond extricating the SAS men. It had been pointed out to her that the US were particularly touchy about their relations with Latin America, and had shown it during the Falklands War, but this had only brought forth a history lesson in Anglo-American cooperation, and how the British had been doing most of the cooperating.

The Americans owed us, and she was confident they would make good the debt. At least, she said she was. Presumably she had *some* fears of an American rebuff, or she would have been on the phone herself, talking direct to the White House.

All this flashed through Holcroft's mind in an instant, flooding his mind with the usual cynicism. 'I think we need your help again, John,' he began. 'What are the chances?'

'Not good,' Stokes said. 'You know what Estrada said on TV yesterday. If we mount another operation he'll have to break off relations . . .'

'Only if the second operation is also a failure,' Holcroft interrupted, half masking the accusation in geniality.

'Could you guarantee your military won't fuck up any particular operation?'

Holcroft winced inwardly at the language. 'I think we could guarantee not to make the same mistake twice in a row,' he said, rather more haughtily than he intended.

'Yeah, well, your guys are doubtless all supermen. The point is, Alan, we're not prepared to put our entire Latin America policy at risk for five men. I sympathize, I hope they make it out. But . . .'

Holcroft heard the mental shrug. 'There is a second possibility,' he said. 'You could simply allow us to use your Panama base facilities to mount the operation ourselves.'

'Same problem,' Stokes said succinctly.

'You got a rather more friendly answer from us when you requested the use of our facilities to attack Libya,' Holcroft said, as unaggressively as he could manage.

'NATO facilities,' Stokes corrected him. 'English soil, I give you that. But you tell me, Alan, did Gaddafi look on the UK

Government as an innocent party because it only supplied the air bases?'

There was no answer to that. 'Touché,' Holcroft replied. 'Well, I tried.'

'I hope they make it,' Stokes said again.

The helicopter touched down in the mountain meadow. Chirlo dropped to the ground and walked across to where an impassive-looking Manomi was doing battle with a mango, tugging at the stringy flesh with his irregular teeth, juice glistening on his chin. The ten *sicarios* he had been leading across the mountains sat and lay in some disarray around him. They all looked like they needed an oxygen tent.

'Well?' Chirlo asked, sitting down next to the Indian.

Manomi smiled, and with a simple contemptuous gesture of one hand passed sentence on his fellow-walkers. 'They will not catch them,' he added unnecessarily.

'But you could?'

Manomi shrugged. 'Probably, but I would not like to bet my life on it. These men can walk.' He popped the mango stone into his mouth and begun to suck on it.

'How far ahead are they?'

Manomi manoeuvred the stone into a cheek. 'Perhaps not so far,' he said. 'They will be sleeping now – they only walk by night.'

'Then why . . .' Chirlo started to ask, but the answer was all around him. These men had nothing left. He was tempted to leave them here.

'If they can keep up the same speed,' Manomi volunteered, 'they will be in San Agustin by tomorrow morning.'

This time they slept through most of the daylight hours, each man taking two hours on lookout and eight hours' sleep.

Wynwood could not quite manage the latter, and in the last hour of daylight, prematurely darkened by their position on an eastern slope, he went to find Chris in the lookout position. The bird-watcher had a smile on his face.

'I saw two of them,' he said, almost dreamily.

'Two what?'

'Andean Condors. They circled the valley up there. Enormous, they were – the wingspan must have been ten feet. Sort of wrinkled-looking heads . . .'

'I know how they feel.'

'And these large silvery patches on the black wings. Incredible,' he sighed. 'But they didn't stay long. I think they must have sensed our presence.'

'I don't suppose they see many people up here,' Wynwood agreed, looking up the pass they had descended that morning. 'No sign of our friends?'

'No. Even if they'd started at dawn and matched our pace they'd still be a couple of hours back. But' – he paused for a moment – 'I was wondering whether we should do something to slow them down even more.'

'Booby-trap the path?'

'Yep. We're still carrying a Claymore. If they lost their lead man it'd slow them down no end.'

Wynwood looked round, thinking it over. The odds against an innocent passer-by being killed seemed pretty remote. But then they hardly knew anything about the place. Maybe in a year, two years, some hiker would come along and . . .

'No,' he decided. 'If we were being really pushed, maybe. But I think we can outwalk this bunch.'

Chirlo stood over Ramón as he made the call.

'Armando, it's me. We have more information about the

gringos. They will probably be in San Agustin tomorrow morning . . . What does it matter how they got there? They walked . . . This is not a joke . . . Good. Now you must contact General Castro in Neiva. Tell him there are five gringo criminals on the run from your custody, and you want them apprehended and returned to Popayán. If he is difficult then you can use our name and offer him whichever you think will work better – money or threats. But only if he is difficult . . . Yes, I understand. I hope you do too, Armando. Chirlo will be handling things in San Agustin personally . . . Yes, the police chief there is an old friend . . .'

Ramón replaced the phone. 'He will do as you asked,' he told Chirlo.

'Thank you, *patrón*. I am sure the murder of his wife has been a great shock to him,' Chirlo added, not bothering to keep the bitter irony out of his voice.

'I'm sure,' Ramón agreed, in a more neutral tone.

Chirlo went back to his own suite, where he restlessly paced the floor for several minutes before allowing himself to sit down with a cigarette. He looked around at all the trimmings of luxury – the fine clothes, the excellent Japanese sound system, TV and VCR, even a couple of expensive paintings he had acquired on a whim in the USA. None of it had ever meant much to him. The fact of it was important, the fact that he had pulled himself up from nothing, from less than nothing – the orphaned boy living wild in the Bogotá sewers who had risen through teenage gangs and worse to become chief hired gun, the *sicario jefe*, of the Amarales. He was proud that he had not gone under, like so many others he had known.

If he had ever thought about the morality of what he did, it would have been simply to dismiss the question. Almost all the men he had killed would have killed him if they had been quicker or brighter or stronger. He was a soldier in a war, in two wars really – the Amarales against the other drug cartels, and the war of the cartels against the United States.

The first was just a straight dispute between businesses – they all knew what they were doing, all accepted the lack of rules, all played to win. The second was just as straightforward. The people of Peru and Bolivia wanted to sell coca leaves, and a lot of Americans wanted to smoke or snort cocaine. The cartels were just middlemen, turning raw material into product and retailing it at a profit on the open market. If the American Government could use force to keep markets open then so could the cartels.

No, it was not where he was that worried Chirlo, but where he could not go. The post of chief *sicario* to such a family was the highest a *mestizo* like himself could hope for. There might be no limit to the wealth he could accumulate, but he could never become one of them. They were Spanish purebloods one and all, each with a beautifully drawn genealogical chart on the living-room wall tracing his descent from the conquistadors.

None of that could be his. All he could have was things, more and more expensive things perhaps, but still things. And his power would always be only that, never true authority. Even as a sixteen-year-old he had seen this emptiness at the heart of his future.

And then he had found Victoria. Now he had lost her, the emptiness seemed so much greater than before.

This time the night's walk seemed easier, but not because their path led mostly downhill – that merely meant a new set of muscles to torture. It was a few good hours of sleep that had made the difference. After the day-long wait outside Totoro, the night's excitement and two long marches, all on only four hours of blissful unconsciousness, their energy reserves had been dangerously low. Now, Wynwood thought, they were fully recovered. Eddie had his jaunty step back, Chris had even seen his birds. All was right with the world, or as right as it could be with a drug cartel on your trail.

Shortly before dawn they reached the forested hills overlooking San Agustin. Only a few lights were showing and it was hard to get any real idea of how big the town was.

The five of them gathered in a circle, barely visible to each other in the still-dark forest.

'The way I see it,' Wynwood began, 'we have to choose now between staying soldiers or going back undercover. And it doesn't seem much of a choice. We can't fight our way out of this country, so there doesn't seem any point in trying. We could present ourselves to the local authorities and hope they're friendly. Or we could go back to being tourists and try and make it to Bogotá, where at least we'll have people to help us.'

'Like you say, boss, there's no choice,' the Dame agreed.

'I don't like the idea of surrendering ourselves to the local military or police,' Chris said, 'at least not until we have some idea whose pocket they're in.'

There were several murmurs of agreement.

'OK,' Wynwood said. 'But if we're going back undercover we have to ditch most of what we're carrying. The MP5s can go in our rucksacks, and we can wear the Brownings, but that's it. The L96 has to go,' he added, looking at the Dame. 'It's earned a decent burial.'

He looked round at them. 'And it's goodbye jungle fatigues, hello your sartorial best.'

'You're not going to wear that shirt again, are you, boss?' Eddie asked. 'There may be fashion police down there.'

It got both lighter and more misty as Wynwood worked his way downhill towards the town. After about a kilometre he came across the first real fence he had seen since Totoro. Since it was high, and stretched into the distance in both directions, Wynwood simply cut his way through it. Climbing a small hill, he found himself suddenly face to face with four figures. For a moment he thought it was a group of men looming out of the mist, but they were statues, man-high stone statues like large chess pieces with flat, playing-card faces. He remembered what Bobbie had told him about San Agustin. He must have broken into the archaeological park.

He continued on his way, more cautiously now, and found some navigational help from the diagrams set up for tourists to follow. Reaching the main gate, he managed to clamber out without attracting any attention from the lighted office off to one side.

From there a road led downhill for a couple of kilometres into the town, eventually becoming a street bound on both sides by houses and bungalow-style hotels. The first real sign of life came from an establishment with the unexpected name of the Brahama Vegetarian Restaurant. Looking in through the doorway, Wynwood could see one European man eating what looked like a pancake.

He went in. The man turned out to be German, and in response to Wynwood's questions about a quiet hotel suggested the one he was staying at himself. It was only two minutes away. He would show Wynwood after he had finished his breakfast.

Resisting the temptation to waste time by ordering himself a pancake, Wynwood made do with a wonderfully hot cup of coffee.

Outside it was now almost full light, and the sun was breaking through the mist. The German, whose name was Klaus, led him round two corners and into a rapidly disintegrating street. A long, one-storey building carried a sign proclaiming it the Residencias El Cesar.

At first sight it did not seem very prepossessing. The large wooden gates were almost falling off their hinges, and the only visible wall looked like it belonged to a barracks. Inside, though, it was a different matter. Klaus led Wynwood down a short passage, turning right onto a verandah that was at least fifty metres long. On one side doors led into a line of rooms, ten or more of them. On the other a balustrade looked out and down over half an acre of tropical vegetation. Butterflies were dancing in the leaves, two donkeys were rummaging in the earth, and a cock, apparently confused by the mist, was belatedly crowing in the dawn.

The owners occupied the far rooms, and the owner's wife, a plump woman whose dress would have seemed appropriate in a Bogotá nightclub, was drinking coffee at the end of the verandah. She showed Wynwood two empty rooms with six beds, the shower and toilet. '*Aguas calientes*,' she said proudly.

Wynwood took the rooms. He could have left the others sitting in the forest while he investigated the situation, but the sooner they came down the better, while the town was still half-asleep. And here in the hotel they would be able to clean themselves up properly – tourists tended not to have their faces covered in dirt.

It took him half an hour to get back to them, this time by a route which skirted round the edge of the archaeological park. Behind him the town was now basking in the early morning sun. Looking back, he could see that it was perched on a sloping plateau above a gorge, surrounded by green hills.

Built to the usual Spanish grid pattern, it was about thirty streets long and six streets wide. Most of the buildings seemed to be of two storeys.

Chris was acting lookout on the forest's edge. The others were half dozing on the forest floor. Wynwood kicked Eddie's foot. 'I've found you a bath,' he said.

An hour later a freshly showered Eddie joined the other four in the room Wynwood was nominally sharing with Anderson. As far as they knew, their passage from the forest to the hotel, spaced out in pairs behind Wynwood, had been unobserved by anyone other than children, dogs and the odd chicken.

It was now 0800 hours, and Wynwood did not think they could count on such invisibility for much longer. 'Andy's the only one they've seen,' he said, 'so he stays in the hotel. In the room,' he added. 'I'm going to try and call Bogotá from the local telephone office . . .'

'Why not from here?' Eddie asked.

Wynwood looked at him pityingly. 'Or we could just run a Union Jack up the TV aerial.'

'Sorry, boss.'

'Like I said, the local office. Depending on what Bogotá says, I'll try the bus station – find out when there's a bus. The rest of you should get out of here, but not together. In ones or twos. And we'll meet back here at noon. OK?'

They nodded.

'Anyone got a book I can read while I'm stuck in here?' Anderson asked.

'*Teach Yourself Plastic Surgery*,' Eddie suggested.

'*South American Birds?*' Chris offered.

Anderson turned to the Dame. 'Some people are interested in birds, and some are interested in *birds*, know what I mean?'

'I'll bring you back a chicken,' Eddie promised.

It was getting warmer out on the street. Wynwood's description of Klaus's banana and papaya pancake had made both Eddie and the Dame feel decidedly hungry, and they made straight for the restaurant. It was more crowded now, with both Colombians and tourists. They took a corner table, ordered pancakes and coffee and sat watching the other occupants, one wary eye on the door.

A bunch of children were going from table to table with a tape recorder, getting all the foreigners to say something in their own language. 'We are Spanish,' Eddie said apologetically, but they were not spared. 'Real Madrid are the greatest football team in the world,' Eddie told them in their own language.

The children left, and a woman appeared in the doorway, demanding that the man at the next table come with her. He argued for a while, then went, leaving half his breakfast still uneaten. No sooner had he gone than two new children appeared, sat down at his table, each with a fork, and demolished the remaining food, occasionally favouring Eddie and the Dame with conspiratorial smiles.

After they had eaten the two men split up, the Dame heading left back up the hill towards the archaeological park, Eddie turning right and walking towards the centre of town. The locals hardly spared him a glance. Most of them seemed too busy playing pool. He could not believe it: in a town as poor and as small as this one he had already walked past half a dozen pool halls. And they were all bursting with activity at nine in the morning.

He walked the length of the main street, past a couple more hotels and a few shops that were obviously aimed at tourists, past a man lying against a wall, his head covered by a poncho.

Eddie presumed the man was sleeping rather than dead. A few yards further on a tethered pig grunted at him – affectionately, he thought.

Eddie walked back through the town and found himself standing in the doorway of one of the pool halls. Why not? he asked himself, and wandered in. He paid for a table and tried a few shots, impressing some of the watching Colombian youths. 'You play me, mister?' one asked in English.

'*Sí, señor*', Eddie replied. He looked at his watch as the Colombian boy broke. Two and a half hours.

The Dame walked on up a rutted road, with only the occasional bar or home on either side. Chickens wandered in circles, a youth went by on a scooter. He noticed clusters of bananas growing upside down on their palm trees, and wondered why he had always assumed they grew the other way.

The road wound steadily uphill past a large, empty-looking hotel. A couple of large birds landed on the asphalt some forty metres ahead of them, and showed no sign of moving as they approached and went past. They looked like vultures. Chris would know.

At the archaeological park office he bought a ticket. There were two separate collections of statues to choose from, one on the open hills, the other in the forest. The latter sounded more appropriate for someone trying not be noticed.

After the clear air of the hills the path through the forest seemed darker than it was. The early morning rain was still dripping down through the trees, competing with the incessant birdsong. The statues had been placed at about five-metre intervals, set back from the gravel path.

The first one was a flat stone bas-relief, hardly human yet nothing else, holding what looked like two bread rolls. The second was recognizably non-human, but no less terrifying because of it. Maybe it was a dog, maybe not. The third was of a human figure playing a musical instrument – or maybe swallowing a snake.

A giant flying insect flew low over the Dame's head and disappeared into the forest. He felt a heightened sense of nature's reality, and it seemed to weaken his own, leaving him a half-helpless spectator, almost in thrall to the stone images. The dripping sound went on, like Chinese water torture. A black butterfly with pale-green patches fluttered by. The path wound on between hanging palm fronds twice the length of a man.

Almost all the expressions on the faces of the statues seemed part-made of pain, and they flickered past his eyes like a parade of grotesques, a line of mirrors, nightmares within the nightmare.

The next one was different. For one thing it was off the path, in a small clearing surrounded by white-barked trees and enormous palms. For another it featured two full, almost naturalistic figures. And they seemed to be fucking each other. The Dame stared open-mouthed at it for a second, then suddenly burst out laughing.

Chris sat in one of the rocking chairs on the verandah and watched the sun slowly rise above the distant hills. Two other guests, a Canadian husband and wife, had emerged, introduced themselves as Tom and Amy, taken showers, and disappeared back into their room. Judging from the sounds soon coming through the wall, they seemed to be enjoying each other's company. It made him think of Molly.

In the tree in front of him a bird appeared. It had a long, black, swallow-like tail, a gorgeous emerald-green breast and a long, thin, black beak. As it hovered frenetically, making a soft humming sound, the beak picked at the tree's crimson flowers.

Chris could not remember ever seeing anything more beautiful. He was still sitting more than half entranced when the man walked past him down the verandah to where the owner's wife was on her fifth or sixth breakfast coffee, and started talking to her in a low, insistent voice.

Her replies were equally inaudible, but a single glance towards him told Chris most of what he wanted to know. The only remaining question was what to do about it.

He was still pondering this when their conversation ended and the man walked back towards him. Chris had his hand inside his jacket, resting on the Browning's grip, but the man walked straight past him, looking resolutely ahead. At this moment the owner's wife chose to disappear through the door at the far end of the verandah.

The man was five metres away from the other end. Chris drew the Browning as he got to his feet, took aim with both hands and squeezed the trigger. The man went down with a clatter.

Chris whirled round but no one appeared to investigate the noise. The owner's wife was still out of sight, the lovers still striving towards a muffled climax. Only the hummingbird had sensed the presence of death and flown away.

He reached the body in five strides, grabbed it by the ankles and dragged it backwards along the verandah and in through the doorway of one of their rooms.

'What the fuck!?' Anderson exclaimed.

'He came for our Poll Tax,' Chris said, closing the door on the outside world and looking through the man's clothes. There was no identification, unless you counted the flick-knife in a pocket and the Walther automatic in the shoulder holster.

Chirlo gazed out into the street from a second-floor window of the San Agustin police headquarters. There seemed to be more gringos than Colombians, and any of the gringo men out there could be one of the ones he was looking for. He had been prepared to look for tidy-looking young men, short-haired and clean-shaven, but Ramón had told him the SAS did not place much importance on external appearance. So any one of these hippie types could have killed Victoria.

And there were so many of them. He could not have them all arrested. No, but all he did have to do was find Anderson. And Anderson would either be with the others or lead him to them.

If he had to put the man's cock through a pencil-sharpener he would lead him to them.

Chirlo looked at his watch. It was only ten minutes since he had sent out the men to check the hotels. The road was blocked. And for all he knew the Englishmen were not even here yet.

He took a sip of the coffee Arevalo's secretary had made for him and lit a cigarette. There was still that empty feeling in the pit of his stomach which had nothing to do with food. And he knew that even killing them all one by one would not begin to fill it.

Wynwood had not had a very successful morning. The woman at the telephone office had been most apologetic but there was a problem with the lines. Both the one running north to Bogotá and the one running west across the mountains were down. It was unheard of that both should be down at once. But . . . Here she had shrugged and smiled prettily and offered the clichéd Spanish response – it would be all right '*mañana*'.

Wynwood doubted it. If the telephone lines were down he did not hold out much hope of the bus station being unwatched. Sure enough, two men he recognized from Totoro were hanging round outside, casting an eye over each European who came to enquire about travel. The Amarales's influence might not stretch to kidnapping them in the middle of San Agustin, but he did not imagine they would think twice about stopping a bus on the open road.

There only seemed one remaining option. He arrived back at the hotel just before Eddie and just after the Dame. They were all treated to the story of the man now stowed under the bed in the corner.

'Time to leave,' Anderson said, 'before someone comes looking for him.'

'Before he starts to smell,' Eddie added.

'The phones are down and the buses are being watched,' Wynwood told them. 'We'll have to pinch a car. Eddie, you're the expert . . .'

'Thanks, boss,' Eddie said sarcastically. It was true, though – he had stolen more cars in his teens than Tottenham had thrown games away. Which was a lot.

'We'll meet on the road outside town,' Wynwood said as he unfolded the map. 'Here,' he decided, pointing to where the road crossed a stream about a kilometre and a half beyond the outskirts. 'Chris, you and the Dame circle round to the north, me and Andy'll take the south. You take a nice car,' he told Eddie. 'Nothing too flashy.'

'I'll look for a Lada.'

'I said a car.'

'Yes, boss.'

Eddie went back to the pool hall and had one last game. He knew it would take the others up to an hour to reach the rendezvous point, and he wanted to be damn sure he would not have to wait for them in a stolen car out in the open.

With about twenty minutes to go he sauntered into the centre of town, keeping his eyes open for a likely prospect. Nothing appeared. He walked on towards a hotel he had noticed earlier that day which offered escorted trips to the nearby ruins for tourists with money. A group of Americans were just setting out on horseback, two blond men and two brunette women. Eddie casually wandered up the alley which ran down the side of the hotel and looked into the yard at the back. There were three cars: a dark-blue Ford Escort, a black Fiat Uno and a red BMW. There were a couple of upstairs windows overlooking the yard, but only a door on the ground floor. No wonder auto-crime is soaring, Eddie told himself.

The BMW was almost irresistible, but he could imagine Wynwood's face when he drove up in it. And the Escort was a hire car with Bogotá plates. The Americans. They had even left the doors open. He climbed in confidently, took off the handbrake and rolled the car silently out of the yard. No one screamed 'thief' at him. In a blind spot by the side of the hotel he stopped and hot-wired the engine.

His watch said he had four minutes. Good timing, he said to himself. Ticka-ticka.

No one seemed to take any notice as he drove out of the town and down a long slope towards the bottom of the valley. He stopped on the nearside of the bridge across the stream, and four men appeared out of nowhere and piled into the car.

'You can't move for hitchhikers in this country,' Eddie sighed.

For a few kilometres they motored along, passing only a couple of cars in the opposite direction, feeling it was too good to be true. They were right. About eight kilometres north of San Agustin they crested a rise and saw the road-block a kilometre ahead in the valley below. Two cars had been parked nose to nose across the road at a place where it was bordered by a wall on one side and a river on the other. At the moment two buses were being inspected, which was fortunate, because it gave Eddie time to halt the car, throw it into reverse and accelerate back up out of sight.

'Did they see us?' Chris asked.

'Don't think so,' Eddie said.

'No way round it?' Anderson asked.

'Nope.'

'Wouldn't help anyway,' Wynwood said. 'Once we're seen they've got nearly 500 kilometres in which to stop us.'

'Plan B, then?' Anderson asked.

'Yep,' Wynwood agreed.

Eddie groaned, and started to turn the car round.

'I hate the fucking *ulu*', he said, using the SAS name for the jungle.

'Don't expect it's overfond of you,' Chris replied.

12

San Agustin and what passed for civilization was disappearing behind them, swallowed by the hills that surrounded it. Their road, already deteriorating, ran uphill towards yet another range of mountains. The last road sign had offered the rather dispiriting information that Florencia was sixty-five kilometres away.

'Where exactly are we going?' Chris asked.

'Like Eddie said,' Wynwood replied, 'the fucking *ulu*'.

'Any particular piece?'

'Give him the map, Andy,' Wynwood said, and waited while Chris found his bearings. 'Once we're over these mountains we're in the Amazon basin and it's all downhill to the Atlantic.'

'About 5000 kilometres' worth,' Eddie said.

Wynwood ignored him. 'If we take the road south from Florencia to Tres Esquinas we'll be on the River Caqueta. From there it's only about two hundred and forty kilometres down river to some place whose name I've forgotten . . .'

'La Tagua,' Chris read off the map. 'And then there's a road to the Peruvian border. About thirty kilometres.'

'Right.'

'Are we going to be any better off in Peru?' the Dame asked.

'No idea. We'll have to talk to Belize. If not, there's always Brazil . . .'

'Which is over 1500 kilometres away.'

'A thousand,' Wynwood corrected him.

'Oh, no problem then,' Eddie said.

Wynwood laughed. 'Where would we be without your cheery optimism?' he asked. 'And I don't want an answer.'

'Yes, boss.'

'Have you always had this natural respect for authority?' Anderson asked Eddie.

'Yeah.'

'What sort of boat do you think we're going to find?' Chris asked. 'Do we have enough money to buy one?'

Anderson grunted. 'Quartermaster's going to love us. We dump all our weapons and then buy a boat.'

'A yacht would be nice,' Eddie observed. 'Maybe we could pick up some luscious cuties en route.'

'The rainforest is full of them. We'll probably have to make do with gang-banging Sting,' Anderson said.

'Jesus!' the Dame exclaimed.

'I doubt if we'll meet him.'

'Who – Jesus or Sting?'

'You could handle a yacht, could you?' Chris asked Eddie.

'A yacht with a crew, yes. But I shouldn't worry about it – I'm sure the boss here is thinking more of leaky canoes.'

'A mind-reader!'

'Seriously, boss,' Eddie said, 'you're not really thinking of canoeing a thousand kilometres, are you?'

'Got any better ideas?'

'Beam me up, Scottie.'

* * *

'Señor Chirlo,' Arevalo said respectfully, despite the fact that Chirlo had his feet on the police chief's desk. 'A car has been reported stolen from one of the hotels . . .'

Pérez came through the door. 'We just found Jorge – dead – in one of the rooms at the Residencias El Cesar. The Englishmen were there this morning – five of them. The owner's wife recognized the description of Anderson.'

'They're gone,' Chirlo said. It wasn't a question. 'Have you checked with your men on the Bogotá road?' he snapped at Arevalo.

'Not yet . . .'

'Do it!'

The police chief returned a minute later. 'They have checked every vehicle. And they haven't seen a blue Ford.'

'And there is no way round the block?'

'No, señor.'

'So where are they?' Chirlo asked himself out loud. He got up and walked across to take another look at the map on the wall. If they were not headed for Bogotá, then where? They wouldn't go back into the mountains, surely? And the only other roads led down towards the jungle. There was no way home for them that way. He turned away and stared into space for a moment, the scar livid on his cheek.

'Every policeman in Huila is looking out for them, señor,' Arevalo said.

Chirlo sighed. He would have to be patient.

An idea came to him. 'Spread the word that there's a thousand-dollar reward for the man who spots them,' he said.

'Yes, chief.'

Chirlo turned his eyes back to the streets, the parade of gringo tourists. The reward would come out of his own pocket, which was only right. In the matter of Victoria's killers he would not want anyone else to pay.

Motoring down the eastern slope of the mountains, telegraph poles flashing past the window, it occurred to Wynwood that the enemy was not the only one who could interfere with communications. They stopped in a deserted lay-by, with more than a kilometre of road visible in each direction, and the Dame shinned up a pole with the wire-cutters.

An hour later they drove into Florencia, a small town close to the feet of the mountains. They had felt both temperature and humidity rising with every one of the last thirty downhill kilometres, and it was now distressingly obvious why most Colombians preferred to live in the mountains. A ten-metre walk in Florencia was enough to stick the shirts to their backs.

They had other, more serious things to worry about. Despite the Dame's work with the wire-cutters, Wynwood had half expected either more roadblocks or an armed deputation of welcome. Neither materialized. In fact the town seemed still becalmed in its afternoon siesta, despite it being nearly five o'clock.

On the journey across the mountains they had compiled a shopping list of what they would need in the jungle, and now they set about trying to fill it. Getting shopkeepers to open up was one problem, finding what they needed in the chaotic shops was another.

They had enough dehydrated food for a week, and collecting and purifying water in the jungle was one of the first things they had learnt during training in Brunei. They were not carrying mosquito nets though, since they had not been expecting to be operating below the altitude at which mosquitoes live. The fair-skinned Eddie was particularly keen that they should make up for this lack of foresight.

After an hour they had filled as much of the list as Wynwood thought they could, and rendezvoused back at the car, which Chris had filled at the petrol station in the centre of town.

He told them the bad news as they drove out along the Montanita road. 'A policeman stood there watching me get her filled,' he said. 'I thought he was going to take a photograph, he was so interested. He asked me where I was headed. I told him San Agustin, tried to act the dumb tourist.'

'That must have been easy,' Eddie observed.

'Would have been easier if I'd had you with me. Anyway, I guess the word hasn't got here yet. But when it does . . . I think Señor Plod will remember me.'

'We'll be on the river by then,' Wynwood said.

'Five men in a boat,' Anderson added.

'The fucking *ulu*,' Eddie said for about the fifth time, though with rather more excuse than the last four. The valley they were now descending was far more thickly vegetated than anything they had seen since the Cauca valley, and the trees were of a different type. Coniferous trees were altogether absent, whereas palms in many shapes and sizes now proliferated among taller deciduous trees of a decidedly unEnglish appearance. They were entering the fringes of the world's greatest rainforest.

'Chirlo wishes to speak with you, *patrón*.'

Ramón put down his magazine and walked slowly across the room to pick up the extension. He had been doing a lot of thinking about Chirlo this last couple of days, wondering whether the family should keep him on. Not because of the discovery that Chirlo had been screwing Victoria – Ramón should have guessed that was happening – but because the chief *sicario* seemed to have been dangerously destabilized by her death.

One thing was certain: if the time did come to dispense with Chirlo's services Ramón wanted a lot of armed help at his shoulder when he handed him the news.

'Yes, Chirlo,' he said into the phone.

'*Patrón*, I have lost the trail of the Englishmen, and I thought you might be able to help.'

Ramón resisted the temptation to tell him to stop wasting his time. 'Of course. But how?'

Chirlo outlined the events of the day, and how the Englishmen had vanished into thin air.

'You say they are not on the road to Bogotá, and they have not doubled back across the mountains towards Popayán?'

'I am certain.'

'Then there is only one possibility . . .'

'Amazonia?'

'Chirlo, we Colombians tend to think that Amazonia has nothing to do with us, even though it is two-thirds of our country. It is just a backwater to us, somewhere where the weather is too hot and humid and a few Indians live . . .'

'This is all true.'

'The SAS are trained in jungle warfare. I forget where – in one of England's old colonies in Asia or Africa. It doesn't matter. The point is they will feel more at home in our jungle than you or I would.'

'I understand,' Chirlo said more thoughtfully. 'But where would they go?'

'Brazil?'

'This is over 1500 kilometres away!'

'So? I tell you, they are taught how to survive in the jungle. And they are not in a hurry. What is to stop them?'

'I am, *patrón*.'

The phone clicked off. It was hardly a respectful goodbye, Ramón thought. Chirlo was either not himself, or his real self was finally breaking through the inhibitions of rank. Either way it did not bode too well for the future.

At the other end of the line Chirlo was busily re-examining the map in the San Agustin police office, Ramón already forgotten. His finger traced possible routes down into Amazonia. There were several, but most of them passed through Florencia.

He spun round on the hapless police chief. 'Get hold of Florencia,' he snapped.

'It is in Caqueta province, chief,' Arevalo said apologetically. 'The lines are the same as for Bogotá. And they will not be mended for an hour or more.'

Chirlo looked at him, trying to repress his growing frustration. Both men knew that the line had been cut just outside the town at Chirlo's instruction, but neither wanted to share the knowledge.

He took a deep breath. It did not matter. If the Englishmen were trying to reach Brazil across Amazonia then time was hardly an issue. He was dealing in weeks, not hours. 'When the lines have been mended,' he told the police chief, 'contact Florencia and ask them to find out if the stolen car has been seen. Anywhere in the province. I will be there in an hour myself.'

'Yes, chief,' the police chief said, managing to repress his sigh of relief. One day with this man had been enough.

They were still about a hundred kilometres from Tres Equinas on the River Caqueta when darkness fell, and the appalling state of the road made their progress slower than it might have been. A third hazard was the stream of heavy lorries travelling in the opposite direction, carrying timber at a pace which suggested the drivers' confidence in their ability to flatten anything they hit. Flashing their lights at them, far from inducing caution, seemed akin to waving a red rag at a bull. The only safe course was to turn out the lights and, if possible, pull off the road. The frequent need to take such evasive action considerably slowed the Ford's rate of progress.

It was 8.30 before they reached Tres Equinas, which seemed to consist of several tumbledown shacks, the sawmill source of the lorries and a hotel which would only have deserved the adjective 'cheap' if the proprietor had paid the guests. This last, which overlooked the river, was also the only source of boats in the village, and Wynwood suspected the worst as the proprietor, none too pleased at being dragged away from doing nothing on his verandah, led them down to the landing stage complaining about the lateness of the hour.

For once Wynwood's pessimism was unjustified. The boats, all identical, looked both river-worthy and considerably better looked after than the hotel or its proprietor. Though shaped like large canoes, they had greater stability in the water and were made of sterner stuff, clinker-built from overlapping planks. There were places for two paddlers, one in the bow and one in the stern, with ample space for two non-paddling passengers and baggage in between them.

The haggling began. At first the proprietor had assumed that they were eccentrics come to rent boats in the middle of the night. The news that they wanted to buy two of them seemed to throw him off his stride, and much bluster was brought forth to cover his confusion.

Wynwood's first reaction was to regret not having simply asked to rent them; his second was to consider just taking them at gunpoint. Still, this would probably have been unwise even if he could have squared it with his conscience – he had no idea what police posts there might be downriver, and he did not want to start a jungle-wide watch for gringo boat-stealers.

A price for two boats was eventually agreed, one which should probably have bought them the hotel as well. They had the choice of which two, and as the patrol's boat specialist, Chris did the choosing.

The owner then offered to show them to their rooms, and was surprised to discover that they intended to set out immediately. Consoling himself with the large wad of pesos in the back pocket of his trousers, he went back to the verandah, muttering '*loco*' to himself at regular intervals.

With this litany vaguely audible in the background the five SAS men loaded their gear aboard the boats. Andy, Chris and the Dame would take one craft, Wynwood and Eddie the other. Since none of them had had more than four hours' sleep in the previous thirty-six, the plan was to get a few kilometres downstream and set up camp for the night.

They eased the two boats out onto the dark river, discovering a strong slow current in the centre of the stream. The river was about a hundred metres across at this point, but widened to almost twice that width before they had gone two kilometres. The jungle came down to the banks on both sides, giving the impression that they were travelling down a chute between two walls, a stationary ceiling of stars above them.

Every now and then what looked like a lighted window would appear in the dark walls to either side, before suddenly shooting off and revealing itself as some sort of luminous insect. The waters were silent save for the swish against their paddles, and the occasional melancholy cry of a bird in the distance seemed to echo all around them.

After only ten minutes or so the darkness relented and a quarter-moon rose above the trees, turning the deep shades of grey into an altogether more enchanting world of silver and black. To Eddie, sitting in the bow of the lead boat, the scene before him seemed more than a touch unreal after the space and light of the mountains and the mad bustle of their journey from San Agustin. He felt like he had been caught in a time warp and transported back to a world still untouched by men. Real or not, it thrilled him to the marrow.

'There's a sandbank about two hundred metres ahead,' Andy said quietly from the boat behind them. As the only non-paddler he had been entrusted with the nightscope.

'We'll see if it has any rooms,' Wynwood said, and steered towards it.

Closer to, the sandbank resembled a swathe of silver dust someone had thrown in the river. It had no rooms, but the remains of a fire showed it had been used before for camping. They pulled the boats out of the water and each man scraped a trench in the sand for sleeping in.

'A fire?' Anderson suggested.

'What do you think?' Wynwood asked.

'I can't see them sending up planes at night to look for us. How would they know it was us anyway? Only if old Trusthouse Forte back at the hotel tells them, and if they talk to him they'll know roughly where we are anyway.'

'There you go, then,' Wynwood agreed. 'I'm going to talk to Belize.'

'Ask them for the football results,' Eddie said.

'This is probably the time to tell you about the candiru,' Chris told Eddie.

'Uh-huh. And what's a candiru?'

'It's a tiny fish, which homes in on piss.'

257

'You're making it up.'

'Nope. And it actually swims up your anus and sticks itself there with barbs so it has to be cut out.'

'Jesus!'

'Why don't you take the boat across and get us some more wood,' Anderson suggested. 'And if you fall in the water try and stay as tight-arsed as possible.'

'OK, OK,' Wynwood said, midway through setting up the PRC 319, 'give me some quiet to think in.' The trouble was, he felt too tired to think straight anyway.

On the other hand, there was not really much need for thought. He told Belize where they were and what their options looked like. Then he requested as much information as possible on what was waiting for the five of them downstream: the navigability of the river, the weather, the numbers and friendliness of the human population, the warmth of their likely reception at the Peruvian or Brazilian border.

Apart from a simple question on the state of their health, the duty officer in Belize restricted himself to acknowledging Wynwood's requests. The latter signed off with a promise to repeat the contact tomorrow at 0800 hours.

By this time Anderson had got a decent fire going with driftwood the Dame had collected on the sandbank, and was in the process of preparing a warm meal from tins they had bought in Florencia. The boat was on its way back with more wood. It was like being a boy scout again, Wynwood thought. He resisted the temptation to start singing 'ging-gang-gooly-gooly'.

They ate their meal, watching the smoke from their fire drift across the stars, and then four of them went to sleep, leaving the apparently inexhaustible Eddie with the first watch.

Just before he slipped into sleep, Wynwood's thoughts were optimistic. He knew they were still in Colombia as the atlases drew it, but he could not help thinking they had escaped from the Colombia of the drug barons. Now it was just them and the *ulu*, and he had won that battle before.

A hundred and sixty kilometres to the north Chirlo took a swig from the can of Pepsi and watched the light plane aim itself between the parallel lines of fires which marked the jungle airstrip. Almost before it had touched down in the bumpy meadow men were extinguishing the fires in the oil drums by the simple expedient of replacing the lids. It was all probably unnecessary, Chirlo thought, but who knew when the satellites up there were taking pictures?

He waited while the plane turned a tight circle and started taxiing back up towards the group of men who were waiting to unload its cargo of coca paste.

The pilot climbed out. As Chirlo had expected, it was the Frenchman Paul Vadim, one of the few men who had worked for the Amarales longer than he had.

'Vadim,' he called out.

'Who wants me?'

Chirlo walked out of the shadows towards him.

'Chirlo,' Vadim said, surprised and somewhat wary. 'You're a long way from home. Is something wrong?' His hand had moved instinctively into his jacket pocket.

'I need you and your plane,' Chirlo said, wondering if Vadim was stupid enough to think he could outdraw and outshoot him. 'I will explain it to you over a beer.'

He and the Frenchman walked along the path past the lab, the filtering plant and the drying structure to the room adjoining the kitchen which had been fitted up to function as a bar.

The fridge yielded two cans of beer, and Chirlo went through the events of the past few days.

'I've never been able to make up my mind which I loathe most – the English, the Americans or the Germans,' was Vadim's only comment.

'They bought two boats at Tres Equinas,' Chirlo concluded, 'and they're somewhere on the Caqueta. I want you to find them, preferably without them realizing you've done so.'

The Frenchman shrugged. 'That won't be easy. The only way you can see what's on those rivers is by flying directly above them.'

'Can't you fly a zigzag route?' Chirlo suggested.

'That would make it less obvious,' Vadim agreed. He had previously thought of Chirlo as just a highly efficient thug. Perhaps he had underestimated him.

It was five in the morning in Hereford when Kilcline woke the CO with the news from Belize.

'Where are they exactly?' Barney Davies asked sleepily, stretching the telephone cord towards the shelves where he kept his atlases. Even as a boy he had always loved maps, and there were now almost fifty atlases of various vintages in his collection. He pulled out the most modern and rifled his way through the pages to Colombia. Why was South America always at the back of atlases, he wondered. Was it that the British had traditionally had less interest in it than other continents?

Kilcline gave him the details again. 'Christ, it looks a long way from anywhere,' he murmured, mostly to himself.

'It is,' Kilcline agreed. 'I've set the wheels turning on the information front,' he said, 'but I thought you'd want to deal with the political stuff yourself.'

'Yes, I'll handle it,' Davies agreed.

'They're transmitting again at 1300 our time.'

'OK. I'll get back to you by 1100.' He hung up, spent a few moments staring at the atlas page, shook his head and went to make himself some coffee. The prospect of more contact with the Foreign Office hardly filled him with the joys of spring. In fact he felt a considerable reluctance to divulge the men's whereabouts to anyone outside the Regiment. But he supposed they had to end up in another country at some point, and it would be better to be greeted by a friendly face than a deportation order sending them back to Colombia.

Eddie sat on the far end of the sandbank from his sleeping comrades listening to the soundtrack of the jungle. It had no recognizable rhythm, unless that in itself was a rhythm; the backing track supplied by cicadas and frogs had the seamlessness of disco, but it didn't exactly set the toes tapping. As for the vocalists, they were a strange bunch, not much given to essaying more than a single croak, howl, hiss or cry. The word 'unearthly' flashed through Eddie's mind, and made him laugh. If the natural earth sounded unearthly they were in deep trouble.

It was just an impersonal sound, he decided. Not threatening, not friendly, just there. Rather like being in London, where these days you couldn't even escape from the hum of traffic in the middle of Hampstead Heath. Just the noise of the world.

Where was there still silence? he wondered. In the Arctic maybe, provided two polar bears were not busy at it on a neighbouring ice floe. He wondered what Lisa was doing. Sleeping, he supposed, since it was about five in the morning in England. Sleeping alone, he hoped. He wondered what she would think if she could see him now. Would she be impressed?

261

In his mind's eye he could see her upturned face in the back of his dad's car, half amused, half nervous. It had been great, but she had been worried that it would not be, that somehow she would not live up to his expectations, or even her own.

The fear of failure seemed to be everywhere, he thought. In sex and love and school and work. Maybe you had to grow up knowing there was no real escape to realize that it was the trying that mattered – stretching yourself, learning new things, going for broke every day of your life.

One day you would lose your bet, but that would not be failure. As long as you were trying you couldn't fail.

13

In the hour after dawn the jungle's backing track seemed to fade, offering each soloist their best chance of the day to be heard. A mixture of cries rent the air – high-spirited, mournful, jaunty, melancholic.

'The heat, the flies, the endless drums,' Anderson murmured, gazing at the dark-green wall of vegetation across the dark green water.

'Sounds like the Brixton Academy,' Eddie said.

Anderson eyed him affectionately. He had grown rather fond of Eddie over the last couple of days, though he could not for the life of him think why. The two of them were reloading their gear into the boats, while the Dame filtered river water through the canvas bag they had looked for and bought in Florencia. It was not as efficient as the Millbank bag they normally used but it would have to do. Once filtered, the water would be sterilized with tablets.

Chris was busy removing as many traces as he could of their night on the sandbank. It was probably a one in a hundred chance that anyone would notice, but it was that chance which the ingraining of good habits was supposed to remove. The SAS did not leave tracks when they could avoid doing so.

Twenty metres away Wynwood was 'talking' to Belize on the PRC 319. Finishing, he collapsed the antennae and walked back across the sandbank to the boats. 'Which would you like first,' he asked them, 'the good news or the bad news?'

'Do we have to have both?' Eddie asked.

'What's the bad news?' Anderson demanded.

'There's a stretch of rapids eighty kilometres downstream, about five kilometres of them, which we'll have to carry the boats past. Tomorrow I guess. There's a portage trail, so the going shouldn't be too difficult.'

'No native bearers?' Eddie wanted to know.

'Only you and the Dame.'

'Ha ha. So what's the good news?'

'It looks like the Peruvian authorities will turn a blind eye to our appearance in their fair country, provided we can get into it without being stopped.'

'That's good news?' Eddie said. 'I was expecting wine and women at the very least.'

'Even a Little Chef with a plump waitress round the next bend would have been something,' Anderson agreed.

'Mmmm,' Chris said, 'I love their cherry pancakes.'

'Have you clowns quite finished?' Wynwood asked politely.

'Yes, boss.'

'Are there any Indians around here?' the Dame asked.

'A few. From the Witoto tribe. But they've been civilized, whatever that means.'

'Bought or killed,' Eddie said dryly.

Wynwood looked at him. Every time he had made up his mind that there really was only cynicism in Eddie's heart, something else would slip out through the protective camouflage. 'Yeah,' he agreed. 'Come on, let's get started.'

They slid the boats off the sand and into the river, and for the next few hours, as the sun climbed into place above them, made steady progress. The river meandered this way and that, but slowly, in giant curves rather than sharp bends, and the wall of forest on either side seemed practically unchanging, as if, like a wallpaper border, it was drawn to a recurring pattern.

If the flora showed little obvious variety, the same could not be said for the fauna. Monkeys chattered and howled in the trees, the occasional alligator snoozed in the shallows, and large fish broke the surface and disappeared again with a splash. Huge blue butterflies floated past like dreams.

And then there were the birds. Chris could hardly believe the variety to be found in any direction he chose to look. There were several species of wading birds, but the ones which drew his attention were the jaburus – white storks almost as tall as men, with red throats and black legs, heads and beaks. They paced up and down the sandbanks with heads slightly bowed, looking for all the world as if they were pondering some deep philosophical problem.

Woodpeckers could be heard and often seen, herons stood watchfully on the banks, hawks circled above the river, kingfishers glided across the water, and bright-coloured macaws flew by, seemingly always in groups of three. The only blots on this tableau of grace and beauty were the flocks of hoatzins, fowls that looked like distant relations of the pterodactyl, and delighted in hissing at the party from the safety of the bank.

The richness of the bird-life contrasted with the almost total lack of any human imprint. The occasional ruin of a landing stage bore testimony to past activity, but no villages came into view, no other boats, no other people. Only a single plane, which flew high across the river behind them, offered visual proof that there were still other humans on the planet.

Wynwood was still wondering about it an hour later. It could have been in this area for any number of reasons, though the most probable was undoubtedly drug-running. And if it had been looking for them it had done a good job of looking like it wasn't. Wynwood mentally shrugged: there was nothing they could do about it if it was, other than keep themselves in a state of constant vigilance.

'Reminds me of my school staff room,' Eddie said in front of him.

Wynwood followed his gaze to where a flock of hoatzins was watching them from the lower branches of a tree. He laughed, and looked back up at the sky. 'Looks like rain,' he said.

He was right. The clouds above grew steadily darker, and finally disgorged themselves just as the five men were pulling the boats up onto the mid-river sandbank Wynwood had chosen for rest and food. Thoughts of seeking shelter lasted about twenty seconds – by which time they were soaked to the skin. They set out receptacles to collect water and sat in the downpour consuming cold the last tins from Florencia.

'I found them,' Vadim said.

'Show me,' Chirlo said, reaching for the map.

'Here,' Vadim said, pointing. 'They were there at quarter past eleven, so . . . well, you can work it out.' He drew on his cigarette. 'Where do you intend to stop them?'

It was Chirlo's turn to point a finger. 'Tomorrow morning, I should think.'

'Couldn't they be there tonight?'

Chirlo shrugged. 'I doubt it, but we will be there just in case.'

'How many of you?'

'Eight men.' Chirlo smiled. 'And an M60 machine-gun.'

The shower had proved as short as it was heavy, and by mid-afternoon the sun had dried them and their clothes as they moved downstream. But towards dusk the sky again darkened and they decided to make a dry camp on the shore rather than risk a cold, wet night on the sandbank.

With the boats secured all five men set to work constructing a waterproof 'basha', using jungle wood – mostly bamboo – to provide the frame, interwoven atap leaves to keep out the water, and various vines and creepers to hold the whole thing together. It was something they had all done before in Brunei, and in not much more than an hour a passable shelter some three metres long and just over two wide had been constructed.

While the Dame prepared some warm food, the others took time to thoroughly clean and dry their Brownings and MP5s. In the jungle, humidity alone could render weapons inoperable, let alone the drenching of a tropical rainstorm.

'Where are we, boss?' Eddie asked.

'About two hours from the rapids by my reckoning,' Wynwood replied. 'So we should get there by 0900 at the latest. Allow three hours for the portage, an hour's rest . . . we should be close to La Tagua by dusk.'

'And then it's what? Sixty-odd kilometres by road to the border?'

'Something like that.'

'Piece of cake,' Eddie said. He looked out through the open wall of the shelter, where the rain was beginning to

267

come down in almost grotesquely large droplets. 'The thought of curried snake for the next thousand kilometres was beginning to get me down.'

'The one I had in Brunei wasn't bad,' Chris said.

They all joined in the discussion, working their way through a long list of things they had never dreamed of eating in pre-SAS days, but which they had eventually found themselves consuming. There was unanimous agreement on the slug's lack of culinary quality.

'McDonald's should try them,' Eddie suggested. 'McSluggets.'

'Just for that you're on first watch,' Wynwood told him.

It rained most of the night, which surprised Wynwood, whose previous experience of rain in tropical areas suggested one heavy shower in the middle of each day. Maybe it had something to do with their proximity to the mountains.

The rain eventually stopped an hour or so before dawn, and for the last hour of his watch Wynwood listened to the maddeningly irregular drip of water coming down through the foliage overhead. A mist rose from the river, which the first light of day turned into an opaque fog. Another ten minutes and the sun began clearing it away, breaking the mist into patches like some wonder detergent clearing pollution from the sea.

As the jungle birds awoke to the sunlight Wynwood woke the others. Within half an hour they had dismantled the basha, done their ablutions, breakfasted and loaded the boats.

They set off in the same order as before, Eddie and Wynwood in the lead boat, the Dame, Chris and Andy in the second. The jungle seemed subdued by the night's rain, and the first hour was spent in an almost supernatural silence. When the men spoke to each other it seemed louder than it should, and the occasional cry of a nearby bird was almost enough to make them jump.

It was out of the general silence that a low murmur became increasingly audible. 'The rapids,' Wynwood said thankfully.

'We must be on the right river, then,' Eddie said.

Six kilometres downstream, just ahead of where a small, heavily forested island bisected the channel, a landing stage had been built to assist in the unloading of boats for portage past the rapids. Since at this time of the year the river was still running low, anyone landing would have to make use of the rusted iron steps which led down to the surface of the water two metres below.

Behind the landing stage several decrepit houses – huts to anyone but an estate agent – were roughly lined up on either side of a dirt road which led off into the jungle south of the river. Inside these huts were now gathered all but two of the twenty or so Indians whose homes they were. Since there were no locks on the doors, only threats and the patrolling presence of five of Chirlo's eight *sicarios* physically kept them there. What would happen when the time came, and the *sicarios* were needed elsewhere, might be problematic, but Chirlo hoped the presence of their headman and his woman on the landing stage, covered by several guns, would give the villagers reason to stay put. These two hostages also had another part to play in the drama Chirlo was hoping to direct, that of a smiling welcome committee for the Englishmen.

The M60 was mounted immediately behind the landing stage, with a line of fire right across the river, just in case the Englishmen were foolish or ignorant enough to attempt the rapids in the boats they had bought. They would certainly die if they tried, but out of Chirlo's sight, which was not the preferred solution.

For the moment the machine-gun was not visible from the river. Four walls of rusty corrugated iron had been rescued from the top end of the village, and recycled into what looked like a simple storage hut. At the pull of a string all four walls would collapse outwards, leaving the gun with a full field of fire.

Chirlo was proud of this idea, but hoped it would not need to be used. With any luck he would be able to get the drop on all five men as they came ashore. Killing them with a machine-gun was, after all, not a great improvement on having the river do it for him. And he wanted to know which of them had killed her.

His men had all been given the positions which they were to occupy the moment the signal was given by the man across the river. He and Fernández were already ensconced inside the door of the first house on the right, which had been built close to the river. The hidden machine-gun, manned by Pérez and Cayano, was ten metres away across the road. Out on the landing stage, as the third point of an equilateral triangle, the two Indians sat in apparent silence.

Had he made any mistakes, Chirlo wondered. The helicopter he had used for ferrying in his men had never been closer than three kilometres to the river, so there was no way they could have heard it. They had no real choice but to leave their boats at this point. They did not have any heavy weapons. He had the superior position.

Looking across the river, he wondered whether he should have put more men on the far bank. At that moment his watchman waved the red T-shirt he was using as a signal. The Englishmen were in sight.

'Get everyone in position,' he told Fernández, 'and remind them – if they fuck up they'll wish they hadn't.'

Coming round the wide bend in the river the first thing Eddie saw, about half a kilometre ahead, was an island in midstream. Then the outer edge of the landing stage emerged from the curve of the right bank.

'People,' he announced succinctly.

'They look friendly enough,' Wynwood said, examining the two Indians through the telescopic sight. One man and one woman, neither of them young. He gave a hand signal to Chris to lengthen the gap between the two boats. He could see nothing suspicious but it was better to be safe than sorry.

They were about two hundred metres from the landing stage when something began to nag at the edge of Wynwood's mind. He took a look back at Anderson, to see if his old partner's fabled sixth sense was picking up any of the wrong vibes, but received only a smile in reply.

'The natives are waiting for their beads,' Eddie said facetiously.

The two Indians had stood up and seemed to be grinning inanely in their direction. Wynwood examined their faces through the scope. There really was something odd about them. They looked, well . . . stoned.

He examined the area behind them, the houses, the corrugated hut. Where was everyone else, he wondered. Where were the dogs? This was the moment in the movie, he thought, when someone says: 'It's too quiet.'

Well, it was. He didn't know why but he didn't like it.

One of the Indians said something indecipherable and beckoned them forward.

That was the last straw. Wynwood hand-signalled Chris to take the other boat away to the left, towards the far bank. 'We'll go in alone,' he told Eddie in a soft voice. 'I'll do the paddling. You keep your eyes open.'

Eddie placed his paddle down and took a firm grip on the MP5 which had been hanging across his stomach.

Wynwood suddenly realized that on one of the visible walls of the corrugated hut the streaks of rust ran up rather than down. With sudden ferocity he propelled the boat forward towards the landing stage.

His scream of 'Take cover' echoed across the river.

Chirlo had watched the separation of the two boats with horror. Why hadn't he foreseen such a simple manoeuvre? And what should he do now? If the two in the first boat landed they would have to be taken, leaving the other three dangerously at liberty . . . unless they could all be taken out by the M60 . . . but they were moving to the other side of the river and he was not that confident in his men's accuracy at such range . . . so perhaps he should open fire immediately on the far boat . . . or else . . .

These thoughts uselessly jostled each other in Chirlo's brain. Accustomed to the split-second decision-making of the slum barrio streets, he lost himself in the luxury of whole seconds in which to make up his mind.

Pérez, in charge of the machine-gun, waited for the order that did not come. In a few seconds the first boat would be shielded by the landing stage, but from where he was the chief could not know that. Logic and fear came together – he gave the word to drop the shields at almost the same moment Wynwood's cry split the silence.

They dropped with a clatter just as Wynwood shot the boat forward towards the cover of the steep bank and landing stage. Pérez sent one stitch of bullets straight through the space where Wynwood's head had been a split second before, then pulled back on the gun and set his sight on the second boat across the river.

In the second boat Chris and Andy responded to Wynwood's cry, but their surge forward was cut off almost as soon as it began. A fusillade of machine-gun fire exploded around them, causing the Dame to curse and the boat to suddenly slow. Chris turned to find the Dame holding a bloody arm and Anderson slumped forward, half his head blown away.

Wynwood's sudden surge forward caught Eddie off balance, and he had only just managed to regain it when the front of the boat rammed into the pilings beneath the landing stage. He reached out an arm and grabbed, somehow keeping hold while the stretch tried to pull his arm out of its socket. The crash had spun the boat's stern to the left, almost catapulting Wynwood into the bank. He managed to keep the MP5 out of the water and gain a hold on the bare red earth of the steep slope.

He could see only sky above the rim of the bank, but a quick look back across the river told its own story. The other boat was running for the cover of the island, but already the man in the back – Andy – had his head slumped forward over his chest, and there was another two hundred metres to go.

The machine-gun fire had stopped, but it could open up again at any moment. There was no choice. Wynwood turned back to Eddie, who was lying forward on the slope on the other side of the landing stage, and gave him the hand signal to advance. Eddie gave him a reproachful glance, then grinned, and started wriggling upwards.

Wynwood did the same. Somewhere up above, two men were conducting a half-whispered argument in Spanish. The gun must have jammed, Wynwood thought. He thanked his lucky stars for the previous night's rain.

He now had his head just short of the top of the bank, and searched with his foot for some point of leverage in the slope. Finding one, he shared glances with Eddie, and they launched themselves up across the lip of the bank just as the M60 opened fire once more. Both landed still rolling, their eyes searching for targets.

Wynwood was only eight metres from the machine-gunners, who were still trying to jerk the gun round towards him when he cut both of them in half with the MP5. Hearing a noise behind and to his left, he twisted round. A feeling like fire running up his arm was followed by the crack of an automatic, and as he opened up with the MP5 a head disappeared round the corner of the building.

Eddie's roll had almost rammed him into the side of the building nearest to the water. In the second he took to decide which way to go, a *sicario* incautiously put more than one eye round the corner and acquired a third in the middle of his forehead. Eddie got to his feet, exchanging the Browning for the MP5, and worked his way round the back of the building. He emerged from the last corner in the same roll, ending up this time in a half-kneeling position with two Colombians not ten metres away.

Having turned everything to disaster with his military inexperience, Chirlo now found himself, for the last time in his life, in his element. As the blond Englishman whirled into view, his revolver raised in both hands, Chirlo simply stepped behind Fernández. It had worked on the streets of Bogotá and it worked now. Fernández absorbed the bullets, his arms flying upwards with the impact, leaving Chirlo space through the armpit to send two bullets into the body of the Englishman. He turned, almost in triumph, to find another Englishman's finger tightening on the trigger.

Chirlo's last thought was of the strangeness of it all: to grow up in one kind of jungle, and to die in another.

Wynwood sank to one knee, his eyes sweeping the scene. In the distance two men were running off down the road; on the landing stage the two Indians were looking at him, almost with curiosity. They had been bait, Wynwood realized, and they were still not sure if they were going to be eaten.

He walked over to where Eddie was lying. One bullet had passed through the heart, another centimetres away. The half-insolent smile seemed younger than before. Wynwood closed Eddie's eyes, and turned to the Indians. 'How many of them were there?' he asked in Spanish.

'Eight,' the Indian man replied. 'Bad men,' he added as an afterthought.

There were two dead by the machine-gun, two more in front of him. Two had run off, and there was the one he had forced back under cover. And there was another slumped behind the corner of the building where Eddie had come up the bank.

'They are all gone,' the Indian said, as if he knew Wynwood needed confirmation of the fact.

Wynwood nodded, and signalled across to Chris to bring the other boat in. As he watched it cross the river his mind played with the hope that Andy was still alive, but his heart was already well into mourning. Behind him the villagers were slowly emerging from their houses. The jungle, shocked into silence by the guns of man, was once more finding its voice.

* * *

275

They buried Eddie and Andy that afternoon, in home-made coffins on the island in midstream, hoping that at some time in the future someone from the British Embassy could arrange for their collection and transport back to England.

The Dame's arm was a mess, but a repairable one, provided they got him out of the jungle before infection had a chance to set in. Wynwood's wound was more superficial, but hurt like blazes just the same.

Leaving, much to the Indians' delight, another large chunk of their gear behind, Wynwood and Chris shouldered one of the boats and what gear they could carry to the foot of the rapids, and by noon next day they were on the road to the Peruvian border. There they found the rough hut on the Colombian side empty of officialdom, that on the Peruvian side full of smiling locals and an irritated man from the British Embassy.

It was over. One Colombian politician had been saved; two SAS men had failed to beat the clock.

Epilogue

Kilcline and Bourne were sharing a lunchtime drink in the Slug and Pellet. The idea was to celebrate Bourne's return, but somehow celebration seemed inappropriate.

'Have you seen Beth?' Bourne asked.

'Briefly. She . . . well, you can imagine.'

Bourne could. He could remember the times his own wife had given vent to her fears of becoming a soldier's widow. Well, Britain would have to be invaded for him to ever see any more real action. He and Lynn were safe. Or as safe as you could ever be in the kind of world they seemed to be making.

He shook his head, as if to shake away the mood. 'It was an amazing achievement,' he said, almost to himself.

'And by the time anyone gets round to acknowledging it, the lads who did it will all be dead,' Kilcline said matter-of-factly.

'We know what they did,' Bourne said. 'And they know, which is what really counts.'

Kilcline managed a smile. 'Your round,' he said.

In the Andes another morning had broken, and Ramón Amarales was enjoying the early sunlight with his usual silver jug of coffee on Totoro's verandah. That morning Miguel was coming out for a meeting to decide who should take the dead Chirlo's position as chief *sicario*. It should not be difficult: there was no shortage of tough and intelligent candidates.

Ramón had a nice surprise for his brother – according to the statement that had arrived the previous day, the balance in their Swiss bank account had just passed twenty million dollars. The Amarales had to be among the richest ten families in Colombia.

And it was down to him – Ramón. Victoria might have been the intelligent one, Miguel the handsome one, but without him the business would never have become as successful as it had.

His great mistake, Ramón decided, had always been to underestimate his own achievements. And his prospects too, for that matter. Victoria was dead, Miguel married to a noisy leech. He had taken their father's ranch and turned it into twenty million dollars. And unless the youths of America and Europe suddenly lost their appetite for artificial stimulation he would double that money in the next five years.

If that was not success, what was?

Chris walked slowly along the Blackwater estuary, thinking it was not much more than a month since he had walked the same path on the way home to find the order to report in. And the next day he had met Eddie at Paddington, and it had all begun.

He remembered the condors in the mountains above Totoro and the hummingbird in the tree in San Agustin and the flashing kingfishers on the river. He remembered the man at the briefing saying Colombia was probably the most beautiful country in the world. Well, he had not seen its equal.

But then there many more countries to see. He stood looking out over the waters shining silver in the sun, not thinking about Eddie or Anderson or the man he himself had killed in

San Agustin – that was all done, all gone, yesterday's world – but about the deep underlying silence of the jungle river in the hour after dawn, the lone screeches of birds he had never heard before.

He was seeing Molly again that evening for the first time since Christmas Eve. She had sounded enthusiastic over the phone, but he had the feeling he was going through the motions, that really he did not want anyone sharing his thoughts and feelings.

Maybe she felt the same. Maybe they could just have fun for a few hours.

'Have you seen today's polls?' Estrada asked Quintana as he came through the door.

'Yes, Rafael,' Quintana said, though he had not. And he did not need to now. If Estrada was in a good mood then they had to be favourable.

'I am going to win,' Estrada said, almost smugly.

'It looks like it,' Quintana agreed.

'And you must take a lot of the credit,' Estrada insisted. 'It was your idea to invite the English in. If Muñoz had simply been ransomed he might have ended up a hero.' He looked straight at Quintana, sincerity written on his face. 'I won't forget it, Luis,' he added.

Estrada had probably been watching some Hollywood tear-jerker, Quintana guessed. He found the thought that his advice had probably secured the man's re-election was almost more than he could bear.

In a Hereford pub Bonnie and Blackie were still trying to decide which women would be favoured with their attentions that evening. There was quite a wide choice on offer, ranging

279

from the teenage gigglers in the corner to the two women in their mid-thirties standing at the bar.

'Bet you they're teachers,' Bonnie said.

'Social workers,' Blackie thought.

'They're over thirty anyway,' Bonnie said. 'So they're probably desperate.'

'I don't know whether they're that desperate,' Blackie said, looking at him. 'Where did you get that jacket – Oxfam?'

'C&A. What's wrong with it?'

'Nothing a good bonfire wouldn't put right. But the wrinklies'll probably like it. Shall we go for them?'

'Why not? There's no substitute for experience.'

Blackie grinned. 'If they think that, you're in trouble.'

'Huh. We've just jumped out of a fucking plane higher than fucking Everest and hang-glided onto a fucking mountain and attacked a drug baron's ranch and got away again. That's experience, isn't it?

'It may not be exactly what they're looking for.'

Bonnie grinned. 'Know what you mean. This is a time for LALO.'

'For what!?'

'Low altitude, low opening, if you get my drift.'

'I do, but I wish I didn't.'

The Dame stood at the heart of the swaying crowd behind the goal at Roker Park. It was half-time, Sunderland were losing, but years of disappointment still could not quench the hope.

The other half-time scores started coming through on the loudspeaker. Tottenham were losing as well, 2-0 at Everton. The Dame knew he would never hear Tottenham mentioned now without thinking about Eddie.

He had been thinking a lot about him anyway in the last few weeks. The trouble was, in one way he had felt very close to him. Hackney was a long way from Sunderland, but they were closer to each other than they were to most places in England. They had a – 'strength' was the only word that fitted – a strength about them that came from knowing hardship, and knowing it as a real community. And from out of this came the strange mixture of pride and bitterness which he knew in himself and which he had recognized in Eddie.

Of course Eddie had been flash, London flash, and where the Dame used silence and reserve to protect himself, Eddie had used jokes and cynicism. But this was just style. What worried the Dame were the differences between him and Eddie. Try to talk to him about England or the Army or politics or religion – anything other than football and women – and he would just say it was all bullshit. Eddie had seemed content to live for nothing but the SAS, and not because of any pride in the Regiment or because he agreed with the jobs it was asked to do. No, he had loved the SAS because, as he had once said, it kept surprising him. It had kept him ticking over, till the clock beat him.

And if one small part of the Dame would have liked to be like that, a brilliant skater on the surface of life, the rest of him knew he never could be. He needed reasons for the things he did, and some judgement at the end of the line. And after what had happened to Eddie, somehow he needed these things more than ever.

Barney Davies sat in his darkened living-room, glass of brandy in his hand, watching the ten o'clock news. The Prime Minister was wrapping herself in the flag again at the dispatch box – something to do with Iraq – he wasn't really paying attention to the details. But the patriotic tone was unmistakable.

281

Nine times out of ten he would have gone along with it, even shared the feelings, if not the belligerency of their expression. But tonight it brought a bad taste to his mouth. He remembered Denis Healey's 'glorying in slaughter', a remark he had thought ill-judged in the extreme at the time, but which now seemed almost fair.

He took another sip of brandy and used the remote control to turn off the TV. What was he complaining about? He had read enough history to know that soldiers had been let down by politicians since time began, so why should he be so upset by one more example of an age-old vice. 'Because,' he murmured out loud to himself, 'this time it was me who had to listen to the utter indifference in the politician's voice.' Not even crocodile tears. Not even a wreath.

Barney swallowed the rest of the brandy in one gulp. Sometimes he wondered why the world was run by people with no sense of honour or obligation.

In the neon-lit room in backstreet Bogotá, the girl in the red dress carefully counted out her earnings from the evening. It was enough, she decided. She collected her English primer from the table and sat with it cross-legged on the floor, rubbing her eyes to keep them open.

Joss Wynwood walked slowly along the dark beach, listening to the waves crashing in from the Irish Sea away to his right. It was a clear night and the lights of Portmadoc were visible in the distance, nestling beneath the dark mass of the mountains beyond.

On his return from South America Wynwood had not gone home to the house he and Susan shared. He wanted to keep it as a place they had been happy in, and so he checked into a small hotel in Hereford and arranged a meeting with her in a restaurant in the town. Both of them had expected a difficult conversation about what was wrong with their marriage and who was to blame, but it was immediately apparent both had been mistaken. There was no point. It was simply over, and both had known it for a long time. So instead they had a strangely affectionate conversation about the mechanics of the split, and parted feeling better disposed to each other than for many years.

Wynwood had decided to take his leave back in Wales, but not with his family. He needed to be alone, and he had always loved the stretch of coastline between Barmouth and Pwllheli, which brought back memories of childhood holidays, of narrow-gauge steam trains and walks in the mountains. This evening he had found a nice pub in Criccieth, enjoyed a game of darts and a few pints, and was now walking back to his Portmadoc hotel along the coast.

Andy had been much on his mind, but he supposed that was natural. They had been like partners for a long time, and the training stint in Colombia had solidified the bond still further. He wondered what Andy would say if he knew that Wynwood was considering quitting the Army.

Why, probably.

I don't really know, Wynwood silently answered his dead friend.

Decisive as ever, I see. He could hear Andy say it, felt the tears rising in his eyes.

He fought them back. It was only the booze making him maudlin, he decided.

Just like the bloody Welsh!

So bloody what. He tried to organize his thoughts for the imaginary debate.

Is it because you were boss and Eddie and I didn't beat the clock?

No. 'I don't think I made any real mistakes,' he said out loud to the sand and the sea. 'You were just unlucky. Eddie . . . Well, soldiers get killed, it's part of the job.'

Is it because you had to kill more people than you were ready for?

'Maybe.' The Cali barrio, the car lot by the Magdalena, the jungle village. The woman at Totoro. There had never been any real choice. 'But I don't think so,' he said.

So what the fuck are you moaning on about? You like the job. You like taking young men and showing them how to make the most of what they have. It's a thing worth doing. And you do it well.

'Yeah,' It was. He did. He accepted all that. 'It's just . . .' he began, and then fell silent again. He had stopped walking, and a flicker of a smile crossed his face as he realized what he would look like to a stranger. A lunatic on a beach, talking to himself. 'It's just . . .'

It's just that you're a maudlin Welsh bastard.

'Just a man,' Wynwood said carefully, 'who wishes that there was no need to bring out the worst in men in order for them to serve the good.'

You could put that in a Christmas cracker!

Wynwood laughed. 'Yeah,' he agreed.

He looked out to sea, listened to the waves. 'Goodbye, Andy,' he said at last, and turned away, walking on towards the distant lights.